The

Anatomy

Lesson

A Kurtz and Barent Mystery

The Anatomy Lesson

A Kurtz and Barent Mystery

Cover design by Steven A. Katz

The

Anatomy

Lesson

A Kurtz and Barent Mystery

by

Robert I. Katz

Also by Robert I. Katz

Edward Maret: A Novel of the Future

The Kurtz and Barent Mystery Series:

Surgical Risk
The Anatomy Lesson
Seizure
The Chairmen
Brighton Beach

The Cannibal's Feast

The Chronicles of the Second Interstellar Empire of Mankind:

The Game Players of Meridien
The City of Ashes
The Empire of Dust
The Empire of Ruin
The Well of Time (Forthcoming)

To Erica, Steven, and Jeffrey

Chapter 1

Two white, protruding fangs peeked out over Nolan's lower lip while a tiny red dribble of dried blood trailed down his chin. His skin was the color of flesh that has lain for many years at the bottom of a grave. His clothes were jet-black and rippling. "It's not bad," he said, and frowned down into a styrofoam cup. "Still a little weak, though."

The ghoul grunted and poured a thick, brown liquid into the bowl. "Try it now."

Nolan dipped his cup into the bowl and sipped delicately, then nodded. "Perfect," he said, and smacked his lips.

"Good." The ghoul took a greenish-looking hand out of a bag and placed it into the bowl, where it floated. "You like?" he asked.

The vampire smiled. "Definitely."

The ghoul smiled back. The ghoul's name was Redding. Redding was almost six and a half feet tall and cadaverously thin, which went along perfectly with his gray skin and decaying features. The vampire looked at him and despite himself, almost shuddered.

"Help me with these, will you?" Redding asked.

Gingerly, Nolan reached into the bag, retrieved more body parts and scattered them strategically around the room. "How about the head?" Redding asked. "Hang it from the chandelier?"

The vampire considered the suggestion, then nodded. "I'll do it," he said. He stood on a chair and attached the head with a piece of twine so that it hung suspended in mid-air a foot below the ceiling. The head's eyes drooped slightly open. They seemed to stare at him accusingly.

"Beautiful," Redding said, "just beautiful."

The vampire examined the head, reached out a clawed hand and fluffed up the red, matted hair. His fangs protruded as a slow smile spread across his face.

Both of them took a moment to admire their work: neatly laid-out platters of hors d'oeuvres, cold cuts and smoked salmon, loaves of bread and soft rolls already sliced, green salad, macaroni salad and potato salad and a pot of baked beans bubbling over a portable heating coil, pretzels, bottles of wine and soda and beer, assorted cakes and pies and sweet pastries and a small cooler set up in the corner of the room with gallons of ice cream inside, and of course the *piece de resistance*, the enormous bowl of rum-laden punch in the center of the table, with a green plastic hand floating on top.

"Beautiful," Redding said again.

The vampire nodded and looked at his watch. "They'll be arriving in less than an hour. Help me set up the VCR."

"You got Nightmare on Elm Street?"

"Yup. And Fright Night and the original Dracula with Bela Lugosi."

"You dog," Redding said.

The vampire shrugged modestly and switched off the light as they left the room.

"I love Halloween," Redding said.

"Trick or treat," the vampire said, and giggled.

Within an hour, the guests began to arrive. Nolan met them at the door, shook the men's hands and pretended to bite the women on the neck. Most of the women responded with mock shrieks. One, a tiny witch with straggly orange hair and a crooked plastic nose, merely yawned. Her name was Carrie Owens.

"So young and so blasé," Nolan said.

Carrie Owens yawned again. "I was on call last night."

The vampire smiled sympathetically. "Go on in and sit down," he said. He waved a hand at the door to the outer office, where Redding had set up bowls of pretzels, potato chips and dip on a corner table between two couches. Fright Night was playing on the T.V.

Carrie went in and flopped herself on the couch. She felt numb. The night before, a fifteen year old had blown off three fingers with a cherry bomb ... not exactly appropriate to the season but there you were, and after the kid was worked up and sent to surgery, a five year old who had swallowed her mother's asthma medication had arrived in the ER, seizing. After that had come a routine stab wound followed by an old geezer brought in by ambulance complaining of chest pain, who promptly arrested. They had worked on the old guy for over two hours. Every time they got a rhythm going, he would wake up for a few seconds and start screaming. Then his heart would fibrillate again, his eyes would roll back and he would go limp as the blood flow to his brain began to fall. In between shocks they pumped on his chest. He was finally stabilized on amiodarone, lidocaine, pronestyl and bretylium drips and sent off to C.C.U. but it had not been a pleasant night for the patient or for Carrie.

On the T.V., somebody was being stabbed in the chest with a wooden stake. Carrie winced.

A man in a pirate's hat flopped down on the couch beside her, a Heineken bottle in one hand and a half-empty glass in the other. His name was David Chao, one of the private surgeons. "Hey, there," he said. "How you doing?"

She yawned again. "I'm tired."

"Rough night?"

"It sucked."

Chao nodded sympathetically. "You here with anybody?"

"I was supposed to meet Angie West but she got stuck in the ER."

Chao cocked his head to the side and gave her a speculative look. "Where's Frank Merola these days?" he asked.

"I don't really know," Carrie said. "And I don't really care."

"Ah…"

Carrie shrugged. On the T.V. screen, an enormous bat was blasted into gouts of ugly-looking smoke by a beam of sunlight. On the other side of Chao, a mummy and a pint-sized Darth Vader flopped down onto the couch, munching pretzels. A devil with a long red tail and an alien in a silver spacesuit came in and leaned against the wall. The little room was getting crowded. A woman dressed in a Tinkerbell costume opened up a window.

"Attention, everybody …"

Nolan stood in the doorway, his cape spread wide, his fangs bared. "Dinner is served."

Carrie rose with an audible groan as the party trooped out and into the next room.

"Very nice," Chao said.

"Yuck," Carrie replied. She was staring at the head hanging from the ceiling. "A little too realistic, if you ask me."

Redding went over to the punchbowl and started to fill the glasses with a metal ladle. People grabbed plates and Redding handed out the punch as the line went by.

Carrie sipped. The punch tasted…strange. She peered into her glass. Floating on the surface was a gray and pink glob, with tiny white strands floating all around it. "God …" she whispered. She looked at all the animated, happy people, talking, eating their food, sipping their wine or beer or punch. One or two, however, were staring uncertainly into their glasses. She walked over to the bowl. Submerged beneath the surface was a human hand.

Redding looked at her with concern. "Something the matter?" he asked.

Carrie plucked a serving spoon from the table, dipped it into the bowl and brought out the hand. It fell off the spoon and dropped to the table, pink and gray and silent, the fingers curled into a shrunken claw. Carrie's stomach did a flip-flop. Redding grinned, looked at the hand and started to say something. He stopped. An uncertain frown crossed his face. Gingerly, he reached out a finger and touched the soft, yielding flesh. It made a squishing sound.

"That looks real," Carrie said in a clipped voice.

"Yes, it does," Redding answered. "It really does. Jesus …"

Carrie leaned over the table and threw up.

Chapter 2

"Cause of death?" Barent asked.

The Medical Examiner squinted down at the head, which was perched on top of the table like an exotic mushroom. The cops were still scouring the room, coming up with more stray body parts

"Hard to tell, actually," the M.E. said.

"Why is that?"

The M.E. looked at Barent as if he could barely restrain his glee, slapped his thigh with an open palm and cackled. "Because they've been embalmed. They're soaked in formalin." The M.E. cackled again, his beady eyes bright. He sounded, Barent thought, like a demented chicken. "This isn't murder, Barent. It's some bright young idiot's idea of a joke."

He picked up a hand and held it under Barent's nose. Barent reared his head back and blinked rapidly. "You smell it?" the M.E. asked.

"Yes," Barent said. His eyes were tearing.

"Formalin." The M.E. smiled in genuine delight at the assortment of body parts. "So far, we've got three hands, one whole torso, one foot, two heads, a liver, a heart and two mismatched lungs. They're from at least three different bodies. I suggest you take a look up in the anatomy lab. You'll find that somebody has pilfered a few cadavers. Like I said, a joke."

"Some joke."

The M.E. shrugged, still smiling. "Reminds me of my medical school days."

Barent shuddered.

The M.E. waved a hand toward the door where the partygoers were clustered outside the room, peering in over the yellow crime-scene tape and grinning. "Look at them," the M.E. said. "They've figured it out for themselves."

The ones who had drunk the punch with the hand in it were generally not so happy.

"Think any of them had something to do with it?"

"Who knows?" The M.E. shrugged. "I critique the performance. You seek out the artist. Happy Halloween."

"Right," Barent said. "Sure."

11

Barent walked over to the doorway with the Medical Examiner, and after the M.E. had pushed his way out, Barent spoke to a tall young man dressed as a vampire. "I understand this is your party?"

The vampire looked around, first left, then right, then grinned sheepishly. "Not exactly. Bob Redding and I organized it."

Barent lifted one edge of the tape. "Come in," he said. Nolan did so and Barent squinted at him. "Don't I know you?"

"Steve Nolan. You met me last year at Easton."

"That's right." Barent nodded. "What are you doing here?"

"I finished my residency in June. I'm on staff."

Barent grunted. Harry Moran, a burly cop in a blue suit and swept back brown hair came up to them. He didn't look at Nolan. "That seems to be it."

The assortment of body parts lay clustered together on the table next to the punch bowl.

Nolan glanced at them with casual interest. He seemed to be trying not to smile. Barent, whose work as a homicide detective had exposed him over the years to more corpses than he cared to remember, had difficulty seeing dead bodies–particularly dismembered dead bodies–as funny. He found himself frowning. "I've been told this was a joke."

"Yeah," Nolan said. "It does seem likely.

"Nevertheless, I imagine that whoever is in charge of the bodies, and also the administration of the medical school, will not be pleased."

Nolan shrugged.

"You have any idea who might have done it?" Barent asked.

"Not a clue."

"I understand that you and your friend Redding put a bunch of plastic body parts around the room."

"That's correct."

The dismembered plastic corpse had been found stuffed in a closet. "Who had access to this room?" Barent asked.

"Damned if I know. I locked the door after we finished setting up but plenty of people must have keys."

"I understand this room is part of the faculty club?"

12

Nolan nodded. "It's usually used for meetings. We generally have a Halloween party here and a Christmas party for the staff, and also a graduation party for the medical students."

"So what you were doing was nothing unusual."

Nolan shook his head. "No."

"When did you finish getting ready for the party?"

"About an hour before."

"What did you and Redding do then?"

"I went back to my apartment for a little while."

"Where is that?"

"Right down the street. The Medical School owns the building. It's faculty housing."

"How about Redding?"

"You'll have to ask him."

Barent grunted again. He was not pleased. Despite his relief that nobody had been killed, he resented being here. Halloween was a lousy time of the year for a cop. This was only the beginning of what would most likely be a long, miserable night, and he resented wasting his time. "You know, it might be just a joke but vandalism, thievery and desecration of the dead are all against the law."

Nolan held up one hand and moved it back and forth, as if weighing the options. "Medical school is a gruesome business. After awhile, you stop thinking of the cadavers as people, or even as dead bodies. After a little while, they're just an unpleasant source of information. I know that sounds insensitive but none of us could survive emotionally if we didn't learn to look at it that way."

"Regardless of your sensitivity or lack thereof, it's still a crime."

Nolan shrugged. "I suppose so."

"This sort of thing happen often? Little jokes with the cadavers?"

"No." Nolan shook his head. "Not at all. The administration is quite aware of the effect such incidents would have upon the school's reputation. Any student who screws around with their cadaver would be instantly expelled. They let you know that."

"Who's in charge of them?"

"The cadavers?"

"Yes."

"Rod Mahoney is the professor in charge of the Anatomy course."

"Where would I find him?"

"Probably at home, watching T.V."

Barent nodded his head and made a notation in his notebook. "I'm going to want to look over the place where they keep the cadavers. Who can take me there?"

Nolan looked at the table spread with Halloween goodies. The crime lab techs were dusting for fingerprints, peering through magnifying glasses and collecting samples of dust from every corner of the room. "What about our party?"

Barent raised an eyebrow. "You can party somewhere else."

"What about the food?"

"You really want to eat it? There's a mummified hand in the punch bowl. Who knows what you'd find in the dip?"

Nolan sighed. "True. I guess the party's over." He shook his head sadly. "Give me a minute. I'll take you up there."

Barent, Harry Moran and Nolan took an elevator up to the Eleventh Floor, where the Gross Anatomy and Histology courses were taught. A faint, decaying odor permeated the entire floor. There were ten classrooms, five on each side of the hall. Each classroom contained four workspaces, and each workspace contained three low tables set against each other in a U with a book shelf running above them, three small lockers, recessed lights set beneath the book shelves and three chairs. Between adjoining workspaces, beneath the tables, were what appeared to be two long metal safes with combination locks on the doors.

"The lockers are for microscopes. The cadavers are kept in there," Nolan said, and pointed to a safe. "Four cadavers in each classroom. Three students to a cadaver."

"Show me one," Barent said.

"I can't. I don't know the combinations."

"Who does?"

"Each student gets the combination to his own cadaver."

"Anybody else?"

Nolan shrugged. "I wouldn't know."

"Mahoney have the combinations?"

"I would think so. He probably assigns them, or one of his assistants."

Barent grunted and turned to Moran. "Give Mahoney a call. Get him here."

"Suppose he doesn't want to come?" Moran asked.

"A crime has been committed. We're not giving him a choice," Barent said.

Rod Mahoney was a tall, thin man, with light, blue eyes behind wire-rimmed glasses. The remnants of his thinning, brown hair were combed carefully over the top of his head and then plastered down. He wore a plaid bowtie in pastel pink and green, a light blue oxford shirt, brown corduroy pants, brown leather loafers and a white lab coat. He wrung his hands as he talked. "This is terrible. Simply terrible. You won't tell the newspapers, will you?"

Fat chance. The media were not exactly the cops' best friends. Barent scratched his head. "It's not our job to keep the press informed."

Mahoney sighed, obviously relieved. "Thank you," he said.

"Dr. Nolan tells me you have the combinations to the safes where the cadavers are kept."

"That's true." Mahoney blinked at Moran, looking like a bewildered rabbit. "I was asked to bring them along."

"Alright, we'll start here. I want you to open every one of them." Mahoney looked even more bewildered. "Is that really necessary?"

Barent wondered. Most likely, the M.E. was correct. It was all just a "joke." Certainly, Nolan seemed willing enough to accept it as such. But something about the whole thing stuck in Barent's craw. Barent wasn't a physician. Maybe he just lacked a sense of humor but a crime was still a crime and fuck Nolan and his amused, long-suffering attitude.

"I think so," Barent said.

Mahoney shrugged, pulled a sheet of paper from his pocket, leaned over and spun the combination. The door swung open. A sharp, pungent odor came from the locker and filled the room. Mahoney reached in and pulled out a low metal table on wheels. As the table rolled out it rose on a spring mechanism and then locked into place, so that the body lying on it was about waist high. The body was male, emaciated and gray, the skin leathery. The features of the face were blank and shrunken together, so that it was

15

impossible to tell what it had looked like when alive. The muscles of the left arm had been dissected neatly out.

Barent swallowed. "Now the next one," he said. "I want to look at them all."

Mahoney frowned. A sheen of sweat covered his face and he blotted his forehead with a handkerchief. "Why?"

"Isn't it obvious? I'm looking for bodies with pieces missing."

"Ah ..."

Barent smiled thinly. Mahoney stepped on a button on the bottom framework of the table and pushed down. The table collapsed slowly and Mahoney shoved it back into its safe, closed the door and spun the combination.

They found what Barent was looking for in the fifth classroom. All four bodies had been mutilated. Two were without heads. Another was missing both hands and a foot. A third body's chest and abdomen had been hacked open, the heart, liver and one lung removed. The fourth table contained only the head and limbs lying together; the torso was gone.

Mahoney looked wilted. He stood with rounded shoulders and a distraught expression on his face. Even Nolan seemed subdued. Moran was pale. Barent broke the silence. "Four different cadavers. Four different combinations. That would imply that at least four different people were in on it."

Mahoney cleared his throat. "Not necessarily," he said. His voice was barely a whisper. "The faculty, the teaching assistants and the dieners all have access to the combinations."

"What's a diener?" Barent asked.

"They're like morticians. The dieners prepare the bodies when they arrive at the school: clean them and preserve them in formaldehyde."

Barent looked at the four tables, the four mutilated cadavers, and grimaced. Already his nose had grown so accustomed to the stench that he could barely smell it, but his mouth tasted foul. "I'll want a list," he said. "Two lists. Everybody who might have had access to the combinations and the names and backgrounds of all four cadavers in this room."

Chapter 3

Kurtz always enjoyed teaching rounds. Chao, evidently, enjoyed them too. Not for the first time, Kurtz congratulated himself on hiring David Chao. Chao had trained in General Surgery at the University of Texas, in Galveston, but his family lived in Westchester and he had wanted to return home after finishing his residency. Not only was Chao good in the OR and a nice guy, but he shared Kurtz' interest in the martial arts. The two of them often spent the evening together, practicing blocks and scissor-kicks, cheerfully trying to knock each other's head off.

"How are you today, Mr. Simmons?" Kaplan asked.

Simmons looked up at Kaplan with a tired expression on his face and barely shrugged. "Okay," he said.

Kaplan smiled widely, choosing to disregard the patient's tone. "Let's see how it looks."

He began to unwrap the bandages from the stump of Simmon's left leg while Patel, Kyle and Chao craned their necks to get a better look. Kurtz stood to the side of the bed, watching. Once the bandage was off, it became obvious that Simmons was not doing 'okay.' The wound had a dusky look and there were small patches of black necrosis around the staple line. Kaplan frowned at the incision, glanced guiltily up at Simmon's face, then looked back to the wound.

"What do you think," Simmons asked in a neutral voice.

Kaplan cleared his throat. "It's probably going to need a little more work."

"You mean more surgery," Simmons said flatly.

"Yes, I'm afraid so."

Kaplan looked around the room, perhaps seeking guidance from Chao or Kurtz, but Chao only looked glum and Kurtz was content to let Kaplan handle it. The situation was unfortunate and uncomfortable but Kaplan was doing about as well as could be done.

"I don't want more surgery," Simmons said.

"The wound isn't healing properly, Mr. Simmons. If we don't clean it up, you'll get infected."

Simmons had diabetes, the brittle sort that was almost impossible to control. Insulin was keeping Simmons alive but periodic injections of insulin were not as good as the body's own finely tuned autoregulation. After years with the disease, advanced diabetics almost all suffered from the effects of prolonged elevations in blood glucose, the most common of which were recurrent infections, peripheral neuropathy and vascular disease. Simmons had had his first toe amputated more than ten years ago. At this point, he had only one toe remaining on his right foot and a below the knee amputation on the left. If the effort to clean up the wound failed, the next step would be to amputate the stump above the knee. A below the knee amp was preferable since a lower leg prosthesis would allow for nearly normal ambulation. If you had to take the knee as well, the patient would never have anything approaching a normal gait.

Simmons shrugged, his shoulders slumping, and turned his head away. When he answered, his voice was ragged. "Whatever you say."

Kaplan swallowed and hesitantly reached out a hand and patted Simmons on the shoulder.

Simmons, Kurtz thought, was not going to do well. They would probably get him out of the hospital this time but he would soon be back and next time it would be a piece of his right foot, or maybe the whole leg. Or maybe he would simply get the almost inevitable myocardial infarction before that happened and peacefully expire. Once they were out in the hallway, Kurtz shook his head. "It's tough," he said to Kaplan. "You do what you can but in the end it's a series of failures. Chronic diabetes is a miserable disease."

Kaplan shrugged, morose.

The next room was more cheery. The case was routine but evidently Kaplan felt that the team needed an infusion of good spirits. Ida Mae Jackson was a middle-aged lady whose umbilical hernia had been repaired the day before. Her rotund abdomen rose high up in the air, covered with white bandages, and she gave them a wide grin from her almost toothless mouth. Ida Mae–she insisted on them calling her by her given name–had been knitting a scarf for one of her many grandchildren, which she put down as they trooped in. "How are you boys doing, today?" she asked.

"Pretty good, Ida Mae," Kaplan said. "Pretty good." All of them, even Kurtz, felt themselves unwind in the face of the woman's simple good cheer. Ida Mae was originally from Alabama and she had never lost her accent. To Kurtz, from West Virginia himself, she was almost a whisper of home.

Ida Mae beamed at all of them. "That's just fine. You boys keep right on doing good work and saving lives. Each and every one of you should be mighty proud."

Chao suppressed a smile and glanced at Kaplan, who rarely needed encouragement to have a high opinion of himself. "Let me look at your incision, Ida Mae," Kaplan said. He put on a pair of sterile gloves and carefully began to peel away the bandages. "Does it hurt very much?"

"Only when I move." Ida Mae seemed to think this comment uproariously funny. She chuckled gleefully and slapped her thigh.

The wound was healing nicely. Kaplan put on a fresh bandage after inspecting it briefly. "It looks fine," he said.

"I knew it would. I'm in good hands."

They trooped out into the hall feeling better. Maybe it was cultural. A New Yorker expected to get better fast and no bullshit. You give a man what he expects, he doesn't feel that he needs to be particularly grateful. It was nice having a patient express some honest appreciation.

The next room belonged to Hector Segura, a courtly gentleman in his mid-sixties who had had half of his face blown away in an assassination attempt by a rival gang of drug dealers. Or so went the story; none of them really knew for sure. Segura had been here for several months and had undergone numerous reconstructive surgeries. For the first few weeks, there had been a twenty-four hour police guard outside his door. But evidently, the threat to Mr. Segura–or the threat that the man represented to the peace and security of the City of New York–had been re-evaluated. Or perhaps a budget cutback somewhere in the police hierarchy had resulted in a reappraisal of priorities. Whatever, the police guard had long since vanished.

"How are you, Mr. Segura?" Chao asked.

You couldn't really see the man in the bed since the sheets were pulled up almost up to his neck and the rest of him was covered with bandages. The bandages wound completely around the right side of his head and most of the left. The only thing that could be seen was one dark eye. Strange, how expressionless eyes were, Kurtz thought. People always talked about how eyes conveyed emotion. Her eyes flashed. His eyes brooded. But it wasn't the eyes, really. It was the flesh around the eyes, the way the cheeks scrunched up, the way the brow crinkled. The eye itself was just a round globe. It never changed at all. It just looked at you. And with his head covered up that way, you didn't have the faintest idea what Hector Segura was thinking.

"I am well," Segura said.

Chao nodded. "Do you have any pain?" he asked.

Segura seemed to hesitate. "No," he said at last.

When Segura had first arrived at the emergency room, the staff had given him the usual full court press but they all assumed that the man was going to die. His right eye was gone, the zygomatic arch shattered, the lower jaw hanging by a thread, the ethmoid sinus exposed and leaking cerebrospinal fluid. The base of Segura's brain could be clearly seen through the hole and blood squirted from the stumps of exposed arteries with each heartbeat. Kurtz had been on call that night and he clearly remembered the scene.

Amazingly, the old man had stabilized with fluid replacement and had suffered neither brain damage nor meningitis. Once it became apparent that he was going to live, they proceeded to rebuild his face. A new jawbone had been carved from one of his ribs, a plastic orbit had been inserted to simulate an eye socket and a muscle flap had been rotated up from Segura's chest to cover the hole. To date, he had undergone nine major operations and would probably undergo at least five more before his treatment was judged to be complete.

Chao glanced down at the chart he carried in his hands. "You're going back to surgery the day after tomorrow."

Segura nodded.

"Do you have any questions about it?"

Something that might have been a smile was apparent through the bandages. "No," Segura said. "I have been through this before."

Chao cleared his throat. "Yes," he said. "I understand." He turned back to the team and glanced at the door. They followed him outside.

"Why didn't you take off the bandages?" Kaplan asked.

"Segura has been here a long time. He knows the difference between work rounds and teaching rounds."

"So what?"

"So the man might resent being put on exhibit for your amusement."

"Amusement?" Kaplan looked incredulous. "Our education is not amusement."

Chao shrugged, evidently unwilling to argue the point. Privately, Kurtz agreed with Chao. He was about to say so when a pretty blonde nurse walked up to him. "Doctor Kurtz?"

He nodded.

"There's a phone call for you at the center desk."

He frowned down at his beeper. "Why didn't they beep me?"

The nurse shrugged. "He said to tell you it was 'Lew Barent.'"

"Barent?" Kurtz looked at Chao and the residents. "I'll see you guys later," he said.

"So then what happened?" Kurtz asked.

Barent had barely picked at his steak. He seemed depressed. "Nothing happened. We packed up and left. It was just a joke, right?" It was the day after Halloween. They were sitting in a diner near the hospital where Barent had asked Kurtz to meet him for lunch. Kurtz had heard about the party and the mutilation of the cadavers, of course. Everybody had. Kurtz didn't blame Barent for being subdued but he was a little surprised. Barent, after all, had seen plenty of dead bodies in his career, considerably more dead bodies than Kurtz had. Still, the way doctors and medical students approached them must seem a little blasé to a cop. Kurtz could still remember his own first day of medical school … the door slowly opening, the cadaver rolling out, the nervous, suppressed giggles. One of his fellow students—a former Navy flier who Kurtz would have figured for nerves of steel—had turned green and almost fainted. They did try to ease you into it, though, at least a little. That first day, the cadavers were lying on their stomachs so you didn't have to look at their faces, and all you had to do was dissect out the occipital nerve on the back of the head, which took about ten minutes. Then you could get out of there and take some time to recover. The second day was easier, and by the end of the week it was just another course, like biochemistry and embryology and genetics.

"How's Betty?" Kurtz asked.

"She's fine."

"Paul, and Denise?"

"Paul is fine. Denise is pregnant."

Kurtz fork stopped halfway to his mouth. He grinned. "Aren't you a little young to be a grandpa?"

"Fuck you," Barent said morosely.

Kurtz grinned, swallowed a french-fry and drained a glass of Coke. Then he picked up the pitcher and poured another. Barent was still working on his first glass and his food lay on the plate, barely touched.

"So what's bothering you?"

Barent gave him a sour look and toyed with his glass. "I don't know. I guess I just don't like bad jokes."

After a moment Barent sighed, raised his soda to his lips and took a long swallow. Kurtz watched him. Barent and Kurtz had gotten friendly almost a year before when Sharon Lee, an obstetrician on the staff at Easton, had been murdered, but the two men had not seen each other in over a month.

"You have privileges at Staunton, don't you?" Barent asked.

"Yes. I do most of my work at Easton but I operate at the school every couple of weeks or so."

"You know Mahoney?"

"Sure. I'm actually pretty friendly with him."

"Really?" Barent's ears pricked up. "Tell me about it."

"Not much to tell. I went to medical school here. I was a little older than most of the other students. Mahoney and I were both vets and we both liked to fish. I see him socially maybe two or three times a year."

"Anything strange about him?"

"Strange?"

"You know ..." Barent shrugged. "Suspicious. Anything that might lead you to think he might have had anything to do with carving up cadavers?"

"Hell, no. He's as straight as they come. And what possible motive could he have? He's a full professor. He's got better things to do than play idiot games."

"I suppose so." Barent put a forefinger on the wet ring that the pitcher of cola had left on the table and drew an X, which he frowned at as if it might contain some secret information. "And I know you know Nolan."

Kurtz nodded. "He was a good resident."

"Think he would have anything to do with this?"

"Nolan ..." Kurtz cocked his head to the side and considered the idea. "Nolan was always a bit of a joker, but it was his own party that got ruined. It doesn't seem likely."

"No." Barent sounded glum.

"Why don't you forget about it? Nobody got killed. Nobody even got hurt. Don't you have any real crimes to solve?"

"Yeah," Barent said. "I do. That's why the investigation's been dropped." He shrugged and grinned wanly. "Who the hell has time for baloney? It was a joke. I can take a joke, as long as the joke's not on me ..." Barent looked at him. "Want to do me a favor?"

"Yeah?" Kurtz said warily.

"You say you're friendly with Mahoney. Give him a call. Talk with him."

Kurtz stopped with his glass halfway to his lips. "What about?"

"Anything at all. Try to get a sense of him. Does he seem worried, upset, pre-occupied? Is anything on his mind, anything he feels like talking about?"

"So you do suspect him."

"No. Not exactly. I don't think it likely that a respected professor of anatomy would suddenly decide to carve up a bunch of cadavers. On the other hand, he must spend a lot of time up there. It is possible that he's noticed things that he didn't feel like telling the police."

"Things," Kurtz said.

"Sure. Have any of the students or the workers been acting strangely? Have there been any other incidents with the bodies, things that maybe he didn't want to tell us? Any disgruntled employees that might feel like playing a little joke?"

"Didn't you ask him all that?"

23

"Of course I did. He said 'No.' Maybe you could see if he tells you the same thing."

Kurtz drained his cola and put the glass down on the table. He shrugged. "If you want."

Barent pulled a folded sheet of paper out of his pocket and passed it across the table to Kurtz. "This is a list of all the people who have access to the cadavers." He grimaced faintly. "All the ones who are known to have access: the students, the faculty, the lab assistants–who are mostly older students who got good grades in the course the year before–and the dieners. We've run a cursory check on all of them. Nothing suspicious."

"Have you talked to them?"

"They've all been questioned but only a few of them by me. I've had more urgent things to do the past few days."

"Oh?"

"Yeah. There was a body floating in the East River with a bullet hole between the eyes and two more in Central Park that had been shot in the back of the head."

"That does seem more your style."

Barent shook his head sadly and took a bite out of his steak. "There are hundreds of murders a year in New York City. Who the hell has time to worry about a stupid joke?"

The look on his face belied his words. Barent was worried. On second thought, maybe pissed-off expressed it better. "Was there anything to tie the cadavers together?"

"Nothing. Two were men and two were women. They were all in their seventies, they all died from natural causes and they all came from different parts of the state."

"I'm not likely to come up with anything new," Kurtz said. "You must know that."

"Of course I know it." Barent grinned sourly. "But maybe you will."

A light shone through the opened doorway of the classroom. Outside in the corridor, the walls were lined with display cases containing an assortment of anatomical oddities, a private collection donated to the school by an embryology professor who had long since retired. There were conjoined twins floating in a glass jar, a tiny malformed cyclops, an anencephalic, the top of its head open, the wispy membranes that should have surrounded its missing brain floating delicately in clear phenol. Kurtz leaned closer to examine an infant with gastroschisis, its intestines hanging in lazy folds outside a nonexistent abdominal wall. Each jar had a small label near the bottom. This one, Kurtz noted, said *New Orleans, 1938*. A long time to be sitting in a jar on a shelf. Kurtz shook his head sadly. Nowadays, the infant could probably have been saved. Not in 1938.

The school tended to discourage casual visitors from coming up here but as a faculty member Kurtz had every right to go where he pleased. Not that he really expected to find anything resembling a clue. He just wanted to get a sense of the place before he talked to Mahoney.

He sniffed and wrinkled his nose. The pungent tang of formalin was just as he remembered it. After a few days of working up here, the students barely noticed the smell but all the freshmen sat together in the cafeteria and people out on the streets often gave them odd looks and then edged away. The odor tended to cling to ones' clothes.

There was a bank of elevators at one end of the hallway and a single door leading to a flight of stairs in the middle of the corridor. The door was a fire exit and was never locked. The doors to the classrooms were also kept open. Medical students tended to study at odd hours (like constantly) and it was not unusual to find one or two of them up here at any hour of the night. Which made it all the more curious that nobody had noticed anything strange going on when the cadavers had been mutilated.

He looked inside the classroom where it had taken place. The students assigned to the room had already been issued new bodies. The lights were on but the room was empty.

Kurtz walked down the hall. Only one classroom, near the end of the corridor, was occupied. A cadaver lay on its aluminum table and a young woman with her hair tied back stood in front of it. She was wearing a canvas apron, long rubber gloves and an intent look on her face, obviously a medical student. Her arms were buried up to the elbow in the cadaver's abdomen. The cadaver had been a woman … an old woman. Gray, furrowed flesh hung loosely off the bones. The eyes were closed, the head shaved. It was still early November. In the next few weeks, after they finished the contents of the abdomen, they would crack the chest and dissect out the heart and lungs. They would go up and split the skull, learning the anatomy of the spinal cord, the cranial nerves, the musculature of the face, the convolutions of the sinuses and the internal structure of the eyes and the brain. By the time the course ended in late May or June, there wouldn't be much left of the cadavers except a few pieces of bone and some unrecognizable bits of flesh.

The young woman was leaning over the cadaver, working intently. She hadn't noticed Kurtz and he saw no reason to disturb her. He padded softly away from the open doorway, glad to be leaving.

Chapter 4

Halloween was even busier for Kurtz than it was for Barent. You could always depend on a good number of stabbings, gun-shot wounds and maliciously stupid accidents. At ten o'clock Friday morning, he was operating on a young man who had inadvertently swallowed a sewing needle. The needle had been inserted in an apple that the patient's son had picked up trick-or-treating. Kurtz managed to retrieve the needle with a rigid endoscope before it perforated the esophagus. After that he had a skin graft on a teenage girl who had been splashed with lye dropped from the top of a building, and after that, a routine gallbladder.

He got out of surgery at three in the afternoon, hungry, and headed for home, an apartment in mid-town that overlooked the East River. When he opened the door, the first thing he saw was Lenore, lying on the couch with a book in her lap. She was wearing a flaming orange jumpsuit and had big gold rings hanging from her ears. She smiled at him and he felt something flutter in his abdomen. "You're home early," she said.

"I finished in the OR and I didn't have any patients to see. You want to get something to eat?"

She put down her book and glanced at the clock on the wall. "It's only three-thirty."

"I was busy in surgery. I didn't get a chance to eat lunch."

She looked thoughtful. "We're supposed to be at the club by six."

"I know. That's plenty of time for an early dinner."

"I feel like I'm betraying my cultural heritage," Lenore said, the expression on her face hovering between amused and resigned. "Jews have never regarded ritualized combat as a respectable human activity."

"They don't know what they're missing," Kurtz said.

Lenore smiled. "Then again, my ancestors didn't believe in boffing the goyim, either."

"Exactly."

He held out his hand. She took it and he pulled her to her feet. She pressed herself against him and he kissed her. "Yum," he said.

She laughed and pushed him away. "We don't want to be late, remember?"

"Maybe a little late. It's fashionable to be a little late."

"You're not serious. I read in a magazine the other day that seventy per-cent of American males get more turned on by violence than by sex. You can't possibly be in the mood."

"Maybe not," Kurtz said. "But now that you mention it, sex and violence together would really do it for me."

She sniffed. "Forget it."

"Anyway," Kurtz went on, "I read in a magazine the other day that seventy per-cent of American women get more turned on by chocolate than by sex."

"Of course we do," Lenore said. "What's so strange about that?"

"So let's bring along a box of chocolates and do it while we watch the show."

"I think," Lenore said, "that you'd better wait until later."

He gave an exaggerated sigh. "Life is full of little compromises."

The temperature was in the sixties, high for this time of year. The leaves were mostly yellow and the remainder were already brown and falling from the trees. There was no breeze at all and the air was moist with a recent rain. They strolled down the street, holding hands, and decided on a little Italian place. They shared a salad and an order of linguine with clam sauce, then caught a cab.

David Chao was sitting in the bleachers, accompanied by a young man and woman, both Asian, whom Kurtz did not recognize. The woman was gorgeous, with golden skin, straight black hair down to her waist and a heart-shaped face. The man bore Chao a strong resemblance. Kurtz and Lenore walked over and Chao rose to his feet. "Richard Kurtz, Lenore Brinkman … these are my cousins, Lily and Chris Chang."

"Pleased to meet you," Chris Chang said. Lily nodded her head and smiled.

"I understand that this is your first tournament?" Chao said to Lenore.

Lenore glanced at Kurtz. "Yes."

Chao was wearing a white pullover top, loose white pants and a black belt. There was a round piece of cloth with the image of a dragon sewn onto the left side of his chest. The bleachers were set up on three sides of a small gymnasium, and were just beginning to fill. Most of the people were dressed in street clothes but perhaps a third were wearing uniforms similar to Chao's. The floor below the bleachers was entirely covered in thick, green rubber padding, upon which a yellow ring was painted. Against the fourth wall stood a table, a time clock and a row of folding chairs where the judges would sit.

Kurtz and Lenore sat down next to Chao and waited. A few minutes later, a young Chinese man wearing rubber gloves, protective headgear, a black belt and a black, sleeveless uniform came in from a side door, walked onto the ring and bounced a few times on the balls of his feet. He was tall for an Asian, well over six feet. He threw a rapid series of punches at the air, bobbing his head, and then folded his arms and stood waiting. A few seconds later another man came in through the same door. This man was white and blonde and wore a white karate outfit, also with a black belt, rubber gloves and headgear. He was even bigger than the Chinese. A referee, a middle-aged black man in a gray robe, inspected each man's gloves and headgear. Both combatants faced each other and bowed. The referee raised his hand, then lowered it abruptly. The blonde man immediately spun into a kick. His opponent leaped back and the blonde's foot swept past his head. As he spun, the blonde stepped below his guard and connected to his side with a fist. The Asian grunted.

"Point," the referee said.

The two men bowed. The referee again held up his arm and dropped it. The blonde man raised both arms above his head and crouched, balanced on one foot.

"Who does he think he is?" Lenore whispered, "the Karate Kid."

"Shh," Kurtz said.

The Asian went in with a front kick to the chest. The blonde moved deftly to the side, trapped his opponent's leg against his upraised knee and connected with a straight punch to the chest.

"Point," the referee said.

"The white guy looks better," Lenore said.

Kurtz nodded. "The Chinese kid's name is Billy Wu. He's pretty good but the blonde is heavyweight champion of his club. His name's Tom Banner. He thinks he's the greatest thing since Bruce Lee. There's talk he may turn pro."

"He is going to turn pro," Chris Chang said. "That's why I'm here."

Chang's eyes were intent, following the action. Kurtz looked at him quizzically.

"Chris is a promoter," David said. "Also an accountant."

Chris grinned. "I started out as an accountant but I gave it up a couple of years ago. There's a lot more money in what I do now."

Billy Wu managed to score a point with a punch to the head but Tom Banner soon ended the bout with a sweeping kick that knocked Wu's feet out from under him. Banner raised both arms over his head, jumped up and down twice and yelled, "Yes!" before giving a perfunctory bow to his defeated opponent. Both men returned to their seats in the bleachers, Wu looking disgusted with himself, Banner smiling triumphantly.

"See what I mean?" Kurtz said. "The guy's a hot-dog."

"But he's a good hot-dog," Chris Chang said. He looked pleased with himself. "I've been talking to him about a contract. It's just about sewed up."

"What do you think?" Chao asked Lenore.

"Too much testosterone for my taste," Lenore said.

Kurtz sniffed and Chao grinned at Lenore, then rose to his feet. "I'm next," he said.

They wished him luck and he descended to the mat. His opponent was a red-headed young man with a yin-yang patch on his chest. Chao and the redhead both donned gloves and headsets at the scorer's table and then walked to opposite ends of the ring. They bowed. The referee held up his arm and dropped it. Chao immediately spun and kicked. His opponent leaned back and Chao's foot swept past his chin. As Chao completed his turn, the redhead moved in and hit him in the ribs with the flat of his palm. Chao grunted.

"Do you know the other guy?" Lenore whispered.

"Jim Salley. He's an aerobics instructor when he isn't practicing his scissor kicks."

"He looks good."

"He is good but I think David is better."

"He ought to be," Chris Chang said with a smile. "He's been taking lessons since he was five. It's too bad David is so into doctoring. I could make him rich if he wanted to fight professionally."

Salley gave Chao a wolfish smile from across the ring. The two men bowed and the referee dropped his arm.

Chao fell to the floor and spun. Salley saw it coming and tried to jump out of the way but he was too late and Chao's kick sent him flat on his back.

"Point," the referee said.

They faced each other again, Salley grinning, trying to give the impression that the takedown was no big deal.

They bowed. Salley spun, jumped and came in. Chao barely moved and Salley's foot went past his head. Chao reached out, tapped Salley on the thigh, just enough to disturb his balance, and connected with an elbow to Salley's abdomen.

"Point," the referee said.

Salley looked grim. They bowed. The referee's hand came down. Salley was more careful this time. He circled slowly to his left, his hands moving in a pattern that was not exactly Taekwondo. It took Kurtz, watching, a moment to figure it out. Pakua, he thought … an unusual style, a little like Wing Chun or Tai-Chi, sometimes likened to a lady dancing. Pakua was an excellent style for defense, not so good for attack. Kurtz had seen it demonstrated a couple of times but he knew of no school in the city that taught it.

Chao stood still as Salley circled, his arms twining in and out. The crowd grew silent. A soft smile crept across Salley's face as he danced slowly across the ring. His attention seemed inward, focused more on the slow, snakelike movements of his arms as they circled around his body than on Chao. He moved left, then changed direction and danced to the right.

Chao stepped in, jabbed. Salley's arms seemed barely to move but Chao's punch was deflected to the side. Chao tried again with the same result.

A shield, Kurtz thought. The arms and the hands become a shield. The weakness of the technique was that it was passive. Kurtz whispered to Lenore, "If he's smart, he'll let Salley come to him."

Evidently, Chao had reached the same conclusion. He stood still, his arms raised in front of his chest as Salley circled closer.

Now. Kurtz leaned forward. Absently, he noticed Lily smiling serenely, as if she had no doubt of the outcome. Chris Chang's face was intent.

Salley's eyes became momentarily focused. His arms moved, blurring.

Chao stepped into Salley's guard, blocking, and deflected the blow down toward his feet, then connected with his elbow to Salley's ribs.

"Point and match," the referee said.

Salley sighed, disappointment evident in his face. The two men bowed and returned to their seats.

"Nice job," Kurtz said.

"What was that," Chao asked. "Wing Chun?"

"I think it was Pakua."

Chao rubbed at the back of his neck and grimaced. "I've heard of it. I've never seen it."

Lenore was looking at Chao as if he were a specimen of some alien race. "That was absolutely amazing."

Chao shrugged. "Thanks."

Lenore turned to Chris Chang. "Do you fight, too?"

"A little," Chris said, and shrugged. "I'm not as good as David. My interest is mainly in arranging the bouts."

"And I know you do," Lenore said to Kurtz.

"Not exactly," Kurtz said. "Not anymore. I just do it for the workout. I stopped competing a few years ago."

"How come?"

"I found that I didn't like getting my face beat in."

Chao snorted. "Richard used to be club champion in the heavyweight division."

Chris Chang looked at Kurtz and squinted one eye. "Sure," he said. "Kurtz … I've heard of you."

Lenore looked at Kurtz as if he were a specimen under a microscope. "You're kidding."

Kurtz shrugged. "I was young and impetuous."

"I see. Not like now."

Kurtz looked at Chao. "You ever hear of Jonathon Dark?"

"Sure. He's terrific."

"He's a jackass," Kurtz said.

Chris Chang shrugged. "A lot of that in this business."

"What are you talking about?" Lenore asked.

"One time, about eight years ago, I was at a match. This guy Dark was in the audience. He was just about to turn pro and he thought he was hot stuff. He was sitting in the bleachers, right under a *No Smoking* sign, and he was smoking, which was pretty unusual for an athlete even back then. One of the kids in my class asked him to put it out. Dark gave him a toothy grin and said, 'Why don't you come on up here and make me?'

"The kid knew who Dark was and he knew when he was out of his league. So he came over to me and told me about it."

"Don't tell me," said Lenore. "You made him put it out? Right?"

"Wrong." Kurtz grinned. "I figured he was out of my league, too. I went and told Master Park."

"Uh-oh," Chao said.

Lenore looked back and forth between Kurtz and Chao. "Master Park?"

"Master Park was the *Sensai*. He retired a few years ago. Korean. He was a little guy with a thick accent and a bald head but they don't come any tougher. He didn't look particularly dangerous but you had to be nuts to mess with him. He comes over to this character Dark and says, 'Sign say no-smoking. Please to put cigarette out.'

"I guess Dark didn't recognize him. Or maybe he did and figured he was even tougher than Master Park. He grins at him and says, 'You gonna make me?'

"Master Park said, 'Rule say no-smoking. Obey rule.'"

"So Dark stretches his arms above his head, looks like he's thinking it over, smiles, and blows a cloud of smoke in Master Park's face."

Chao shook his head sorrowfully. "I bet that wasn't smart," he said.

"No. It wasn't. Master Park knocked out four of his front teeth."

"Are you serious?" Lenore asked.

"Absolutely. Master Park must have been pretty pissed off. He did it with a head butt. Suddenly Dark is unconscious on the floor, there's blood all over the place and one of Dark's upper incisors is sticking out of Master Park's forehead."

"Yecch," Lenore said.

"You bet. They take Dark back into a dressing room and a few minutes later he starts to wake up but he's disoriented. He doesn't know where he is but he does know he's been in a fight. He starts thrashing around, cursing and breaking the furniture. So somebody comes and tells Master Park and by this time, he's got no patience left at all for Jonathon Dark. He comes into the dressing room, blood is running down both of their faces, and he starts to pound the guy's head against the floor until finally Dark realizes that he's beat and decides to stop fighting."

"I see," Lenore said. "And this is the experience that led to your decision to stop competing?"

"Hell, no," Kurtz said. "I competed for about three years after that. I'm just giving you an example."

"That's a very interesting story," Lily said.

Chao and Kurtz were both smiling. Lenore looked back and forth between them and said, "I think it's one of the most ridiculous stories I have ever heard in my life."

Kurtz smiled back at her. "Well, I thought so, too. The man should never have used a head butt. A *sensai* is supposed to have more dignity than that."

"I wasn't talking about the head butt and you know it."

"I suppose," Kurtz said. He smiled wider. "But you probably shouldn't try to figure it out. It's one of those *guy* things."

Lenore sniffed. "Maybe Mother was right."

"About what?"

"When she told me that all men were alike."

"Of course she was," Kurtz said.

Chapter 5

"I was taking my anatomy lab final and I could tell I was kicking ass. Even when I was a freshman I knew I was heading for surgery and I really wanted an A in anatomy."

Kaplan had great hands but he talked too much and his favorite word was *I*. Kurtz held the retractors and said nothing as Kaplan cut the branch of the vagus nerve that led to the stomach, carefully over sewed the ulcer and began to close.

Patel had grown up in Bangalore and gone to Medical School in New Delhi, but despite any cultural differences, he seemed to know exactly how to deal with Kaplan. He grinned at Kurtz from under his mask. Chao shook his head.

"Yes?" Patel prompted. "What happened then?"

Kaplan had his eyes fixed on the patient's abdomen and didn't notice Patel's smile or Chao's amused disdain. "They had specimens set up along the whole hallway, one to a hundred. You went from one specimen to the next, trying to identify each structure. I was really into it. I had almost reached the end and I knew I was doing great. There had only been one or two things that I wasn't sure about–there was half a brain with a pin in it and I wasn't quite certain whether the pin was in the globus pallidus or the putamen and there was a dissected pelvis with a tag on a ligament that could've been either the lacunar or the pectineal, but other than that I knew I'd been perfect. Anyway, I get almost to the end and there's this head sitting on a tray with a little yellow thing dissected out under the jaw and I look at it and I think immediately, sublingual nerve–alright!"

"Put your sutures a little closer together," Kurtz said.

Kaplan gave him a wounded look. Kurtz smiled.

"Anyway," Kaplan went on, "I came out of the test feeling great. I knew I had aced it."

He shook his head and grinned in wonderment. "It wasn't until about an hour later that I suddenly realized, Jesus Christ, that was a head sitting there on that tray."

"So?" Patel said.

"What do you mean, so?"

Patel winked at Chao and said, "I don't get it."

"I mean, it was a *head*–a whole human head just sitting on the tray!"

"You already said that. What about it?"

"But don't you think that's gross?"

"Oh," Patel said. He shrugged. "I guess so." He shrugged again.

Kurtz sighed. After this case, he had half dozen patients to see in the office. Kurtz had made an appointment to drop in on Rod Mahoney later in the evening. Barent had briefed him as well as he was able but none of it was news to Kurtz. "Mahoney is fifty-five years old. Undergraduate at University of Illinois, Masters and Ph.D in anatomy from Loyola. He's been at Staunton for six years. Before that, he was at University of Pennsylvania. Staunton apparently offered him more money and his own lab and he was promoted to Full Professor three years ago. Mahoney served one tour of duty in Vietnam–1970 to 1972. He's been married for twenty years to the former Claire O'Brien, a paralegal he met in graduate school. They have two children, Kevin and Clarissa, both of them in college."

Barent squinted at the paper. "A speeding ticket in 1987. No other criminal record."

"Not much to go on," Kurtz said.

"Nope."

Roderick Mahoney lived with his wife in a small split-level in Brooklyn, not far from Prospect Park. The neighborhood had once cherished ambitions of becoming a second Soho or Tribeca, full of art galleries and coffee houses and the yuppies who frequented them, but ambition had succumbed to the sad reality that there were only so many coffeehouses, art galleries and yuppies to go around, and most of these preferred to be in Manhattan. The neighborhood was still peacefully middle-class, but the aborted Renaissance had long since vanished, and the run-down communities to the east were steadily encroaching.

Kurtz arrived at Mahoney's house soon after dark and parked his 2001 Toyota Camry on the driveway next to the front yard. The yard was tiny, barely more than twenty square feet of short grass bounded by a white, wooden fence, more of a trellis to support the rose bushes of which Mahoney's wife was so fond than a serious attempt to keep out the neighbors. Kurtz walked across the lawn and up to the front door and knocked. A woman with large green eyes, graying blonde hair and a thin figure answered the door. She smiled when she saw Kurtz. "Richard," she said. "How are you? Come right in."

"Hello, Claire," Kurtz said. The living room was just as Kurtz remembered it. The furniture was Early American, all original pieces, plain but very expensive. A hand-woven rug covered the floor. A fire was burning in the hearth.

Kurtz sat down in a rocking chair and stretched his legs.

"And how is Lenore?"

Kurtz and Lenore had gone out to dinner twice with the Mahoney's. Claire Mahoney had been an Art History major in college and worked part-time in a gallery downtown. Lenore worked as a graphic artist and in her spare time sculpted bronze figurines, mostly of animals. Claire and Lenore had a lot to talk about.

"She's fine," he said.

Claire smiled at him. "I hear a rumor you're engaged."

Kurtz supposed you could call it that but he wasn't quite willing to concede the point, not in public. "Almost," he said. "Not quite."

"Richard," a voice said. Rod Mahoney stood by the entrance to the room. He looked pretty much the same as Kurtz remembered him, maybe a trifle thinner. Kurtz rose to his feet and they shook hands.

"I'll leave you two alone so you can talk," Claire said. "We should get together again soon."

"That would be nice."

Claire left the room and Mahoney sat down in a chair across a low wooden table from Kurtz. "Chess?" Mahoney asked. He was already opening a chessboard and setting up the pieces.

Chess was Mahoney's great pre-occupation, that and the war in Vietnam. Mahoney talked about Vietnam rarely and only when he had a drink in his hand and only to his friends; such conversations tended to be draining for both Mahoney and his listeners. Most of Mahoney's platoon had been wiped out, not in a major offensive but one by one, in a series of jungle incidents. One had had his legs blown off by a land mine. One had been shot in the back of his head by a sniper. Two had died in a surprise assault while walking down a jungle trail. One had fallen into a concealed pit and been impaled on wooden stakes. Another had been stabbed to death in the middle of a supposedly friendly village by a twelve-year old boy. Mahoney himself had been hit in the chest by shrapnel, spent three months recovering and was, for a brief time, not expected to survive.

"Chess?" Kurtz said with a resigned grin. "Sure."

The pieces were made of some sort of pulverized stone, mixed with epoxy and pressed in a mold. Both the white and the black pieces were scattered with glittering flecks of gold, blue, red and green. "It's a cheap thing we brought back from a vacation in Central America. Probably made in Taiwan." Mahoney looked at Kurtz. "You want white or black?"

Kurtz shrugged.

"Take white," Mahoney said. "I'm feeling generous."

Kurtz knew how the pieces moved but that was about it. Mahoney won the first two games in fifteen minutes each, then shook his head. "You're not any better than you used to be."

"That's true," Kurtz said.

Mahoney frowned down at the chessboard. "When I was a kid I wanted to be the next Bobby Fischer. Man, the way he beat Spassky, it galvanized the nation. Us against the Bear. Individuality and Free Enterprise versus the godless specter of Communism. Of course, the godless specter produced every world champion for the last hundred years except for Fischer, but so what? For once, we were beating them at their own game. A made for TV event if there ever was one, except for the fact that chess is basically a bore to watch. Not a lot of action in chess. But they actually made it exciting. Remember Shelby Lyman? Nobody ever heard of the guy before or since, but what a commentator! Jesus, he fairly vibrated over every move. Even if you didn't understand the implications yourself, he could make you believe you were inside the players' heads. Of course, after the match was over, chess retreated back into its usual obscurity."

Kurtz had heard this litany before. "You should have continued playing," he said. "You really love the game."

Mahoney smiled wistfully. "Not much money in chess. Of course, Kasparov is a millionaire but he's pretty much the only one."

"Even so, a man has to follow his star."

"Really?" Mahoney looked thoughtful, frowning down at the board. "Do you think so? And what if a man's star leads him off the end of a cliff?"

"Then I guess you could say he made a mistake."

"Exactly." Mahoney shook his head and gave a sad sigh. "Chess is no way to make a living and if you don't devote pretty much all of your time to the game, you'll never get good enough to go anywhere with it. It's funny, when I was a kid, I used to think that sometime around your teenage years, you would somehow receive the knowledge of what you were meant to do or be in life. I mean it. I actually thought it was just a part of growing up, like puberty, that you would wake up one day and realize, I'm going to be a doctor, or a lawyer, or a cop, and the knowledge would be obvious and inevitable and absolutely right. I can't tell you how disappointed I was to realize that it didn't work that way, that you have to decide these things for yourself."

"Where I grew up," Kurtz said, "it was just naturally assumed that you were going to do whatever it was that your father did."

"A different version of the same thing. Destiny. But destiny doesn't exist."

Over two thousand years ago, Heraclitus had written that character was destiny. You were what you were and you could never, ever escape it. Your choices were programmed into your genes, the concept of free will, an illusion. "I don't know," Kurtz said.

"You know it doesn't." Mahoney shook his head sadly. "But it wasn't just jobs and career. How about women? The idea that there somehow exists a 'Miss Right' for every man and a 'Mr. Right' for every woman is just a variation on the same theme. This is a myth that's engrained in American culture and it's total baloney. By the time a man settles down, he's probably met at least a dozen women who he could have married if circumstances had been different.

"I'm fifty-five years old," Mahoney said. "I think about that sometimes. When I was young, I was just living my life. You wake up in the morning, you do whatever it is that you do, you go to sleep. One day turns into another. Now, I look back and I can hardly believe it. How did I wind up here?"

Kurtz nodded. "I understand."

"All those choices," Mahoney said. "Every day there are choices. It's not just jobs and careers and women, either. It's everything. Why didn't I become a fighter pilot? Why didn't I climb Mount Everest?" Mahoney shook his head. "Ah, well …"

Kurtz suddenly remembered Barent, and the fact that he had an ulterior motive here. "Tell me," Kurtz said. "Are you speaking theoretically, or in particular?"

"What do you mean?"

"Is something going on that I'm not aware of? Are you suddenly dissatisfied with your work? Is Claire getting on your nerves?"

Mahoney grinned wanly. "One's wife always gets on one's nerves. It's part of their job." He shook his head. "No. I am perfectly satisfied with my wife, and I still like my job, despite the fact that it doesn't pay as much as I would prefer. I'm just …" Mahoney shrugged and frowned down at the chessboard. "I don't know."

"Yeah." Kurtz nodded his head. "I guess nobody else knows either." He shrugged. "I don't know what to tell you. You just have to muddle through."

"Such wisdom," Mahoney said. "I'll try to keep it in mind." He glanced down at the board. "Another game?"

"Sure," Kurtz said.

Chapter 6

As had become all too usual since his daughter's wedding, Barent felt a lot like a second thumb, definitely superfluous if not actively in the way. Paul, he was sourly gratified to note, seemed to feel exactly the same as Barent himself. Paul was sitting at the head of the table, picking at his roast beef, while Betty, Denise and Gloria Janus, Paul's mother, chatted excitedly, their heads so close together that the men could barely hear a word of what they were saying.

Bill Janus, Paul's father, ate his food with a fond smile on his face, obviously not bothered by this systematic exclusion. Every once in a while he glanced at his son and his smile grew wider. "More roast beef?" he asked.

"No," Paul said. "Thanks."

"Lew?"

Barent quickly swallowed. "Uh, yes," he said. "Please."

Bill Janus passed him the tray. "Potatoes?"

"Sure."

"First grandkid, isn't it?" Janus said.

"Yeah," Barent answered. "How did you know?"

"You got that look. Like you don't exactly know where you fit in and you don't like it."

Barent looked over at the women, still excitedly buzzing, and grudgingly smiled. He had had pretty much the same feeling last year during Denise and Paul's wedding, when his sole appointed role was to sign the checks and stand around in a tuxedo, looking proud. This time, he was even more peripheral. "You're right," he said.

"It's our third. Paul's sister had twins just last year. Jesus, you'd of thought it was the second coming, the way they carried on."

Barent cast a bewildered glance at the women.

"Yeah," Bill Janus said. "Men don't understand these things. It's one of the sacred mysteries. Don't let it worry you. It always happens."

"I'm only the father," Paul said. "Don't mind me."

"For the next eight months, you're part of the furniture. Sit back, smile and do what you're told. Just be glad they're all happy."

"Oh, boy," Paul muttered.

Was it like this when his own kids were born?

Betty's mother and sister had seemed to be around all the time. Now that he thought about it, the only thing he could really recall about Betty's first pregnancy was one time when Betty had gotten a craving for lobster. Barent hated lobsters. He couldn't look the ugly things in the face. Even dead (especially dead) on the plate, they seemed to be leering at him, daring him to eat them. Also he resented the toothy grin on the fish store owner's face every time Barent showed up. The guy thought he had found a real mark and there was nothing for Barent to do but (as Bill Janus had just said) smile. Luckily it had only lasted a few days and after that for about a month all Betty had wanted was Wendy's hamburgers. Not Burger King. Not McDonald's. It had to be Wendy's. At least they were cheap.

The phone rang and Paul immediately rose to his feet and went into the kitchen to answer it. He came out a moment later and said, "It's for you, Lew."

Barent went into the kitchen with a sinking feeling. He was off duty and Harry Moran was the only one who knew where he had planned to be tonight. He picked up the phone and listened, grunting softly at the appropriate places. "Alright," he finally said. "I'll meet you there. A half hour."

He put the phone back down with a sigh and looked back into the dining room. He had a sudden burst of fondness for all of them, even his wimpy son-on-law. They were a rock of stability in an uncertain world. They were his world, come to think of it.

Sadly, he shook his head and picked up the phone again to call Richard Kurtz.

The apartment was quiet when Kurtz arrived home and he thought at first that Lenore had gone out. Then he went into the kitchen and immediately saw the two stuffed lobsters and a sheet of paper lying on the counter with writing on it. The note read, "I'm in the bathtub. Want to join me?"

Kurtz would.

Lenore's golden hair was pinned on top of her head so it wouldn't get wet. The sunken tub was otherwise full of bubbles up to her chin.

"Hi," she said. A bubbly hand rose up and a bubbly finger beckoned. She grinned slowly. Kurtz grinned back. He couldn't help himself. A year ago, Kurtz had been full of angst that he had difficulty defining, even to himself. Lenore had taken care of that.

He undressed while Lenore watched with a little smile on her lips. He tested the water with a toe. "Jesus, that's hot."

"Too hot?"

He eased himself in and slid down facing her. "I'll manage."

"I'll just bet you will."

He felt something barely perceptible along the soles of his feet and he shuddered deliciously.

"Is my big surgeon ticklish?"

"Stop that," he gasped.

"Are you sure?"

Her fingers began to creep up along his leg. "Are you very sure?" He tried to grab her hand but it skittered out of reach.

"Two can play that game," he said.

He reached for her and she gasped and suddenly they were side-by-side in the tub. "Would you believe that I never made love in a tub before I met you?" Lenore whispered.

"Your education was neglected," he said. He kissed her and she kissed him back hard.

"Let me get on top. Otherwise you'll drown me."

Kurtz had no objections and within seconds they were moving back and forth together. Lenore had an intent look on her face and her eyes were closed, fiercely concentrating. Finally, she gave a little cry and stopped moving and her eyes peeped open. She smiled lazily. "How was that?"

"Pretty good," he said. He was gasping for air. "But I think we can do better."

"Always room for improvement." She breathed deeply. "Give me a minute to catch my breath."

He wrapped his arms around her and held her tightly in the hot water. "Don't take too long."

She snuggled up to his side, grinned at him mischievously and said, "Did I mention that we're going to my parents' for Chanukah?"

He looked at her. She smiled. "Oy, gevalt," he said.

She smiled wider. "Now, how shall we do it this time?" She looked thoughtful. "Maybe from behind."

Kurtz loved lobster. Lenore had picked up two big ones, already stuffed with bread crumbs and crab meat. She put them under the broiler while Kurtz dried his hair. Life was good, Kurtz thought. Life was in fact pretty damn terrific. He and Lenore had been together for nearly a year. They hadn't officially moved in together. She still kept her little apartment on the Upper East Side but she spent most of her time here. He thought about that as he got dressed. Why hadn't they set a date yet?

They talked about it now and then but there was a tiny core of reluctance at the center of Kurtz' soul, a reluctance that Lenore seemed, frankly, to share. Maybe it was because both of them had been burned before. It was not that Kurtz had any doubt about his feelings for Lenore. He was crazy about her. What it was, he supposed, was that the present was so good. Close to perfect, in fact.

The lobsters were sweet, the wine lightly chilled. There were French Fries and coleslaw on the side and a chocolate mousse for dessert. They sat around the table in silk bathrobes and stuffed themselves. Every once in a while Lenore's robe slipped open to reveal the tops of her quivering breasts and once a pink nipple peeped out. Kurtz felt like a king. "Where did you get all this?" he asked.

"I picked up the lobsters from the fish store around the block. The mousse is from Balducci's."

"It's great."

"And easy. Don't forget easy."

New York was an easy place to live if you had money. Kurtz had been poor for most of his life and he hated extravagance. On the other hand, he liked to live well.

"How did you pay for it?"

"I put it on your credit card."

"Good."

Kurtz could afford it. She couldn't, at least not very often. That was the deal. For the time they were together, Lenore chipped in what she could afford and Kurtz took care of the rest.

They were half way through dessert when the phone rang. Kurtz looked at it and groaned.

"You're not on call, are you?" Lenore asked.

"No."

"Then let it ring."

"I can't."

Surgeons didn't ignore phone calls. In the end, it was irrelevant whether you were on call or not. Maybe a plane had gone down at Kennedy. Maybe a drug deal had turned into a riot. You never knew when you might be needed and if you were needed, you had to go in.

He rose to his feet and put the receiver to his ear. "Hello?"

He listened for a few moments, then his breath hissed in through his teeth and he felt himself nodding. "Alright," he said. "I understand. I'll be there."

He hung up the phone, dazed, the rich dinner sitting suddenly like a leaden weight in his stomach.

"What's up?" Lenore asked.

"I have to go."

He shuddered, feeling a sudden anger so intense that his voice trembled. "That was Lew Barent. It's about Rod Mahoney. He's been murdered. Barent says he's been ripped to pieces."

Chapter 7

The little street where the Mahoneys lived was filled with police cars and curious spectators. Kurtz parked his car down the block, then worked his way through the mob and up to the barrier set up around the driveway, where a beefy patrolman with short gray hair stood guard on the other side of the yellow crime scene tape.

"My name's Richard Kurtz. Detective Barent asked me to come by."

The patrolman gave Kurtz a non-committal look, glanced down at a clipboard and then back to Kurtz, as if wondering what the brass could be thinking. "Come on in," he said.

Flashbulbs went off in his face as Kurtz walked up to the house. Great. His picture would be in all the papers by morning. Half his patients would instantly assume he was a murderer.

The door was unlocked and Kurtz walked inside. Claire Mahoney sat in the tiny living room, flanked by two women in police uniforms. She clutched a white handkerchief in her fist and rocked slowly back and forth, tears leaking down her face. Kurtz hesitated. One of the policewomen caught his eye. She gave a tiny shake of her head. Kurtz nodded reluctantly and walked on to the back of the house. Barent was leaning against the wall in the hallway outside the study, staring off into space. He barely smiled when he saw Kurtz. "Glad you could come."

"What happened?"

"Easier to show you."

He opened the study door.

Blood covered the walls. A cluster of severed arms and legs were tangled together under the window. Mahoney's headless torso sat propped upright in a chair, clothed in a black jacket, white shirt and bowtie, the shirt and jacket stained with blotches of red. The head sat all alone in the center of the desk, facing the doorway like a gruesome mask. Mahoney's penis had been severed and stuffed in his mouth. He had a very long penis. It dangled down his chin, the head sitting on the desk and pointing at the door like an obscene tongue. Mahoney's sightless eyes seemed at first to be eerily wide open. Then Kurtz noticed that the eyelids had been removed. They were sitting on the desk next to Mahoney's head, two little white

46

strips of flesh fringed with black lashes. Bloody stripes had been painted on both cheeks.

"Jesus," Kurtz whispered.

Barent silently nodded. After a moment, he said, "The wife discovered it. Evidently, she screamed, then had enough presence of mind to close the door and dial 911."

Kurtz nodded. He couldn't take his eyes off Mahoney's head.

"Remind you of anything?" Barent asked.

"Of course. The Halloween party."

Barent nodded in doleful satisfaction.

Three men in shirts, ties and long black aprons came up to Barent from the hallway. "Can we start in now?" one of them asked.

"Yeah," Barent said. He looked at Kurtz. "I was just waiting for you to show up. I wanted you to see it."

"Why?" Kurtz asked.

Barent gave a wan grin. "I'm not exactly sure. I suppose I figured you might have a few ideas."

"Well, I don't."

Barent sighed and gave a slow shake of his head. "Neither do I, not offhand. Or rather, I have plenty of ideas but none of them necessarily tie together." He shrugged. "Then again, it's early and you got to start somewhere. Are you in or out?"

Kurtz looked back at the body parts scattered about the room. Rod Mahoney had been his friend. "I'm in," Kurtz said.

Barent nodded. "I thought you would be."

"Every once in a while," Barent said, "you get a crime like this, one where the victim is not only murdered but mutilated, and it turns out that the motive was to send some sort of a message. Some of the drug cartels are big on that. But it's rare. Almost always, you get a crime like this, it's personal."

"I remember you telling me once that most crimes are committed by friends or relatives of the victim."

They were sitting in a small bar a few blocks away from the scene of the murder. A pitcher of beer sat on the table between them. Both men had a full glass but neither had touched it. Kurtz felt frankly nauseous. The lobster and the wine he had drunk earlier were churning in his stomach.

"You don't look so good," Barent said.

"I don't feel so good."

Barent frowned and looked away. He seemed to have difficulty looking Kurtz in the eye. "Maybe I should have kept you out of it."

"No. It's alright. Believe me."

"I hope so. Your young lady will probably not be pleased."

"She'll manage. Lenore is tough."

Kurtz smiled fleetingly, then touched his lips to the edge of the glass and grimaced.

Barent said, "Sometimes the motive is so personal and idiosyncratic that it has little or nothing to do with the actual victim. The violence with which the crime was committed indicates violent emotion but sometimes that doesn't tell you anything useful because the emotion is expressed randomly rather than focused on a particular individual."

"You mean the guy who did it is crazy."

"Yeah. Sometimes you find a motive that makes sense, or at least a sort of sense: the victim stole his girl, or he got a job that the killer wanted, or he robbed him of some money. Sometimes it makes less sense but at least there's a discernible relationship: he beat him in a spelling contest back in Third Grade, maybe. But sometimes it makes no sense at all. Sometimes it's just crazy. And sometimes the victim has no relationship at all to the criminal. Sometimes the victim is just a random target.

"Then again, maybe he's crazy like a fox. At this stage, all the speculation is bullshit. We just don't know yet."

Bullshit or not, Kurtz was determined to speculate. It gave at least the illusion of doing something to solve the crime. Fleetingly, Kurtz thought of what his medical colleagues would have said if they could have seen him here. He was a surgeon, a respected practitioner of the medical arts. What business did he have getting involved in a murder (another murder)?

The fact was, however, that getting involved in murder, even if his involvement was only peripheral to the case, was coming to feel distressingly natural.

"If the criminal is a lunatic," he said, "wouldn't you expect that there would be others?"

"A serial killer?" Barent morosely nodded. "Yeah. There almost always are. And there haven't been, not that I know of. Guys who do this sort of thing tend to do it in the same way every time, like a ritual. They're fulfilling a psychological need that is very specific. Nuts, maybe, but specific. There are murders every day in New York. There haven't been any others like this."

"How about the Halloween party?"

"I don't know." Barent frowned down at his beer. "What these things are all about is the killing. Carving up bodies that are already dead and ruining a stupid party is a completely different kettle of fish. The Halloween party may have set the killer off–it may have given him the idea–but most likely, the obvious explanation there is the correct one. It was just a joke. We have to look into it, of course, but personally I doubt they're related."

"The press will assume differently," Kurtz said. "The resemblance will be hard to get away from."

"The press may be right. I'm only giving you my opinion."

"And maybe there have been similar murders but not in New York. Maybe the killer has moved here from somewhere else."

"Could be. The FBI will know."

"And maybe this is only the first," Kurtz said.

"Maybe." Barent shook his head and grimaced. "But whichever it is, it's not likely to be the last."

Chapter 8

Kurtz was not allowed to be present when the police interviewed Claire Mahoney. No matter what his interest in the case, it wouldn't have been proper. The unfortunate fact remained that Claire, as well as being the bereaved party and the principal mourner, was also the primary suspect. Not that Claire Mahoney had any motive that was immediately apparent, but the simple odds did say that the wife of a murder victim had a greater chance of having committed the crime than anyone else.

Her story seemed unassailable, however. "I arrived home from shopping," she said. "I found him ..."–she shuddered and her eyes leaked tears–"like that."

Barent's voice was gentle. "Did you always go shopping at that particular time, Mrs. Mahoney?"

"Usually I did. Why do you ask?"

"It makes it easier for a criminal if he knows that the victim will be alone."

Or he simply doesn't care, Barent thought. If Claire Mahoney hadn't been out shopping, maybe she too would now be dead and in pieces.

She nodded and clutched her handkerchief.

"Were there any signs of forced entry? Were any of the windows broken? Or any of the locks?"

There weren't, and Barent already knew it, but he had to ask. "No," Claire Mahoney said.

"Was the door locked or unlocked when you arrived home?"

"It was locked," she said.

"You're sure?"

"Yes. I'm certain."

"Were there any signs of a struggle in any of the other rooms? Anything broken? Anything knocked to the floor?"

"No," she said. Her voice was dull. "Everything looked ... normal."

All of which proved nothing but was definitely interesting. It meant that Mahoney had either let his murderer into the house, in which case he must have known who he was, or that the murderer had a key–or that Claire Mahoney was lying.

"So when you arrived home, you had no suspicions that anything was wrong?"

She shook her head.

"What did you do when you arrived home?"

"I put away the groceries. I had bought ice cream. If you don't put it in the freezer right away, it melts."

"You put away the groceries, and then what?"

"I sat down in a chair by the front window to read a magazine."

A copy of *Time* was sitting on the small table next to the easy chair by the window.

"And then what?"

"I began to prepare dinner."

The table in the dining room was set for two. A bottle of *Concha y Toro* Cabernet was open on the table. A chicken and two sweet potatoes had been roasting in the oven. They were burned.

"And you hadn't seen Dr. Mahoney in all this time?" She shook her head.

"Was that unusual?"

"Not at all. He often came home from work and took a nap before dinner."

"But you knew that he was home."

"His car was in the carport and the bedroom door was closed. I just assumed."

Barent nodded. "At what time was dinner ready?"

"About seven."

The call to Barent at his son-in-law's house had come at seven forty-three. He had noted the time.

"And you went into the bedroom to wake him?"

"Yes."

Claire Mahoney's face tightened and she closed her eyes. "I'm sorry, Mrs. Mahoney," Barent said.

She swallowed. "That's alright, Detective," she said in a faint voice. "I realize that you have to ask your questions."

He nodded encouragingly.

"I went into the bedroom to wake him a little before seven. I wanted him to have time to wake up and wash his face before we sat down to eat."

"But he wasn't in the bedroom," Barent said.

51

"No."

"And then what?"

"I looked in the study. It seemed like the most logical place for him to be, if he wasn't sleeping."

"Did you actually go into the room, Mrs. Mahoney?"

"No. As soon as I opened the door, I saw …"

Her breathing grew ragged and she seemed to sway in her chair for a moment before catching herself. "I saw him. Or what had been done to him. I closed the door and I ran to the phone."

"You called 911."

"Yes."

"Did you call anyone else?"

"No."

"And what did you do then?"

"I ran out of the house. It occurred to me then that whoever had done that to my husband might still be lurking about. I didn't want to be inside."

When the police arrived, they had found Claire Mahoney standing in the front yard. The two responding officers had reported that she was pale but composed. She had answered their questions politely in a subdued voice and then led them back inside before going to pieces.

"What time was it that you arrived home?"

"About five-thirty."

"And at what time did you leave to go shopping?"

"A little after noon."

"That's a long time to be food-shopping."

"I wasn't only food-shopping. I went downtown to Sak's. I bought a scarf and a new pair of gloves. I did the food-shopping on the way home."

A scarf and a pair of gloves with Sak's labels and price tags still attached were sitting on the kitchen counter.

"Mrs. Mahoney, do you have any idea who might have done this to your husband?"

"Absolutely not," she said. "How could I?"

Barent didn't feel it necessary to explain the most obvious answer. "Did your husband have any enemies that you knew of?"

She gave a quick, crooked smile, as if she found the question bitterly amusing. "Enemies, Detective? Do you mean the sort of enemies that might have murdered him and then carved him up into little pieces? No. He didn't have any enemies."

Barent hated this part. It was inevitable. No matter how hard you tried to be gentle and considerate, you always wound up offending them. The husband (or wife, or son or granddaughter) was dead. And in the process of trying to discover the truth, it was inevitable that the suggestion would be made that maybe, just maybe, the victim might have done something (somewhere, sometime) that gave someone–maybe a lunatic, but *someone*–the idea that he deserved it. Also, of course, it was inevitable that sooner or later the spouse would get the idea that maybe the police–despite their calm tones and sympathetic demeanor–suspected them (which they did).

"Mrs. Mahoney, you have already stated that you have no idea who might have killed your husband."

"No," she said, and gave him an indignant look. "I do not."

"Then you don't know what sort of enemies he might have had, do you? Whether you knew them or not, he pretty obviously had them."

She stared at him for a long moment and then her eyes wandered away. She seemed to be thinking about it and Barent waited patiently. "No," she finally said.

"Mrs. Mahoney, so far as you know, was your husband a secretive sort of man?"

"Secretive?"

"Did he talk much about his work? His hobbies? The things that he did? The people he knew? Or did he keep them to himself?"

"I don't think he had any secrets. We talked all the time."

"Would you say that his mood had changed at all lately? Had he seemed depressed or worried about anything?"

She hesitated. "No," she said. "Not at all."

He looked at her, considering. Unless she was a very good actress, this was the first thing she had said that was untrue. "Are you sure?"

"Yes," she said.

He waited, saying nothing. After a moment, she began to fidget, and then asked, "Why are you looking at me like that?"

"You seemed doubtful."

Now she would either admit it or get angry again.

She frowned and stared out the window. There wasn't much to see. The night was cold and cloudy. A row of streetlights cast a clear, white light on a row of small houses across the street. The crowd had dispersed. "He seemed preoccupied," she said. "I wouldn't say he was depressed but something was on his mind."

"He didn't speak about it?"

"No. I assumed that he would when he was ready to. He always had in the past."

"In the past?" he said.

She smiled fleetingly. "It was never anything very serious. Should he hire a new lab tech? Were the questions on the anatomy exam too difficult? Where should we go for our next vacation? What type of car should we buy? We led very ordinary lives, Detective."

Her voice seemed to suddenly break and she clutched her handkerchief. "We were happy."

Maybe they had, Barent thought. And maybe they were. But nobody's life is as routine as all that. Everybody had problems. Everybody had crises that might have been routine but were important to them. He scratched his head. Claire Mahoney seemed again to be on the verge of tears and it was already late. In a day or so, she would feel more like talking. Barent had seen it many times before. Now she was stunned, the situation unreal. Give her a few days, the reality would have sunk in and if it had been a good marriage, she would want to talk. She would be desperate to talk. Talking would be the only way left to hang on for a little bit longer to the life that she no longer had. "Alright, Mrs. Mahoney," he said. "I'm sorry to have bothered you. Perhaps we'll talk again in a few days. By then, hopefully we'll have gotten to the bottom of all this."

But somehow, he doubted it.

Barent was present at the news conference but thankfully he was not called upon to speak. The Commissioner and the Mayor expressed the usual official outrage and assured the public that everything was being done that could be done.

"I have no doubt that we will find the person responsible for this despicable murder," the Mayor said. The Commissioner was standing right behind him, looking stern.

Sure, Barent thought. Easy for you to say.

"The sympathies of the entire city go out to the bereaved family. We wish them to know that we will not forget them in our prayers."

What's with this *we* stuff?

Barent had read someplace that King Edward the Eighth once said, "The only ones entitled to use *We* are the King and a man with a tapeworm."

Well, this was America and the Mayor of New York was nobody's king.

The Mayor moved off the podium and the Commissioner strode up. "We're urging the neighborhood to keep calm," he said.

Urge away, Barent thought.

"The Medical Examiner is already working with the victim's remains and the technicians at the police lab are processing everything that was found at the site. The Mayor and the City Council have authorized me to announce that there will be a twenty-thousand dollar reward for information leading to the arrest and conviction of the murderer of Professor Roderick Allen Mahoney. We're asking anybody who might have such information to come forward. That's all. Thank you."

The Commissioner smiled grimly and stepped down. The members of the Press milled about uncertainly, then headed for the door.

Message delivered. We care. The boys in blue are on the case and the City can sleep soundly. Everybody knew it was strictly pro forma but you had to go through the motions. The public expected it. And the reward might help.

Barent sighed. It was going to be a long night.

Chapter 9

Kurtz had been through this once before and he knew what was expected of him. Barent's idea of Kurtz' role was that the younger man would act as a resource, a consultant on the professional world in which the victim had lived and worked. That was how it had been the last time, when Sharon Lee was murdered and that was how it should be this time; Kurtz had enough objectivity to realize it. But the realization did nothing for his mood. This was the second time in less than a year that violent death had invaded Kurtz' universe. (All the knifings and shootings and trauma victims that he took to the OR didn't count. They weren't personal.)

Two times was two too many. He resented playing a role on the sidelines.

Unfortunately, he thought, that was the role he was going to play. Barent and Kurtz were both professionals, and in certain ways the professions of policeman and physician (especially surgeon) were similar. They were both hierarchical, at least during the years of training. Surgical residencies were often described as military organizations. You started at the bottom, doing scut and taking orders from everybody, including the nurses, desperately trying not to fuck up. As you got a little older and began to have some idea of what you were doing, your responsibilities as well as your authority increased. By the time you got to be a chief resident, you had a whole group of junior physicians under your command and the attendings were beginning to give you a little respect. And then you became an attending yourself, supposedly an independently acting practitioner, but you were still a junior attending and the senior attendings and the chief of the service and the chairman of the department and the departmental quality assurance director and a whole bunch of others (most certainly including the nurses) had the right to poke their noses into how you were doing things.

Kurtz had been in the military. He had been a clerk for CID, the investigative branch of the service. He had for a brief time even considered going into police work as a career. He knew how Barent ticked, he knew where he himself fit in and he wouldn't have dreamed of screwing up his friend's investigation because his ego chafed at the size of his own role. But he still resented it.

56

"A brandy for your thoughts?" Lenore said. She handed him a medium-sized snifter of Courvoisier X.O. and sat down in a chair across from the couch.

"Son-of-a-bitch," he muttered.

She gave him a look of guarded sympathy and swirled her own brandy in the palm of her hand. "You've got a lot on your mind. Would you rather I left?"

"No," he said quickly. "Not unless you want to. Just don't expect me to talk about much tonight."

She smiled. "I can do that."

He smiled back. She tucked her legs under her, curled up in the chair and picked up a book. Kurtz brooded. He had not seen very much of Rod Mahoney on a regular basis, at least not after working hours, but they had had lunch together maybe once a month, whenever he had a case on the schedule at Staunton.

"You never got to know Rod very well, did you?" Kurtz said.

Lenore looked up from her book. "He seemed nice." She shrugged. "When we were together, I was mostly talking to his wife."

"And now it's too late." Kurtz shook his head sorrowfully.

Lenore put down her book. "What was he like?"

"He was nice, just a nice, normal guy. He liked his family. He liked his work. I remember him talking about how awe-inspiring human anatomy was, how every fiber and bone and muscle fit neatly together, how all the organs did just what they were supposed to do. He used to laugh at the irony. Most people think of their own insides as horrible, or at least ugly. Rod thought they were beautiful. Rod didn't have a lot of problems. He didn't have a lot of ambitions, I think mostly because he was happy with what he had. Some of that came from the war."

"Vietnam?"

"Yeah. Most of his platoon was killed. Rod was badly wounded. I think he came to the conclusion that he was lucky to be healthy and alive and that feeling never left him. The other night was the first time I ever heard him sound depressed or uncertain."

Lenore nodded silently. After a moment, when it became apparent that Kurtz had nothing more to say, she picked up her book.

So who might have murdered Rod Mahoney and why had it been done?

The bottom line was that Kurtz hadn't a clue, and there wasn't a single thing he could think of that might be useful. Sitting around and feeling cranky was not Kurtz' preferred mode of action but it was all he could do right now. Barent would call him when there was something he could help with and that was simply that.

Barent was interviewing suspects, or pursuing clues, as he liked to think. There were the Mahoney's two children, both of them now home from school to attend their father's funeral. Rod Mahoney had also left a sister, named Evelyn Richter, with whom he was not on good terms, and a brother-in-law that Claire Mahoney had described succinctly as "a jerk." In addition to these tag-ends of the family, there were a series of co-workers, lab assistants, dieners, fellow faculty members, all of whom had known the murdered man and none of whom had an immediately apparent motive.

Barent started with the sister and brother-in-law. They lived in a one bedroom apartment on the Eighth Floor of a building not far from Times Square. He had phoned ahead and verified that they would both be home; nevertheless, when Barent and Harry Moran arrived, they found only the sister. She was a small woman, plump, with a baby face and straight brown hair. She was forty-three years old but looked at least ten years younger. "Jay had to go out," she said. Her voice held an aggressive whine. "He said he couldn't stay inside for a minute longer, what with all the tension lately."

She looked back and forth between Barent and Moran, evidently expecting them to be impressed with her husband's sensitivity. "He'll be back soon. Come on in."

The apartment was uncluttered. There were only a few pieces of furniture but what there was seemed expensive, a leather couch and loveseat, a low coffee table made out of carved driftwood and a high definition TV against the opposite wall. The two policemen sat down on the couch. Eveleyn Richter plopped down on the loveseat, her short legs barely touching the floor, and looked at Barent.

"We're very sorry about your brother, Mrs. Richter," he said.

She nodded her head, taking these routine condolences as her due.

"We have a number of questions that we have to ask."

"Sure," she said. "I understand."

"Did you see your brother very often."

"No, not lately. We used to but we argued a lot. It was better to keep the relationship more casual."

She seemed matter-of-fact, as if the estrangement from her brother was just one of those humdrum facts of life.

"What did you argue about?" Barent asked.

"Money," Evelyn Richter immediately said.

"Ah …" Barent said. Moran, whose preferred persona was one of perpetual boredom, gave Barent a slight, wolfish smile.

"What about money?" Barent asked.

"It was our father's money. He had cancer. He knew he didn't have very long to live and he transferred all of his money into Rod's name. For tax purposes, you understand."

She looked at Barent brightly.

"Go on," Barent said.

"After he died, Rod was supposed to give me half."

"You mean he didn't?" This was too good to be true, a motive dropped into their laps like a plum falling from a tree.

"Of course he did," Evelyn Richter said. "Rod would never do a thing like that. He gave me every penny."

"Oh." Barent glanced at Moran. Moran shrugged. "Then what was the argument about?"

"He didn't like the way I spent it. He kept telling me I should invest it. I should save it for a rainy day. But how could I invest it? I have expenses." She looked around the apartment and smiled vaguely.

"I see," Barent said. "What do you do for a living, Mrs. Richter?"

"I have a teaching certificate."

"And where do you work?"

"I'm between jobs just now. I've been looking." Her face became suddenly wary. "Now don't you start."

Barent looked at her.

"It's my life and I'll do what I want with it. Rod was just like Daddy, always telling me what I was supposed to do. I don't need to hear it from you."

"I'm a policeman, Mrs. Richter," Barent said. "I'm not your father."

She nodded but still looked suspicious.

"And your husband? What does he do?"

"He's a building contractor."

A building contractor … a building contractor could mean damn near anything, from janitor to all-purpose handyman to Donald Trump. "And where does he work?"

"He works for Gaddison Realty. They're Downtown."

Gaddison was a large outfit. Barent knew them very well and had never heard that they were anything but reputable. "Mrs. Richter, do you know of anybody that might have had a motive to kill your brother?" Barent asked.

"Certainly not."

Evelyn Richter squared her shoulders and gave Barent a fierce look, a look which immediately dissolved into uncertainty. "You don't think I did it, do you?"

He was about to offer the usual diplomatic denial but before he could open his mouth, Evelyn Richter laughed incredulously and slapped her knee. "You do, don't you? That's really amazing. You think I killed my own brother. I can't believe it."

She looked, actually, as if she were savoring the notion. "No, Mrs. Richter," Barent said. "We don't think you killed your brother."

In fact, Barent was neutral on the point. Maybe she had and maybe she hadn't, but whether she had murdered her brother or not, Barent was already prepared to state in court that Evelyn Richter was a bubblehead. "We have no idea yet who might have done it. We're trying to gather information, that's all."

She still looked doubtful and seemed about to say something but right then, the front door opened. A man perhaps two inches shorter than Barent's five foot ten walked in. He wore a light brown trench coat and a fedora that looked expensive. He saw Barent and Moran, raised his eyebrows and walked over to the couch.

"Honey," Evelyn Richter said. "These are the policemen, Detective …" She stopped and looked uncertain.

"Detective Barent," Barent said. "And Moran."

"Jay Richter," the man said, and held out his hand. "Sorry to run out on you before but I needed a little fresh air. I hate being cooped up inside. What can I do for you?"

"We were wondering if either of you knew who might have had reason to dislike Rod Mahoney."

"Rod?" Jay Richter wrinkled his nose as if Rod Mahoney was a name he had heard only rarely and in some forgotten context.

"Rod Mahoney," Barent said. "Your brother-in-law."

"Yes, of course." Richter appeared suddenly irritated. "Why should we? We hardly saw him once a year. I really know nothing about him, except that he taught anatomy at Staunton."

"Did he ever lend you money, Mr. Richter?"

It was a shot in the dark but it seemed to find a target. Richter cleared his throat, suddenly realized that he was still wearing his coat. "Excuse me for a moment," he said. He went over to the hall closet and hung up the coat and hat. "Cold outside today," he said. He walked back over with a bright smile, rubbing his hands together. "Now then," he said. "What was your question?"

"I asked if Rod Mahoney had ever loaned you any money."

"No," Jay Richter said. "Never. Why do you ask that?"

Evelyn Richter was staring at her husband with her mouth partly open. He smiled at her and she closed her mouth.

"I understand that you work for Gaddison Realty," Barent said. "What do you do?"

"Mostly purchase supplies," Richter said. "Plumbing, mostly."

Barent wrote *plumbing* neatly in his notebook and peered at Jay Richter. "And when was the last time you saw Rod Mahoney?" he asked.

Richter blinked, the sudden change in subject seeming to unsettle him. "I don't know … Easter?" He looked at his wife, who was staring at him with silent fascination.

Evelyn Richter seemed suddenly to realize that she had been asked a question. "I think so," she said. "We went over for supper. Yes. It was Easter."

"I assume that you've spoken with him more recently than that?"

Evelyn Richter said, "I talked to him every few weeks or so, on the phone."

"And what did you talk about?"

61

"Oh, you know …" She shrugged. "Whatever."

"Had anything been bothering your brother lately, Mrs. Richter? Did he seem pre-occupied, maybe even upset?"

"Rod?"

She squinted her eyes, concentrating. It occurred to Barent that Evelyn Richter did not spend much time thinking about the problems or the feelings of people other than herself. "I don't think so …"

You win some, you lose some, and some get rained out. These two, Barent thought, were not going to be any help at all, at least not deliberately. "Thank you, Mrs. Richter," Barent said. "Mr. Richter. You've been very…cooperative."

Evelyn Richter looked uncertain. Barent figured that uncertainty was her standard condition. "We'll speak again," he said.

Jay Richter frowned, then forced a smile. "Of course," he said. "We'll do anything we can. Just give us a call."

Barent smiled back. "I'm sure you will," he said. "We'll talk when I know more."

Elvira Pang, that was the name of the associate professor who had taught the anatomy course with Rod Mahoney. Elvira Pang was a good-looking woman of Chinese ancestry, perhaps thirty-five years old, maybe a little older. "I give about a quarter of the lectures."

She hesitated, then said, "Rod gave about a quarter, too. The rest are given by a lot of different people, surgeons and internists mostly. We have a cardiologist talk about the functional anatomy of the heart. Some of the orthopedists talk about the muscles and bones. We used to have an ENT surgeon talk about the larynx but we eased him out a year or two ago. He used to go on and on about the wonders of the cricopharyngeus, the arytenoid cartilage and the thyro-hyoid membrane and bored all the students to tears."

Barent held up a hand. "I don't think this is exactly what I need to know."

Elvira Pang looked at him uncertainly. "You said to tell you about Rod's work."

"What I meant was, how did Dr. Mahoney spend his day? What was his routine? Dr. Mahoney, in particular."

"Oh." She wrinkled her nose. "Well, he would arrive in at the office, usually around 8:30. He'd get a cup of coffee, sit down and do paperwork, usually until 10:00 AM. The lectures most days are from 10:00 to 11:00. He attended almost all the lectures, even the ones he wasn't giving himself. After the lecture, he had office hours until noon. Students could come in and talk with him if they had problems or just questions. At noon, he would go for lunch. In the afternoons, he would either proctor the lab sessions or go to his own lab."

"What does research in anatomy consist of?"

She shrugged. "In the old days–I mean a couple of hundred years ago–most of it was comparative. How one organ or structure in the human body is analogous to a similar organ in a different animal. Some of that still goes on, but today, most of it is functional, and most of that is biophysics. How bones and muscles exert stress, how the heart manages to beat two billion times over the course of a lifetime before it wears out. Things like that."

"And what was Dr. Mahoney's research?"

"To tell you the truth, he didn't really have anything going at the moment. Rod's last published first-author paper was about three years ago. These days, he mostly teaches and helps other people with their own projects."

"Is that usual?"

"For a senior professor who already has tenure?" She shrugged again. "Sure."

"And this was the routine that he followed every day?"

"Wednesday afternoon, there was no lab session. Usually we had a course meeting on Wednesdays to discuss how things were going, any students who seemed to be having trouble, how the lecturers were working out."

She shrugged again. "Stuff like that."

"Who is 'we'?"

"Rod, myself, and the lab assistants."

The lab assistants were second and third year medical students who had gotten A in the course, and a few post-docs. They changed every year, as the students went on to clinical rotations and then graduated. The names of the current crew were Joe Higgins, Melanie Costin, George Krane and Howard Clark. Barent already knew that from the Halloween incident. They were all pale, pasty-faced and bewildered. None of them had a criminal record. "Were there any personality conflicts among this group?"

"Conflicts?"

"Did everybody get along?"

"Oh. Sure."

"No problems at all?"

Elvira Pang smiled faintly. "It's an anatomy course, not high finance. We do the same thing every year. It's pretty routine."

"Dr. Mahoney was murdered on a Tuesday. Was there anything at all unusual about that day?"

"Not in the slightest."

"What time do the lab sessions start?"

"One o'clock."

"On the day that he was murdered, did Dr. Mahoney proctor the lab session, or did he go to his own lab?"

"He went to his lab."

"You're sure?"

"Yes. I remember."

"Alright. Now, how about the students. Any problems?"

"Not really. Some are smarter than others but medical students are all smart. There are always one or two who struggle with the material but nobody has actually flunked the course in a couple of years."

"Getting back to the lab assistants, has there ever been a problem with any of them?"

She wrinkled her brow and thought about it. "Maybe three years ago, Rod had to fire one of them. He was stealing equipment from the lab and selling it."

"What was his name?"

She had to think about it. Finally her face cleared and she said, "James Gallagher. I'm certain of it."

"What happened to him?"

"I don't know."

She didn't look too interested, either. Professors, medical students, lab assistants … a pretty bland bunch, all-in-all. Not the usual thieves, murderers and druggies that a policeman had to interact with on a daily basis. Barent supposed James Gallagher, wherever he was, might have a motive to dislike Rod Mahoney but that was really reaching.

"So far as you know, Dr. Pang, did anybody have a reason to dislike Professor Mahoney?"

She answered instantly. "Not at all."

"He had no enemies that you know of?"

"Enemies?" She looked at him incredulously. "He was an anatomy professor. What do you mean by enemies?"

Put that way, the question did sound a little ridiculous. "Dr. Pang," he said, "somebody murdered Professor Mahoney. Whoever did it was not likely to be his friend."

"No," she said. "I guess not. But I haven't the faintest idea who might have done it."

Barent sighed. No, he didn't suppose that she did. And neither, at this point, did he.

Gary Dixon had been identified by Claire Mahoney as her husband's closest friend. He did not at first glance seem to be the sort of man that a mild mannered academic would be friendly with. He was large and hairy and he had an amused glint in his eye. He wore a bandana around his forehead and a sleeveless, black t-shirt with a Harley-Davidson logo on the front. He owned a motorcycle store, which was empty of customers at the moment. Barent and Dixon were talking together at the counter next to the front door. Big bikes with chrome trim and black vinyl seating lined both sides of the room.

"Rod ..." Gary Dixon shook his head sadly. "He was my Lieutenant. I was a Sergeant. In Vietnam, you know?"

"I understand," Barent said. "I was at Quang Tri."

"Yeah?"

Gary Dixon looked at him with a bit more interest. "Rod was a good officer. He really cared about the men. It tore him apart when any of them got hurt."

"I understand that there were a lot of injuries in your platoon."

"It was war, but yeah, I would say that we had our share." Gary Dixon smiled cynically. "Maybe more than our share."

"Did you see him often?"

"Maybe every month or so we'd get together, play chess, have a beer, talk about old times."

Chess … Dixon looked like a Hell's Angel. He didn't look like a guy who would play chess. "I understand that Dr. Mahoney was a very good chess player. How good are you?"

"Pretty good. When I was a teenager, I had a 2200 rating. That's just below Master. I stopped playing seriously when I got older. The game took too much time and there's not enough money in it. I still follow it."

Just goes to show, Barent thought.

"When was the last time you saw Professor Mahoney?"

The door opened and a small man dressed in a blue suit walked in. He blinked at Barent and Dixon uncertainly. "I understand that you have a Suzuki GS-550 for sale?"

"Yep. It's in the back." Dixon turned to Barent. "Excuse me."

"Take your time."

Dixon conducted the little man to the back of the store where an enormous motorcycle stood alone on a raised platform. Barent thought that the man's feet would barely reach the pedal. The man inspected it carefully and then asked Dixon a few questions that Barent couldn't hear. The little man nodded and the two of them began to walk back to the front of the store. "Okay, let me see what I can do. I'll talk to you tomorrow."

"That's alright," Dixon said, "but if anybody comes in and makes me a firm offer, I'm going to have to let it go."

"I understand that."

The little man nodded his head decisively and pushed open the door, not looking at Barent as he went. Dixon walked back to the counter, smiling broadly. "That Suzuki is a classic. I got a real good buy on it. Now," he said, and rubbed his hands together, "where were we?"

"The last time you saw Rod Mahoney."

"Oh. Yeah." Dixon stopped smiling. "It was about two weeks ago. We had a beer."

"What did you talk about?"

"Not work, I can tell you that. I didn't understand his and he didn't care about mine. We talked about old times and politics and

66

the families. That's what we always talked about. And we played a couple of games."

"During your recent conversations, did anything seem to be bothering Professor Mahoney?"

Dixon shrugged. "I don't think so. Not that I could see."

"Did he seem pre-occupied?"

Dixon squinted his eyes, obviously giving the question careful consideration. "Maybe. Rod was always a quiet sort of guy. If anything in particular was on his mind, he kept it to himself. He did seem maybe a little quieter than usual."

"Did anybody dislike him, that you know of?"

Dixon shook his head. "No way."

"No way, nobody disliked him or no way, you don't know?"

"Both. Who would dislike Rod? There was nothing to dislike."

Barent sighed to himself. Rod Mahoney, the universal nice guy. Only trouble was, somebody had disliked him enough to bludgeon him to death and tear his body to pieces. "Maybe," Barent said. "But somebody must have."

"I'm sorry," Dixon said. He shook his head. "But I don't know who."

The door opened and a small Asian woman walked in with a little girl in tow. Barent thought they looked Vietnamese. Dixon smiled at them both. "My wife, Trann," he said. "And this is Trixie."

"How do you do?" Barent said. Trann smiled at him. Trixie gave him a suspicious look.

"Daddy," Trixie said, and tugged at Dixon's pants, "are we going to Friendly's? Mommy says we can go to Friendly's for dinner."

Dixon sighed and looked imploringly at his wife. "Friendly's?" he muttered.

Trann held her hands up helplessly. "She got all A's on her report card. She wants to go to Friendly's to celebrate."

"All A's, huh?" Dixon sighed. "I guess that means we have to." He said to Barent, "I hate Friendly's."

"Me too," Barent said.

Chapter 10

Harry Moran and Artie Figueroa had each made over a hundred phone calls and had paid five personal visits to people whose stories seemed at least possible and another four to some others who could not be reached by phone. One of these had resulted in violence when it became obvious that they were being handed a line of bullshit and Moran had had the bad sense to openly laugh. The subject, a large, bald-headed guy who looked like an unemployed truck driver and was obviously coked up to the gills, took a swing at Moran. Moran, who had a black belt in Shotokan, slipped the punch and kneed the character in the groin. This resulted in another hour's waste of time taking the idiot downtown and booking him.

This was the trouble with rewards. They sometimes resulted in useful leads but inevitably brought swarms of human cockroaches out into the light. You knew before you even started that ninety-nine calls out of a hundred were going to go nowhere, were inspired solely by the hope of putting one over on the cops and then skipping out with the loot.

For two days, they answered the phone, put in legwork and came up with nothing.

For Kurtz, the two days were busy but routine. Kurtz went to the OR in the morning and saw patients in the afternoon. Barent did not call.

The day after that, at 10:20 AM, Kurtz was just finishing up in surgery. The patient was named Anna Krenskie, an elderly lady, well-spoken and intelligent, with a devoted, supportive family, but like a lot of people who might have been expected to know better, she had denied her symptoms until it was too late. She had been passing blood in her stools for months before she had reluctantly mentioned it to her husband. Mr. Krenskie had asked his physician, a urologist, for advice and now Mrs. Krenskie was in the OR with a new colostomy and mets to the liver.

"Seventy-three," Kaplan said, and shook his head.

Patel gave a slight nod but said nothing. His hands continued to put sutures, one after another, into the subcutaneous fat. Kyle, who was an intern and not the talkative sort, hovered over Patel's hands with a scissors and cut the ends of each suture as Patel finished tying it.

"My grandmother went this way," Kaplan said. "Some people are more afraid of doctors and hospitals than they are of cancer."

"I don't think that's it, exactly," said Kurtz. "I think it's just that they're so afraid of hearing the bad news that they can't bring themselves to face it."

"That was it with my grandmother," Kaplan persisted. "She came from the old country. She was a tough old broad and she'd had plenty of bad news in her life but she hated hospitals. A hospital was a place you went to die. She wouldn't get near one. My dad had to practically drag her."

"And then what?" Kurtz asked.

"She died six months later–at home. She insisted."

Kaplan's grandmother had been a wise woman, Kurtz thought. Home was better. Hospitals were uncomfortable places at the best of times. The food was bland, the beds were hard. There were always noises coming from the hallways, making it impossible to get any sleep. The staff, no matter how dedicated they might be, tended to treat the patients like idiot children and the patients, frightened and demoralized, sometimes acted as if they were. Far better to go at home with your family around you. Keep your dignity.

Kaplan stapled the skin and Patel and Kyle put on the bandages. Kurtz went out to the locker room to get dressed. Five minutes later, he was strolling out toward the ER entrance when a voice came over the loudspeaker, "Code M, Fourth Floor. Code M, Fourth Floor."

Code M was hospital jargon for somebody running amok, usually a psych patient or somebody overdosing on uppers or PCP. The M stood for *manpower*. Kurtz stopped and scratched his head. The Fourth Floor was only two floors above the OR and contained nothing but some administrative offices and a hallway full of call rooms for the residents. There shouldn't have been any patients up there.

It was none of his business, though. Kurtz began slowly to walk toward the doors leading down to the street at the end of the hall. Then he stopped again and grinned and headed for the stairs.

The Fourth Floor had originally been built as a patient unit. A cluster of low desks stood behind a partition that had been intended as a nursing station. Behind the partition was an open area for the staff to work and behind that were two small rooms, one to serve as a lounge for the nurses to sit in and have a cup of coffee and a sandwich, the other as an equipment and medication closet. Now, both rooms were used for storage, packed with cartons and crates. A row of doors lined the hallway past the nursing station. They were all closed.

A group of frightened looking young men and women clustered around the elevator bank, talking among themselves and staring grimly at a large, brown haired man with enormous, hulking shoulders, wearing an orderly's uniform, who was standing in the center of the nursing station. He was holding a pretty, red-haired woman, who Kurtz vaguely recognized as a nurse on one of the floors. She was cursing, flailing her arms and trying to struggle. The man held her casually in the crook of one arm, seeming to pay her exertions little attention and staring at the people by the elevator.

Where the hell was Security?

Kurtz had taken the main stairway to the floor below and then come up the back stair to the Fourth Floor. The door at the head of the stairwell had a glass panel set in the center, at a comfortable height of about five feet. Wherever the action might be taking place, Kurtz could plainly see that it was not within view of the stairwell. Cautiously, he had pushed the door open. He could hear what sounded like a group of buzzing voices and one, a woman, crying out,

"Goddamn it, let me go! Damn it, Hickey, please let me go!"

Hickey. Kurtz didn't know anybody named Hickey.

The hallway in which Kurtz stood was at right angles to the main hallway leading to the elevators. The two hallways formed a T. The nursing station stood in the center, with an entrance onto both hallways. Kurtz inched his way down the corridor and cautiously peered around the edge of the wall.

Their backs were to him. The woman was struggling, trying without success to pry the arm from around her waist, occasionally kicking at the man's legs. Hickey was impervious. He seemed to be catatonic. He stood still, his breath wheezing, staring straight ahead at the opposite wall and the people milling about.

The woman appeared to be in no immediate danger but that was an illusion. It was impossible to tell what was going on in Hickey's brain. At the moment, he seemed content to hold his captive. A minute from now, he might decide to snap her neck.

Kurtz' options were limited. He could stand still and wait for Security–but once they arrived, what were they going to do? Hickey didn't seem to be in any condition to reason with. Kurtz could step out from behind the wall and hit the man on the head. The problem with this plan was that he had nothing but his fists to hit him with and Kurtz' fists weren't half as hard as Hickey's head. He could grab Hickey from behind and try to overpower him. Kurtz had no doubts about his ability to accomplish this. But could he accomplish it without the man's captive being injured?

What he needed was a distraction, something to take Hickey's mind off whatever the hell he was thinking, or even better, something hard to hit him with. Behind him, near the door to the stairwell, was an alcove containing two fire extinguishers, one red and one silver. Silver fire extinguishers contained water. A red one with a black rubber cone attached would contain carbon dioxide while red with a black hose meant mono-ammonium phosphate, a dry powder that would smother any sort of fire short of burning metal. This one had a hose. Hospital regulations required that you sit and listen to a lecture on fire safety at least once a year. Make sure you use a fire extinguisher appropriately, that was part of the message. A couple of years before, a neurosurgery patient's drapes had caught on fire, ignited by an electrocautery. An over-eager rescuer had sprayed mono-ammonium phosphate into the patient's open skull. Carbon dioxide was a gas and might have been okay but mono-ammonium phosphate is stored under pressures of several hundred pounds per square inch and the unfortunate patient's brain had been turned into jelly.

Kurtz walked back, removed the fire extinguisher from its holder and hefted it. Not exactly an M-16, he reflected, but it ought to do.

He cradled the fire extinguisher under his arm, stepped out from behind the wall, pulled the pin, aimed the hose at the middle of Hickey's back and squeezed the handle. A white cloud whooshed out of the cylinder. Hickey gave an inarticulate cry. His hands flew up and the red-headed nurse stumbled to the floor. Hickey whirled around, roaring. Calmly, Kurtz sprayed him in the face. Hickey shrieked, clapped his hands to his face and charged forward. As Hickey stumbled past, Kurtz stepped deftly to the side and swung the fire extinguisher. It cracked into the side of Hickey's head. Hickey's shrieks stopped abruptly. He fell to the floor and lay still, moaning.

Kurtz turned to the nurse, who had risen to her feet and was watching Hickey warily. "Are you alright?"

Her eyes flicked to Kurtz' face. "Yeah," she said. "Thanks."

"What happened?"

"That asshole tried to rape me." She gave Hickey a contemptuous glance.

Kurtz scratched his head. Offhand, he didn't see anything that might have stopped him. "Tried?" he said.

"Yeah." She gave a wan smile. "He tried alright, but he's drugged out of his mind. He couldn't get it up."

A drug overdose was hardly a homicide, but at this point, everything having to do with the medical center was automatically assumed to be related to Rod Mahoney. Barent got the call and showed up in the ER an hour later. Hickey was tied up in a strait jacket and strapped to a stretcher. His face was red and he was panting hoarsely. Kurtz leaned against the wall, his hands in his pockets, looking pleased. A small man in a white lab coat was waving a sheet of paper under Kurtz' nose. "Scopolamine," he said.

"What did you say?" Barent asked.

The little man looked at Barent suspiciously. "Who are you?" he asked.

"Detective Lew Barent," Kurtz said. "This is Rick Hanson, the head of the clinical laboratory."

"Pleased to meet you," Barent said.

Hanson seemed doubtful. He looked back and forth between Kurtz' blandly smiling face and Barent's. Kurtz, he obviously felt comfortable with. Kurtz was one of them, a physician. Barent was something alien to Hanson's sense of order. Reluctantly, Hanson said, "Scopolamine is a naturally occurring anti-muscarinic. It's related to belladonna and henbane. Scopolamine readily crosses the blood-brain barrier. It can cause a whole variety of neurologic symptoms."

"Scopolamine … there was a mnemonic," Kurtz said. "Dry as a bone, red as a beet …" He shrugged. "I forget."

"Tight as a drum and mad as a hatter."

Kurtz grinned. "Right."

Hanson looked again at Barent and scratched his chin. "Scopolamine isn't the only thing he's got floating around in his blood. There's also heroin."

"Heroin plus scopolamine …" Barent looked momentarily thoughtful, then nodded to himself. "Polo," he said.

Hanson blinked at him. "Polo is a game that rich people play on horses."

Barent grinned. "In December of 1995, over fifty people were hospitalized in New Jersey after shooting up heroin laced with scopolamine. The street name for the stuff is 'polo.'"

Hanson gave a small shake of his head. "I didn't know that. The patient has needle tracks all up and down his arm but I've never heard of anybody deliberately abusing scopolamine. We figured the heroin was contaminated."

"Adding scopolamine is supposed to give heroin an extra kick," Barent said. "Too much of it can be fatal."

Hanson shrugged. "It almost was."

"When will he be able to answer questions?"

"Probably right now," Kurtz put in. "There's an antidote for scopolamine, a drug called antilirium. They were getting ready to give it to him when you arrived."

"Good," Barent said. "Let's go talk to him. Either of you care to speculate how many other guys are shooting themselves up with the same lousy stuff?"

Hanson pursed his lips. "I hadn't thought of that."

"Well, think about it," Barent said. "Think about it hard."

Chapter 11

Hickey blinked twice, shook his head and came awake as expected. After figuring out where he was and who he was talking to, he clammed up completely and refused to speak any further without a lawyer being present. His lawyer arrived within a half hour, a thin man with a sharp nose, named Jeffrey Leonard. He asked for a few minutes to confer with his client, a request which the police had no choice but to grant. He came out of Hickey's room a short time later and announced that Hickey would answer none of their questions. Barent was not surprised. So far, the hole that Hickey had dug for himself was shallow. He could claim temporary insanity and nobody was going to dispute it with the levels of scopolamine that he had floating in his blood. Once he started naming names, he would be in too deep to back out.

Twenty minutes later, Kurtz and Barent were sitting in Kurtz' office. Kurtz was in a good mood. Barent was not. "What are you smiling at?" he asked.

"Am I?" Kurtz leaned back in his chair, put his arms behind his head and stretched. "I figure I did pretty good. Knocked out the bad guy, saved the damsel in distress. It's not my fault if the schmuck won't talk."

Barent grunted. "One day, you're going to get yourself into something that you can't get out of."

"The guy could have killed her. What else was I supposed to do?"

"Wait for Security?

Kurtz shrugged. "I was there. Security wasn't. Turns out that a psych patient in the ER went nutso at about the same time. Security was dealing with him."

Barent shook his head. "So alright, you did pretty good. But your friends would appreciate it if now and then you walked away from a fight instead of into it."

"Jesus, you sound like I'm wandering the streets just looking for trouble. I'm not the one who started it."

"But you have to be the one to finish it, don't you? And anyway, you don't have to go out looking for trouble. It always seems to find you."

Kurtz put a meditative look on his face. "I think it was Thomas Jefferson who said, 'All that is necessary for the triumph of evil is for good men to do nothing.' Or maybe it was Edmund Burke. You figure the police are doing such a terrific job of combating evil?"

Barent set his lips in a mulish line and said nothing. After a few moments of silence, Kurtz asked. "How's the investigation going?"

Barent looked at him. "So far we're nowhere, but that's to be expected. There are plenty of people we still have to talk to."

"How about the neighbors? Any of them see or hear anything?"

"One old lady who lives across the street thought she saw somebody ringing the doorbell. Then again, she's a little nearsighted and not too swift. She wasn't even certain of the house."

"Not exactly encouraging."

"You're right. She thought it was a man, dressed in a suit and hat but she couldn't describe him, couldn't even say if he was white or black."

"Just one?"

"She only saw one. She wasn't paying much attention."

"How about a car?"

"She didn't notice a car."

"There aren't any subways in that neighborhood. Anybody coming from outside would have had to drive."

Kurtz stared off into space. The Mahoneys' little neighborhood was a fairly common one for Brooklyn, an assortment of tree-lined streets full of small houses, all with their own yards, the sort of neighborhood you could find all over America but which the public never thought of in association with New York City.

"Have you talked to the neighborhood kids yet?"

"What neighborhood kids?"

"The public schools let out for lunch. Kids sometime come home and then go back after they eat. Maybe one of the kids saw something."

Barent stared at him. "Well, aren't you the little Sherlock."

"Sorry. Just trying to help."

Barent pulled out a cigar, stared at it ferociously and then shoved it back into his pocket. "Yes, for your information, we've talked to the kids. We've talked to every kid, mother, father, aunt, uncle and hermit who lives on the goddamn street. Nobody saw a thing except the one woman."

"Sorry," Kurtz said again.

Barent was not mollified. "You know, Richard, dragging you into things turned out okay last time, but we were both lucky. If anything happened to you, Lenore would never forgive me, and I would never forgive myself."

He looked serious. Kurtz was honestly touched. Also a trifle miffed. "I've been living away from home for a long time. You're not responsible for what I do."

Barent looked at him grimly for a moment, then gave a grudging smile. "I know," he said. "It just makes me nervous, having you around. You're not a cop. I can't escape the feeling that you don't belong."

"What you really mean is you can't escape the feeling that I don't know what I'm doing."

"That, too."

"I'm not going to argue with you. I'll just tell you again, I'm not going to screw up your investigation but our friend Hickey, allow me to point out, had nothing to do with the investigation. If anybody has a beef with me, it's Hospital Security, 'cause they're the ones I showed up. And not for the first time, by the way."

"Okay," Barent said. He held his hands up. "Peace. I'm sorry."

After a moment, Kurtz grinned. "So how about the man in the suit?"

Barent grinned back. "We're looking for him. Believe me, we're looking."

During the next two days, fifteen people were brought into the Emergency Room, raving out of their minds on a combination of heroin and scopolamine. Thirteen of these were residents of the neighborhood surrounding the medical center. Two were employees of the hospital; a lab technician in the blood bank and a maintenance worker on the same ward where Hickey had served as an orderly.

Twelve of the fifteen were as circumspect as Hickey. Three were willing to talk. All three fingered a nursing student named Marcia Rice as the person who had sold them the contaminated heroin. They picked up Marcia Rice the next evening at her apartment. She turned out to be tiny, with scrubbed cheeks, corn-colored hair and a high-pitched voice. She was crying as Barent and Moran walked in to interview her.

"I didn't do it! I didn't do anything!"

She didn't look like a typical drug-dealer but then most didn't. "Your name is Marcia Rice?" Barent asked.

"Yes," she said, "but I didn't do it!"

"You didn't do what, Miss Rice?"

She stared at him angrily through her tears and said, "I didn't do anything. I don't even know why I'm here. Isn't that against the law? Don't you have to charge me with something?"

"We have twenty-four hours in which to charge you, Miss Rice." Barent looked at her. She seemed honestly terrified. They had already determined that Marcia Rice had no previous record. She was nineteen years old, got good grades and was highly thought of by her teachers and classmates. "You have been read your rights, haven't you, Miss Rice?"

"Yes," she said.

"Then you know that you don't have to answer any questions without a lawyer. Do you want a lawyer, Miss Rice?"

She hesitated. "I don't need a lawyer," she said. "I didn't do anything."

Barent glanced at Moran, who shrugged. Some of them tried to play it that way and for some of them—even some of the guilty ones—it was barely even an act. They did it but they didn't think about it. They needed the money and if they didn't do it, then somebody else would. Or they only dealt with people of quality and nobody was getting hurt, anyway. Or it was a matter of civil rights and nobody else's business. Any rationalization at all would do. Some of them did it almost in their sleep. Selling drugs was so far removed from their normal activities and their conception of themselves as decent human beings that it became like a waking dream. Almost unreal. You asked them about it afterward, they could barely remember doing it.

"We have three people who claim that you habitually sold them heroin, Miss Rice."

"They're lying!"

"All three?"

"Yes!"

Barent sighed. "I doubt the judge will see it that way, Miss Rice. These people don't even know each other. They have no reason to lie."

She stared at him, her lower lip trembling.

"If you cooperate, it will go better for you," he said gently. "Believe me."

She stared at him a moment longer and then started to cry again. Barent handed her a tissue, which she took without a word and clutched to her face. After a few minutes her sobs lessened and she whispered something that Barent couldn't hear.

"What was that, Miss Rice?"

"Jerry," she said. She raised her face and said it again. "Jerry Rubino. He told me to do it."

"Who is Jerry Rubino, Miss Rice?"

"My boyfriend," she said.

Some boyfriend, Barent thought.

"Where does your boyfriend live, Miss Rice? And what does he do, other than deal heroin?"

Jerry Rubino was a computer consultant. He lived in a high-rise apartment not far from Lincoln Center. At least he used to live there. The Rice girl's testimony was enough to get a search warrant and the building superintendent supplied them with a key. They showed up with ten men in bullet-proof vests and didn't bother to knock but they were too late. As soon as the key turned in the lock, they realized it. The air was stale and carried the unmistakable scent of rotting flesh. One of the cops, a rookie, turned green and sat down in a chair in the kitchen. They found Jerry Rubino lying in the bedroom, duct tape wrapped neatly around his wrists and ankles, bound and gagged, with a bullet through his head.

Chapter 12

Barent and Harry Moran sat on the couch in Kurtz' apartment, balancing cups of coffee on their knees. Kurtz enjoyed seeing them this way, the steely-eyed defenders of the law, looking domestic.

Lenore walked in from the kitchen carrying a tray. "Cake, anyone?" she asked. "How about a cookie?"

The coffee cup seemed very small in Moran's ham-like fist. He stopped with it halfway to his lips and said, "Yes, thank you." Lenore placed a slice of cake and two chocolate chip cookies on a small white plate and handed it to him.

"Lew?"

"No, thanks."

Lenore was wearing sneakers, a pair of old blue jeans and a faded denim shirt over a pink Danskin top. She seemed to be enjoying the conversation. She smiled as she lounged back into the couch and sipped her coffee.

"Jesus," Kurtz said. "It's like a cliché, you know?"

"What do you mean?" Barent asked.

"Drugs. Cocaine. Heroin. It's like life in this city revolves around nothing else. You turn on the TV, all you see is drugs. Somebody gets shot on the street, nine chances out of ten it's related to drugs."

Barent gave him a smile. "So where have you been the last twenty years?"

"It seems like it's worse than it used to be," Kurtz said.

"It is worse. The war on drugs is a joke. They ought to legalize it; fewer people would get killed."

"Is that the official position among the police?"

"You'd be surprised. A lot of cops feel that way. Look, you get burned out after awhile. You get, if you'll pardon my lack of moralistic fervor, cynical. Junkies are not your average upstanding citizens. Let the animals kill themselves in their dens. Who cares? I don't. What I care about is when some nice kid gets it in a drive-by shooting or some nice woman gets robbed at knifepoint to support some shithead's habit and he just happens to slit her throat as an afterthought because it's easier to do it that way and not have to worry about being identified. If it was legal, then it would be cheap.

If there was no money to be made, then the scumbags wouldn't be in the business. The only ones dying then would be the junkies and who cares about them?"

"Their mothers?" Kurtz said.

Lenore widened her eyes. "You wouldn't forget about their mothers, would you, Lew?"

"Their mothers ..." Barent made a disrespectful sound between his teeth. "So, okay, maybe their mothers. But maybe not even their mothers. You can bet they've put their mothers through the ringer more than once, and their fathers and sisters and brothers, too. But even supposing that they happened to be relatively decent people who simply got stuck with a nasty habit, your chances of getting them off the stuff and into rehab are a hell of a lot better if it got treated like a disease instead of a crime."

"Geez," Kurtz said. "You're a bleeding heart."

Kurtz himself had thought for years that legalization was the only logical way to deal with the drug problem but he would never have expected a cop to see it that way.

"No. I'm a realist. I believe in solving problems, not making them worse. The way we deal with drugs in this society is making it much worse, believe me. The last people on Earth who want drugs legalized are the dealers. It would eliminate their profit.

"Now in this case, it seems pretty obvious that Jerry Rubino either fucked up or he was set up. If he was set up, then most likely somebody is trying to muscle in on somebody else's business. And if that's the case, within the next few days we're likely to have a full blown gang war going on."

"I didn't know my life was going to be so exciting when I got involved with a surgeon," Lenore said. "Most doctors are so staid and boring."

Kurtz grinned at her. She grinned back. Moran allowed a faint smile to drift across his face. Barent rolled his eyes.

"Well," Kurtz said, "a simple little bullet through the brain is a lot neater than being chopped to bits."

"True. But if you think Jerry Rubino and whoever killed him ties in somehow to Rod Mahoney, then we haven't been able to make the connection."

Kurtz shrugged. "They're the only two murders I've been involved with lately. It's only natural that I would look for a relationship."

"Don't look too hard. You'll get eyestrain."

"Mr. Segura?"

Segura, as always, was sitting up in bed, reading. The bandages wound neatly around the top of his head and most of his face. "Good morning, Doctor."

The voice issuing from behind the bandages was precise. It contained only the hint of an accent, something in the way it rolled the r's and elongated the vowels.

The magazine lay carefully folded in Segura's lap. His hands were still. However violent Segura's personality may have been before half his face got blown away, he had learned patience while in the hospital. "I was wondering," Kurtz said, "if you might give me some information."

The one eye looked at him, expressionless.

"I've been told that you might have some knowledge of how the drug business works."

The one eye blinked. Segura said nothing.

"I'm not asking you to reveal anything that might be incriminating. I'm interested in the mechanics of the process. How the stuff gets from there to here."

"Why?" Segura's voice sounded amused.

"Some strange things have been happening lately."

Kurtz told him. Something in Segura's posture, the set of his shoulders, the motionless way he held his head, conveyed interest.

"These things are indeed strange," Segura said when Kurtz had finished. His voice sounded detached. "Your policeman friend may have been right about one organization moving in on another's territory but in my opinion, the other explanation that he suggested is more probably correct. This person Rubino, the one who was selling the heroin?"

Kurtz nodded encouragingly.

"It seems likely to me that Señor Rubino took advantage of the opportunity to make more money than was prudent. Such things happen quite often. He cut the heroin with scopolamine, hoping to make his supply go further. He miscalculated the dose. His activities came to light. He was killed by his own suppliers. There is no necessity to invoke a gang-land conspiracy."

Segura seemed to slump down in the bed. He looked tired. "I know little of heroin. Heroin does not come from my country. My people ..." He shrugged. "They do not deal in heroin. In the old days, almost all of the heroin entering this country came from Anatolia, from the mountains of Turkey. Opium was smuggled first into Europe, primarily Marseilles, where it was refined into heroin. You have heard of the French Connection?"

Kurtz nodded.

"The Turkish government was determined to wipe out the trade and they were at least partially successful. Today, most heroin comes from Asia, from the poppy fields of the Golden Triangle."

Kurtz hadn't known this. Barent, presumably, did. "Who does deal in heroin?"

"The Sicilianos, what you call the Mafia. Hong Kong. Vietnam. Cambodia. The Chinese. And of course, Afghanistan. After the fall of the Taliban, the warlords of that country see heroin as a way to easy cash." Segura shrugged again. "Anyone with connections in that part of the world. Anyone who can tap in to the supply."

Rubino ... not a Colombian name, according to Barent. Rubino had come from Queens, a third generation American with roots in Naples and Milan.

Segura, who had continued to watch him, said, "Why do you want to know these things, Doctor? This has nothing to do with the practice of medicine. This is not your business. You should not get involved in it."

Now where had he heard that before?

"I have no intention of running a one-man crusade," Kurtz said. "I'm only curious."

"Curious ..." Segura sighed. "A kilo of heroin fetches more than a million dollars on the open market. The price of cocaine is less than a tenth the price of heroin. Heroin is tasteless and almost scentless, a simple white powder. It is very easy to smuggle heroin into this country. You asked me how the stuff gets from there to here?" Segura shook his head. "There are a million ways. It comes in by plane. It comes in by boat. It comes in labeled as shipments of stereo equipment, or antiques, or curry powder from India. It is pulled from the sea in fishing nets and lobster pots. In smaller deliveries, it arrives in the false bottoms of luggage and the handbags of little old ladies.

"You should not be so curious, Doctor. Heroin is very big business and people will do terrible things to preserve it."

The sheet stirred. A thin, white hand rose up to touch the bandages on Segura's face. "Look at me and learn wisdom. Stay out of things which do not concern you. Let your policeman friend deal with this."

"Do you think that he can?" Kurtz said tightly.

"Perhaps. Your friend, his business is finding murderers. Perhaps the police can solve the murder of Professor Mahoney and even that of Jerry Rubino. About this I have no idea. But they cannot stop the traffic in drugs and neither can you. Your friend knows this. You should know it, too."

For long minutes after Kurtz had left, Hector Segura brooded. This was not good, he thought. This was not good at all. This sort of business could definitely put a crimp in his plans. Hector Segura, despite his injuries (perhaps, in part, because of them) had very large plans. Finally, he sighed and picked up the phone by the side of his bed and dialed a number. The voice that came on was one that he instantly recognized. "I wish you to take a message to Vincent DeNegri," Hector Segura said.

Chapter 13

The report from the FBI arrived the next day. Four years ago, a day laborer in Boise, Idaho had been chopped to bits by another man who suspected that the victim had been having an affair with his wife. The murderer was still in jail. A year before that, a woman was raped, burned to death and dismembered by a gang of three rogue bikers on the outskirts of Seattle. The bikers had all been caught and given thirty years to life. One of the bikers had written a book about his abused childhood and misspent youth. It had garnered him critical acclaim but the family of the dead woman had attached the proceeds and the judge had not been moved to leniency. There had been no other murders similar to that of Rod Mahoney anywhere in the United States during the past ten years.

"What do you think?" Barent asked Moran.

Moran, who had flipped through the folder as soon as Barent finished it, shrugged. "Nothing."

"No," Barent agreed.

The autopsy report on Rod Mahoney and the final report from the crime lab had both arrived two days before. They had been a bit more useful. Mahoney had been killed by a single blow to the head. The instrument of death had been the proverbial blunt instrument, round and about an inch in diameter, most likely a crow bar or a piece of plumbing pipe. The jagged edges of the wounds on his arms and legs indicated that he had been dismembered by hand-held instruments not designed for the purpose, most likely a wood-saw, some sort of small knife and a hatchet. There were no flecks of rust in the wounds, which meant that the tools were either new or were well-maintained. All of the blood was Mahoney's. The murderer had worked carefully but an adult male cannot be dismembered without scattering a lot of blood. Most of it had pooled on the carpet but there were droplets all over the furniture and the walls. There were five distinct footprints, all made by the same pair of men's running shoes. They were Reebok DMX, a reasonably expensive but popular brand.

A small spatter of blood high up on one wall gave strong evidence that Mahoney had been standing when originally struck. The angle of the blow on the top of his head indicated that the murderer was probably above average height, about six feet, or perhaps an inch or so taller. The depth of the footprints in the carpet indicated a weight of perhaps one hundred ninety to two hundred pounds. The depth of the wound in Mahoney's head indicated a man of great strength in the arms and shoulders.

The murderer had worn leather gloves. There were prints all over the room. The prints from a glove were just as distinctive as the prints from a finger. If the police ever ran across these particular gloves again, they would know it. Most likely, however, both the gloves and the tools were at this moment at the bottom of a landfill, maybe the shoes as well. Barent doubted they would ever find any of them. They told you some things, though. Aside from the height and the weight and the fact that the guy was strong, they told you that he was probably well off. The gloves were real leather, not synthetic. The shoes were a standard brand but not cheap. And of course, there was the fact that the murderer was working alone. Unless, Barent reminded himself, there had been others standing lookout.

A few dried blades of grass had been found among the footprints on the carpet. The grass was Bermuda grass, a type found primarily in warmer climates and commonly used on golf courses.

So what did they know?

Above average height, strong, probably well-to-do. Not a pro. A pro would never have done it alone, even with a lookout. Too risky, and it would have taken far too long. A pro would have shot Mahoney and been done with it, and if for some unknown reason a pro had wanted to kill somebody and then chop him to bits, he would have used power tools, not wasted his time hacking the guy's arms and legs off. And the tools … Not too many people living in the city had any use for a wood saw and a hatchet, which means the guy lives somewhere else, either the suburbs or out in the country, unless he bought the tools especially for the purpose. Also he was probably recently returned from a trip to a warmer climate. And maybe he likes golf. That was a fair amount. It was certainly a hell of a lot more than they had before.

And then there was the crime itself, the nature of it. Despite speculation that the murderer was simply crazy, the other explanation was beginning to make more sense, especially in light of what was now evident. Whoever had murdered Rod Mahoney, had done it for personal reasons, which meant that he had known Mahoney and had good cause–at least in his own twisted mind–to hate him. The fact that Mahoney had let him into the house lent credence to this theory.

Barent put down the folder on Manoney and picked up the autopsy report on Jerry Rubino. It was not as helpful. No footprints. No glove prints. No signs of a struggle. Jerry Rubino had died with an enormous level of heroin in his blood. Whoever had killed him had found a victim almost incapacitated by dope and in no condition to put up a fight. The bullet had been a standard nine-millimeter steel jacket, the sort most crooks these days were using.

Jay Richter was only five foot eight. Not the right height, though he did wear good clothes …

Barent sighed. "Let's go interview some suspects," he said. Moran looked at him and grinned. "You bet."

"You're looking good," Kurtz said. Nolan had put on some weight. His pants were neatly creased. His tie was expensive and his face no longer had that lean, pale look.

Nolan smiled in satisfaction. "Being an attending is better than being a resident."

"I'll say."

Nolan nodded crisply and looked down at his menu. "What's good here?" Kurtz asked.

The Faculty Club was an incredible anachronism for a hospital. It had waiters and a menu that changed every month and the chef had trained at the Culinary Institute of America. Staunton liked to do things with class. Founded only in 1957, it was the youngest of New York City's medical colleges, located on Manhattan's West Side a few miles downtown from Columbia-Presbyterian, which it regarded as its main competition. Easton, where Kurtz did most of his cases, was Staunton's second largest teaching hospital, and all of the physicians at Easton had faculty appointments at the medical school as well.

"I don't know," Nolan said. "I've only eaten here once. I can't afford the prices."

Actually, Kurtz thought, the prices were quite reasonable. The club probably received a subsidy from the school. A waiter in a tuxedo appeared at their table. "Gentlemen, have you decided?"

"I'll have escargot," Kurtz said, "and then Dover sole." Nolan ordered a Caesar salad and a hamburger. "How about some wine?" Kurtz asked.

"Sure," Nolan said. "I don't know too much about wine. Why don't you order."

By the time he finished his residency, a surgeon could tell you the fine points of every Chinese restaurant and pizza place within miles, particularly the ones that delivered. Within a few years, as their wallets expanded along with their practices, most of them metamorphosed as rapidly as possible into self-styled gourmets–a perhaps understandable reaction to all those years of eating junk. Kurtz ordered half a bottle of Chassagne-Montrachet 1998.

"I understand this is where the famous Halloween party took place," Kurtz said.

Nolan winced. "Not exactly. There are some rooms down the hall that they reserve for private meetings and medium-sized conferences. They wouldn't let us in here. We might damage the china."

"I heard it was quite a party."

Nolan gave a little snort. "It didn't last too long. Your old buddy Barent shut us down."

The waiter arrived with the wine and showed Kurtz the label. Strictly speaking, it was against the rules to serve alcohol in a hospital. They got around that by locating the club in the Administration Building of the Medical School. Kurtz nodded. The waiter popped the cork, which Kurtz sniffed, and then poured a thimble full into a wineglass. Kurtz raised it to his lips, sipped and then rolled it around his tongue. "Very good," he said. The waiter poured the wine and then left, taking the empty bottle with him.

"This is good," agreed Nolan.

"Better than formalin with a twist of human flesh?"

"Jesus, you really want to talk about that, don't you?"

"Yeah."

"Why?"

"Curiosity."

Nolan sadly shook his head. "So much for my reputation as a wild and crazy guy. A lot of people thought I had something to do with it."

Kurtz grunted in sympathy. "Who do you think did?" he asked.

"Damned if I know."

"Speculate. Who do you think?"

"Most people figure a bunch of medical students. Personally, I doubt it. All four cadavers in the classroom were mutilated. The students only have the combinations to their own cadavers, so it would have had to have been at least four of them working together. And once their own cadavers had pieces missing, it would make it a lot harder to learn the material. They would have to go look at somebody else's body, which is a pain for everybody. Why do that to yourself?"

Kurtz nodded. It made sense. The waiter placed a salad in front of Nolan and a round tray with six snails in garlic butter in front of Kurtz. The butter was still bubbling.

"And then Mahoney gets murdered," Kurtz said. "Interesting timing, wouldn't you say?"

Nolan frowned and seemed suddenly surprised to see the piece of lettuce on the end of his fork. He placed it in his mouth and chewed it. "People have noted the coincidence," he muttered sourly.

"Hell of a coincidence."

Nolan swallowed, looking morose. "I suppose you're right."

"So tell me, was the room with the buffet table locked?"

"You mean after Redding and I left? Yes. We didn't want some joker to come in and steal all the food."

"And who would have had access to the key?"

"Plenty of people. Security must have copies. The locksmith ... I imagine the manager here must have one." Nolan shrugged. "Probably more. I wouldn't know." Nolan fixed him with a beady eye. "Why are you asking all these questions?"

Kurtz smiled. "Like I said, I'm curious."

Nolan snorted.

The waiter arrived with their main courses and the two men dug in. Kurtz was hungry and evidently so was Nolan. Neither of them said anything more until they had almost finished.

"You like it here?" Kurtz asked him over coffee.

"Sure. What's not to like? I'm doing what I was trained to do and I'm getting paid for it."

"That doesn't necessarily mean you have to like it."

Nolan looked at him as if he had a screw loose. "It's surgery," he said.

Which was exactly Kurtz' point. Nolan was still young, still full of the old fire and brimstone. Give him an abdomen full of pus and a set of sharp scalpels and he'd labor all day and all night long, as happy as a clam.

"Any problem getting your cases on?" Kurtz asked.

"Not too much. I have to schedule a few weeks in advance."

Not bad for a junior guy. The older, busier surgeons had first dibs on OR time. It was like that everywhere. New staff members usually had to settle for time on Friday afternoon or Saturday morning, the hours when everybody else wanted to be off. The fact that Nolan didn't might mean that the OR wasn't as busy as it used to be, back when Kurtz was a resident. There were a lot of hospitals in New York and with managed care moving steadily in the competition for patients was furious.

Kurtz looked moodily at Nolan over his coffee. The younger man was staring out the window at the Palisades across the Hudson. He had a satisfied smile on his face and Kurtz almost chuckled. Let the kid enjoy it, Kurtz thought. School's out. Time to play. After everything Nolan had been through in the last few years, the opportunity to be his own boss, work seventy hours a week and get paid for it must seem almost like a vacation. Of course he wasn't really a kid. Nolan must be in his early thirties, but in surgeon's terms, he was still wet behind the ears.

"Anybody around here who doesn't like you?"

"Me?" Nolan looked surprised. "What do you mean?"

"Anybody who might have had a motive to ruin your party?"

Evidently the idea had never occurred to him. Nolan shifted in his seat and grimaced. "Jesus," he said. "No way."

"How about Redding?"

Nolan considered the idea for a moment, then shrugged. "I seriously doubt it."

"Well," Kurtz said. He sipped his coffee and looked out at a seagull flying over the river. "Life is full of little mysteries, isn't it?"

"Yeah," Nolan replied. "I suppose you could say that."

Bob Redding was an ER doc. ER's were occasionally staffed by a private group of physicians but more often the doctors who worked there were employees of the hospital. The possibilities for getting rich working the ER were limited but as medical specialties went, it was a popular job. You didn't have to worry about the pension or the malpractice insurance. The hours were regular and the night-call limited.

"What percentage of the business in here do you think is drug related?"

Redding puffed up his cheeks as he thought about it. "Percentage?" He shook his head. "I couldn't really say. Probably not a lot but it's constant, you know? We get at least one shooting or stabbing a night and most of it is probably related to drugs. At least it is if you consider that either the guy who did it or the guy who got it or both are probably using."

Kurtz hadn't spent a lot of time down here in the past couple of years. For the moment, it was quiet. There weren't any police cars or ambulances lined up outside and the nurses were sitting behind their monitor screens, drinking coffee.

During his residency, Kurtz had known the place well. A surgeon-in-training spends a number of months covering the ER. It was great experience. Sometimes you even got to ride the ambulance when they needed a physician at the scene and when you got back to the hospital, you followed the patient into the OR and then into the ICU, participating in their care every step of the way. It had been casually assumed that most of the shooting and stabbing victims were high on something. The tox screen didn't always come back positive but there were a lot of drugs that could only be picked up by specialized tests and frankly, it didn't matter. Most of the patients were intubated and on ventilators for a day or so after their surgery and by the time they were ready to come off ventilatory support, any drugs that might have been in their systems were gone.

"Would you say that the incidence has gone up recently?"

"How recently?"

"The past year?"

Redding thought about it. "I couldn't say."

"The past month?"

"The past month? Definitely. This thing with the scopolamine … "

"No," Kurtz said. "I mean aside from that."

"I don't know." Redding looked at Kurtz with narrowed eyes. "Why are you asking?"

"No reason, really." Kurtz smiled. "I'm just curious. You think the thing with the Halloween party and the business with the scopolamine could have anything to do with each other?"

"Are you kidding?" Redding looked at him skeptically. "Why would they?"

"Why not?"

"Why not?"

Redding seemed to think that repeating a question in a sarcastic tone of voice constituted an answer. "Look, I was as upset as anybody by the way that turned out. It was my party that got ruined. But nobody figured that for anything but a stupid joke. How could it be related to bad heroin? Even if it was a hospital employee peddling the stuff."

"I don't know," Kurtz said.

"Well, I don't either," Redding answered.

"Where were your parents from, originally?" Kurtz asked.

Kurtz and Chao had different block booking times in the OR. Since OR time was a surgeon's most jealously hoarded commodity, the rest of his practice had to be arranged around those precious hours when he could actually get to operate. Kurtz and Chao ran on schedules that were largely independent but which intersected at fixed points. They did teaching rounds together every Monday morning and they were in the office together every Thursday afternoon.

At the moment, they were taking a lunch break. Kurtz' office contained a mica covered desk, a set of battered easy chairs that Kurtz could not bear the thought of throwing out, a comfortable old couch, a small glass covered coffee table, an abstract painting on the wall opposite the window and an enormous black filing cabinet containing patient records. A small white refrigerator that at the moment contained nothing but a loaf of bread, a container of orange juice and jars of peanut butter and jelly was hidden inside a closet.

"My mother was from Hong Kong. She had just completed school and was taking a vacation in New York when she met my father. His parents had emigrated a long time before that and he was in Business School at NYU. Why?"

"Have you ever been back there?"

"To Hong Kong?"

A small box of Chicken McNuggets and a package of fries sat on the table in front of Chao. He picked up a nugget, dipped it in barbecue sauce and bit off half of it. His jaws worked stolidly as he thought about it. "Once, when I was a little kid. It was a complete and utter drag. My grandfather was rich. You ever hear of Northwind Manufacturing?"

"Can't say that I have."

Chao nodded, unsurprised. "Neither have most people. It's a holding company. It owns pieces of other companies: electronics, Chinese pottery, jade, all sorts of stuff. My grandfather owned Northwind. They do some business in the States. They have a branch office in Chicago."

Chao picked up a French fry, dipped it in barbecue sauce and popped it in his mouth. "Anyway, he had this mansion with servants all over the place. Hardwood floors, antiques, French wine and Cuban cigars. And not a thing to do that a little kid would find interesting. My mother, she was one of five sisters. My mother and my aunts had one large room to themselves when they were growing up. They had two brothers who each had a whole wing of the mansion. The classical Chinese viewpoint didn't put a lot of value on girls. The old man did take care of them, though. When he died, my mother got quite a windfall."

"What happened to your aunts?"

"Two of them came to America. One is in London and one stayed in Hong Kong."

"How about your uncles?"

"They run Northwind. They're rich."

"It must be nice, being rich," Kurtz said.

Chao shrugged, then stifled a yawn behind his palm.

"Rough night?" Kurtz asked.

"The usual." Chao shrugged again. He had been on call the night before. Chao was not so long out of his residency. To Chao, "the usual" truly sucked. A few years before, a woman named Libby Zion had come into an emergency room and died, supposedly after being mistreated by a resident. The fact that the resident had been working his tail off for two days straight and was completely exhausted figured prominently in the ensuing investigation. After that, New York State had passed legislation making it illegal to keep residents in the hospital for more than twenty-four hours. This was supposed to prevent mishaps caused by overtired hands and minds, which it might have done except that, within a year, the surgical specialties had managed to get themselves exempt from the new regulations. They claimed that surgical training was so difficult that without those endless nights on call, the budding young surgeons would never get sufficient experience to learn their craft and the public health would thereby be endangered. The fact that paying for additional personnel was expensive did not ostensibly enter into the debate. In any case, it was slavery as usual where surgeons were concerned.

"Have you ever heard of the Golden Triangle?" Kurtz asked.

"Sure. It's an area of Cambodia, Laos and Vietnam where opium poppies are grown. Why?"

"This business with the scopolamine ..."

Chao puffed out his cheeks thoughtfully and ate another fry. "You know anything about the Triads?"

Organized crime had been moving into Chinatown lately. There had been a number of stories in the papers. "I've heard of them," Kurtz said. "They're Chinese gangs, aren't they?"

"More than gangs. They're like the mafia. Supposedly, the Triads have been in existence for over two thousand years. Supposedly, they control a large part of the heroin traffic."

Segura had mentioned the Chinese. "I didn't know that," Kurtz said.

"I'm not sure there's anything to know. My parents are pretty well-to-do. I never spent much time in Chinatown but we have relatives who did. Every once in a while, you'd hear rumors."

Kurtz looked at him.

Chao looked uncomfortable. "You mention the mafia to an Italian kid, he tends to get upset. It's a stereotype. Chinese feel the same way about the Triads."

"Sorry."

Chao shrugged. "I'm the one who brought it up." Then he grinned. "Do you like Chinese food?"

"Sure. Who doesn't?"

"My mother is having a dinner party next week. She asked me to invite you."

"Really?"

Kurtz was surprised. Kurtz had never met Chao's parents. "Why?"

"She's been wanting to have you over for a long time. Chinese are very conscious of hierarchy. Not only are you my boss, but we do karate together. To the traditional way of thinking, the fact that you spend time with me outside of the job is a mark of special recognition. It's like you're my patron or something."

Chao was as American as apple pie but his mother was from the old country. The foreign residents were often startled by America's free and easy ways, Kurtz reflected. Patel, for instance, called everybody senior to him "Sir," which tended to make Americans uncomfortable, at least at first. Once they got used to the idea, most of them seemed to enjoy it. "That's very nice of her. When would this party be?"

"Saturday night."

Chao grinned. "I'm bringing Carrie Owens."

"Carrie Owens … Little blonde? Pretty? Works in the ER?"

"Yeah. She was at the Halloween party. She drank some of the punch with the dead hand in it and threw up all over the buffet table. It stimulated my protective instincts."

"Good luck," Kurtz said. Offhand, Kurtz couldn't recall any plans for Saturday night. "Can I bring Lenore?"

"Of course."

"Let me talk to her, see if she has anything planned. I'll get back to you tomorrow."

"Sure," Chao said.

Chapter 14

Since there were now two murders to investigate, Barent and Moran decided to split up. For the moment, Barent wanted to concentrate on Rod Mahoney. Harry Moran took Arnie Figueroa with him and left to follow up on Jerry Rubino.

Mahoney's two children had arrived home from school the day prior to the funeral. They were still home. Barent knocked on the door of the small house and Claire Mahoney answered it. She nodded him in, her face wooden.

"How are you today, Mrs. Mahoney?" Barent asked.

She shrugged. "Coping, thank you."

"Are your children here?"

"Yes. Please come in."

Barent followed her into the living room, where a young man with brown, tousled hair and a lanky frame sat talking with a blonde young woman who looked a lot like him. They both stood up as Barent entered the room. Claire Mahoney introduced them, then asked Barent, "Would you rather I left, Detective?"

"If you don't mind."

She shrugged her shoulders and wordlessly walked out. Clarissa and Kevin Mahoney stood looking at him, their expressions wary. Barent sat down in a straight-backed chair. "Please sit," he said.

Mahoney's two children exchanged wordless glances and sat down. Kevin cleared his throat and said, "Have you made any progress yet?"

"Not really," Barent said. "It's still early."

Clarissa frowned at that but said nothing.

"You were both at school when it happened?" Barent asked. One rarely interviewed two suspects at a time. For one thing, being alone tends to put people off guard, make them at least a little nervous. For another, it makes it easier to check any inconsistencies in the stories. In this case, however, Mahoney's kids were pretty low on the suspect list and they went to schools that were five hundred miles apart, so there wasn't a lot of question about their stories jiving. Barent had already checked with the schools and the airlines and made certain that they had both, indeed, been where they claimed.

Clarissa nodded and Kevin shrugged and said, "Yes."

"When did you last see your parents?"

"I was home for a weekend about a month ago," Clarissa said.

"I haven't been back since the school year started," said Kevin. "That was early September."

"Did you notice anything strange about your father, at that time?" Barent asked Clarissa.

Clarissa frowned. "No," she said. "Not at all."

"Your mother tells me that your father seemed pre-occupied lately, as if something had been on his mind." This wasn't exactly what Claire Mahoney had said but a little creative license was part of the job.

She shook her head. "Not that I noticed."

Barent turned to Kevin. "How about you?"

Kevin seemed bewildered. "No."

They both looked like they meant it. "Had he been having any financial difficulties lately?"

Kevin scratched his head and Clarissa rolled her eyes. "Does that question bother you?" Barent asked.

"It seems pretty far afield," Clarissa said. "My father was not exactly a jet-setter. Look at this house? Does it look extravagant to you?"

The house did not look like the house of people who lived beyond their means, which was irrelevant. Plenty of people had second and third houses, and cars and jewels and mistresses stashed away in unlikely places. "That's not exactly the point," Barent said. "Lots of people live frugally and still have money problems. Sometimes they lose their job. Sometimes they make a bad investment. Sometimes they lend money to a relative and don't get it back."

Kevin grinned briefly and Clarissa looked annoyed but settled into her chair. She stared out the window, frowning at the street. After a moment, Barent said, "Well?"

"I think that Dad might have loaned money to my Aunt Evelyn," Clarissa said.

"What do you mean, *think*?" put in Kevin. "He definitely loaned money to Aunt Evelyn."

Barent already knew this but in never hurt to confirm a story. "Have you any idea how much?"

Kevin hesitated. "I don't think it was very much. A few hundred."

"A few hundred *this* time," said Clarissa. "Over the years, who knows? Probably thousands."

"Did she ever pay any of it back?"

"Maybe." Clarissa shrugged and looked vaguely disgusted. "Dribs and drabs. Aunt Evelyn is one of those people who can never quite get their shit together."

Clarissa Mahoney was … what? Nineteen? Barent looked at her moodily. "How about your uncle?" he asked.

Clarissa made a rude noise. "A jerk," she said.

"Anything specific?"

Kevin looked thoughtful. Clarissa gave another shrug and allowed her eyes to drift out to the street. After a moment, she said, "Not really. He just seems like a phony. Whenever they came to visit, he would make a big fuss over us, give us hugs and kisses and talk about Paris and Rome and all the famous people he knows and the big business deals he's got in the works. But somehow none of them ever turned into anything and he never remembered Christmas or our birthdays."

Not exactly major criminal behavior, Barent thought. "I see."

Clarissa grinned. "It sounds a little petty, put like that. Doesn't it?"

"A little," Barent agreed.

"I've got no reason to suspect that either of them would be capable of murder, if that's where this conversation is leading us."

Barent looked at Kevin. "How about you?"

"Me?" Kevin seemed startled. "I always liked Aunt Evelyn. She's completely helpless in the real world. I feel sorry for her. Uncle Jay is a jerk but it's a long way from being a jerk to killing a member of your family."

Maybe, Barent thought. Maybe not. So far, he had a possible motive for the Richters to have done it, which was more than he had on anybody else.

"I have a few more questions," he said, "and I don't want you to take them the wrong way."

He looked at them. Kevin looked wary. Clarissa met his gaze and reluctantly nodded.

"Alright."

Barent shifted his weight in the chair and leaned forward. "First of all, did your parents have a happy marriage?"

"Definitely," Kevin said. "Mom and Dad did everything together. Dad was crazy about her."

"Did either of you ever have any reason to suspect that your father might have been having an affair?"

Clarissa sniffed. Kevin grinned. "Dad?" he said. "I doubt it."

"Clarissa?" Barent said.

"No way," she said shortly.

"Alright, one last question: can either of you think of anybody, anybody at all, who might have had reason to dislike your father?"

They both thought about it, concentrating on the question. After a few moments, Clarissa said, "There was a lab assistant, a year or so ago. Dad had to fire him."

"Why?"

"I don't know."

"Kevin?"

Kevin nodded slowly. "Clarissa's right. I'd forgotten about that."

"Do you remember any of the details?"

He shook his head. "No."

"How about the name?"

Kevin stared into space and squinted his eyes. Clarissa shrugged. Finally, Kevin said, "Gallagher …?"

"That sounds right," Clarissa said.

Elvira Pang had already told them this. James Gallagher had been traced to a small college in Minnesota, where he taught biology. The local police had been asked to investigate. They had come up with nothing. James Gallagher was recently married to a graduate student in Sociology. He had a good reputation at the school and he and his wife seemed happy. They had not left Minnesota for at least six months prior to Rod Mahoney's murder.

"Thank you," Barent said. "Thank you both."

"Rubino …" Arnie Figueroa said. "Where have I heard that name before?"

"Michael Rubino?" Moran said. "Does that ring a bell?"

Arnie thought about it for a moment, his eyes narrowed in thought, then slowly nodded. "Yeah," he said. "I think so."

Moran grinned. Michael Rubino had been a middle-level member of the Lucchese family. Five years ago, an anonymous tip had led the cops to Michael Rubino's body, buried under twenty tons of landfill at the Staten Island dump. He had been strangled. "His father?" Arnie asked.

"Uncle."

It was a cold, gray morning. The weather reports were predicting rain for later in the afternoon. Moran was driving. "Rubino worked for a company called Comm-Link. Ever heard of it?"

"No.

"A couple of refugees from Motorola got together with some guys from Apple and Novell and decided to ride the cutting wave of wireless communications. They're supposedly doing well."

"Where did Rubino fit in?"

"That's what we're going to find out."

Moran pulled over in front of a medium sized skyscraper and parked the car in an empty space by a hydrant. He pulled down the sun-visor with the NYPD logo on it and they walked in. The lobby was crowded with people wearing business suits, mostly men. The few women all seemed to be wearing glasses and understated makeup and had pre-occupied looks on their faces.

Must make them seem more serious to the business bureaucracy, Moran thought.

They took the elevator to the Fifteenth Floor and walked down a carpeted hall to a doorway that said, *Comm-Link Associates*. Inside, a pretty young woman with swept up brown hair and coral lipstick was seated at a shiny, metal desk. "Can I help you?" she asked.

"Detective Moran and Detective Figueroa," Moran said. "We're here to see Mr. Bryant."

She didn't hesitate. "Of course," she said. "Mr. Bryant is expecting you. Go right in."

Past the desk was a wooden door with a frosted glass panel and an antique brass doorknob. Moran grasped the knob and opened it. A harried looking face looked up from a pile of papers covering the middle of an enormous mahogany workstation. On one corner of the desk sat a PC, pictures of multi-colored fish slowly swimming across the screen. "Mr. Bryant?" Moran asked.

"Yes?" Bryant said. He seemed bewildered. "How can I help you?"

"Detective Moran. And Detective Figueroa."

Bryant's face cleared. "Oh, yes, of course. Sit down." He pointed to two chairs on the opposite side of the desk. "Let me just clear a space."

With Moran and Figueroa sitting, the piles of papers on the desk almost obscured Bryant's face. He picked up two stacks, tucked them under each arm and placed them on a small table next to the desk. "There," he said, and beamed at them both. "That's better. Now, what can I do for you?"

Bryant had wispy blonde hair, myopic blue eyes and pink, round cheeks. He looked like a middle-aged cherub.

"Jerry Rubino," Moran said. "We understand that he used to work for you."

Bryant's smile vanished. He gave Moran a hurt look. "Yes. Jerry did good work, when he showed up."

"What exactly did he do?"

"Jerry was a programmer. He had a real talent. Unfortunately, he called in sick quite a bit, almost always on Monday or Friday. I had spoken to him about his work habits more than once but it didn't seem to have done much good. If he hadn't died, I was probably going to have to fire him."

"What sort of programs was he working on?"

"Networking. It's our business. We take personal computers of all types and tie them together into LANS–local area networks. Jerry was working to tie the older variety of PC's, the ones without voice capability, into a voice activated system."

"How would that work?"

"All personal computers come with expansion slots. You design a hardware modification, pop it in, and write the software to make it work."

Not much of an interface between voice activation and heroin, Moran thought. "How was he doing?"

"The project is going pretty well. Jerry was not the only one working on it."

"Was he the only one selling heroin?"

Bryant's face seemed to freeze. "I beg your pardon?"

"You do know that Jerry Rubino was selling heroin?"

"The newspapers mentioned it," Bryant said stiffly.

"People who deal one drug often deal others. Heroin ... cocaine. The thing about cocaine, it has a certain *cachet* among the intelligentsia. A quick snort, your brain works faster. You feel good. It's neat and clean and doesn't involve anything painful or bloody like needles. Computer people ... they like to think of themselves as being very, very cutting edge. What do you think?"

"I think that you're making ridiculous suggestions. You have no evidence at all for what you're saying."

"No?" Moran leaned back in his chair, stretched and allowed a happy smile to creep across his face. "Tell me, where does the funding come from to run your business?"

Bryant stared at him.

"Start-up companies need money. You don't pay people with promises."

"Our business has been profitable for the last three years of operation, and our funding is a matter of public record," Bryant said.

Moran shrugged. "Maybe I'm wrong," he said. "I've got a suspicious mind. You've got this guy who you admit doesn't do a lot of work. He deals heroin. He gets shot dead in his apartment, gangland style. You say you were going to fire him but you *didn't* fire him. All of this suggests to me that maybe you *couldn't* fire him, that maybe Jerry's presence here was part of the cost of doing business."

Bryant's breath hissed in between his teeth. "I think you had better leave," he said.

"Are you sure?"

Moran made no move to rise from his chair. "You said your funding was a matter of public record. We have reason to believe that Jerry Rubino had connections to the Lucchese crime family. Under the RICO statutes, the government could seize a corporation that was operating as a front for organized crime."

"That's ridiculous!" Bryant said, and pounded the desk with a fist. "God damn it, you can't come in here and make threats like that!"

It seemed to Moran that Bryant really meant it, which was good for Bryant but not so good for the investigation. Moran sighed and pasted a regretful smile on his face. "Look," he said. "I'm investigating a homicide. I'm not interested in shutting down your business. I just want to know why Jerry Rubino got shot in the head."

"I don't know why Jerry Rubino got shot in the head," Bryant said. "I don't know anything about heroin or cocaine or organized crime. And our funding comes from Citicorp. And if you try to claim otherwise, I'll sue you."

Moran turned to Figueroa. "What do you think, Arnie?"

Arnie, who had sat quietly through the conversation, suddenly grinned. "I think we should talk to Jerry's co-workers."

"Fine," Bryant said. "Talk to anyone you want."

He punched a button on his desk and spoke into it. "Miss Robbins, the gentlemen"–his lip curled as he said the word–"who are with me want to talk to some people out on the floor. Please prepare passes for them."

He turned back to Moran. "Will that satisfy you?"

"Yeah," Moran said equably. "I appreciate your cooperation."

Bryant sniffed, and said nothing.

Arnie Figueroa smiled. Moran frowned and rose to his feet. "Well," he said to Bryant, "have a nice day."

Chapter 15

"When I was in college I had a good friend named Jennifer Wing," Lenore said. "She got married a couple of years ago. I was invited to the wedding."

It was Saturday morning. Lenore's head was resting comfortably on Kurtz' shoulder. Her hair was tousled and they were both breathing hard. Kurtz and Lenore had woken up a half-hour before and had just finished making love, which was pretty much what they did on Saturday mornings.

"So?"

"You ever go to a Jewish wedding? Or an Italian wedding?"

Offhand, Kurtz couldn't see the connection. "Sure," he said. "What about it?"

"Lots of food, wasn't there?"

"Sure," he said.

Lenore nodded wisely. "Jennifer's wedding was the same."

"Don't weddings always have a lot of food?"

Lenore looked at him sadly and twirled a finger in his chest hairs. "Where have you been all your life? Of course they all have food, but if you're Jewish or Italian, it's not considered polite to send a guest home until they feel like they're going to explode if they eat another bite. Every Jewish or Italian wedding I've ever been to had so much food, your head could spin just looking at it."

"And Chinese weddings are the same as Jewish and Italian weddings?"

"The one I went to was. I think it has to do with family, the way the Chinese and the Italians and the Jews see themselves as part of an extended family."

It occurred to Kurtz, not for the first time, that Lenore's mind was always working, ferreting out associations that other people would never see. "What does this have to do with anything?"

She gave him a look that said the connection should have been obvious. "Culture is a larger reflection of the family. The way a society is organized reflects the way that its families are organized."

"You're saying that Chinese have close families," Kurtz stated.

"Absolutely."

"Like the Jews and the Italians."

"You bet. Actually, so far as I'm aware, the only ethnic groups that don't are you cold-blooded Northern types. It's probably why the British had an Empire. They were compensating for the fact that their parents sent them to boarding school and otherwise ignored them."

Then again, Lenore did sometimes say things just to see if she could get away with them. She smiled at him and Kurtz drew a deep breath. "What exactly are you talking about?" he asked

"I'm talking," Lenore said patiently, "about Chinese food."

"What *about* Chinese food?"

"At my friend Jennifer's wedding, they must have had twenty or more courses, traditional Chinese dishes. They were served one at a time. You would eat one dish, the waiters would bring out another. You finished that, they'd bring out another. Almost all meat. Peking Duck, Garlic Chicken, Lobster in Chili Sauce, Szechuan Beef, Shrimp with Ginger. I guess that in China, only the rich could afford a lot of meat, so serving all that meat was a way of one-upping the relatives and friends."

"So?"

She smiled at him. "Don't eat much today. When we go to the Chao's?"

"Yeah?"

"I bet there'll be enough food to kill an ox."

"Paul does not need help washing the car," Barent said.

"Of course he doesn't." Betty nodded wisely. "That's just an excuse."

"An excuse."

"Didn't I just say that? Is there an echo in here?"

Barent glanced at her out of the corner of his eye but kept most of his attention on the road. "An excuse for what?"

"An excuse for a little attention. He's feeling neglected."

"I wonder why," Barent said.

Betty sniffed. "*Men* … a woman gets pregnant and *you* turn into big babies."

Offhand, Barent could think of a number of rejoinders to that one. He picked the safest. He cleared his throat.

Betty grinned at him. "So alright, women do tend to get a little sappy when a new baby is on the way."

After thirty years of marriage, Barent knew when to keep his mouth shut. He nodded his head judiciously and concentrated on driving.

"Denise is starting to get nauseous," Betty said.

"Oh, boy," Barent said, and shuddered.

"Hopefully she won't get it as bad as I did."

Most women didn't. Betty had been sick as a dog for one whole trimester. "I can see why Paul is feeling a bit overwhelmed."

"So help him wash the car," Betty said. "And don't be sarcastic."

"Me?" Barent was offended. "When have I ever given the little wimp a hard time?"

Betty gave him a guarded look. "I'm warning you."

"Alright, alright," he said. "I'll keep my mouth shut."

"Good," she said. "See that you do."

Barent, actually, was just as glad of the opportunity to get away and do something brainless for a little while. There had been a few leads but no breaks so far in the Mahoney case.

Comm-Link Associates seemed to be a completely legitimate business. As Bryant had said, their financing came from Citicorp. They had no known connection to organized crime and their products were highly regarded within the industry. As for the man in the suit who had been seen wandering around the Mahoney's neighborhood, he might as well have been a phantom.

Jerry Rubino's father had died a few years before. He had no brothers or sisters. His mother was from the old country. She wore a black dress with a kerchief over her head and spoke English with a thick accent. She seemed to regard the police as being somehow responsible for her son's murder and refused to talk to them.

He sighed. Betty, who knew his moods well, glanced at him sideways and said nothing.

Paul and Denise lived in a converted brownstone near Pelham Parkway, in the Bronx. They rented a ground floor apartment with a one-car garage. When Barent pulled up to the curb, Paul's car was already parked in the driveway. Paul leaned against it, his hands in his pockets.

"I'll go into the house and see Denise," Betty said. "Remember, behave."

Barent growled inaudibly as they got out and Betty, after greeting Paul with a peck on the cheek, headed for the front door.

Paul looked at Barent sourly. He looked tired, Barent thought. "I want you to know that I didn't ask you here," Paul said.

"Huh?" Barent said.

"I am perfectly capable of washing a car without your help. Denise set this up. She thinks that if you and I spend a little time together, we'll end up putting aside our differences and turn into the best of buddies."

Barent blinked at him.

"Let me tell you something," Paul said. "They call it *morning sickness* but Denise has been throwing up for three days straight and I'm not in the mood for your snide little cracks. I really don't care what you think about stockbrokers and I don't care what you think about me. If you've decided to give me a hard time, you can get back in your car right now and get lost."

Barent grinned. He couldn't help himself. He cleared his throat and reached up and scratched the back of his head.

"Well?" Paul asked.

"I wouldn't think of it," Barent said. "Why don't we wash the car and pretend that we're the best of buddies?"

Paul grunted. "Fine," he said, and went to turn the hose on.

An hour later they were leaning against the car, chatting amiably. "The Knicks don't have a chance," Paul said. "Look, every team that's won the championship in the past twenty years has had at least two go-to guys, guys you could depend on to put the ball in the basket. Even Chicago, the year they first won it. Everybody said they only had Jordan but Pippin and Horace Grant were both up-and-coming. The Knicks have nobody. That's it."

Barent agreed with him. He nodded dourly. "Yeah. Give them credit, though. They've got guts.

Paul shrugged. "You need guts but you also need talent. The Knicks don't have enough of it."

Barent lit up a cigarette and then held out the pack to Paul, who shook his head. Barent took a long, satisfied drag and let the smoke dribble out his nose. "The Yankees might do it, though," he said.

Paul nodded. "They usually do, now that they've got Torre and Steinbrenner has learned to back off a little."

Just then, Betty came out of the house. "How are you two getting along?" she asked.

"Fine," Barent said. "Just fine. What else?"

She looked back and forth between their faces and smiled innocently. "Denise is taking a nap. Why don't we get going? I have some shopping to do before dinner."

"I thought you were staying," Paul said.

Betty looked uncertain. "I don't know if Denise is up to it."

Paul shrugged. "She'll enjoy the company. It might take her mind off her stomach. I can cook."

Betty thought about it for a moment, then smiled. "Okay, then. But I'll cook."

Chapter 16

Kurtz and Lenore left Manhattan at 5:00 PM by the West Side Highway to the Bronx and then took the Sawmill Parkway up to Westchester County. By the time they arrived at the Chaos split-level home in Chappaqua, the sky had turned black. Chappaqua was a well-to-do suburban community, where the upper middle class could afford to live in tiny three bedroom houses and the rich could afford four. Kurtz didn't get it. If you had all that money, why would you want to crowd yourself in this way?

Of course, in the city you had even less space, but in the city, you had The City. Around here you had to drive two miles just to buy a newspaper.

The street was crowded with cars. Kurtz found an empty space and parked. They walked up to the front porch and Kurtz pressed the buzzer. The door was opened almost immediately by a slim woman with a round face and shoulder-length black hair. "Yes?" she said.

"Mrs. Chao? I'm Richard Kurtz and this is Lenore Brinkman."

"Yes, yes," she said with a smile. "Come in. Come in. I take your coats?"

A Chinese man clutching a cocktail glass came up to them and shook hands. "Happy to meet you," he said in unaccented English. "I'm Herb Chao, David's father."

He was dressed in gray slacks, blue jacket and red-striped tie. His shoulders were narrow and he had a substantial middle-aged paunch. His hair hung over his collar. He had sideburns. The whole effect was weirdly outdated, as if Herb Chao had tried too hard to fit in during the sixties and then given up. "Follow me," he said. "The guests are in the den."

The den was down a flight of steps. It was a large room with stone flooring, a pool table in one corner, a bar and sliding glass doors leading to the backyard. One side of the room was walled off by a black, wrought iron railing. On the other side of the railing sat an easy chair and two white couches around a low coffee table. A platter of cheese and crackers and another platter of hors d'oeuvres were set out on the table. A crowd of about ten people were holding drinks and talking. "Feel free to help yourself," Chao said. "I've got to give my wife a hand with the food."

"Sure," Kurtz said. "Thanks." He turned to Lenore. "Can I get you a drink?"

"A glass of white wine?"

"Okay."

When he got back from the bar, he found Lenore discussing Impressionist art with a woman named Lisa, who designed stage sets for off-Broadway productions. The two women seemed quite engrossed in their conversation and so after handing Lenore her drink, Kurtz sat down on one of the couches and filled a small plate from the platter of hors d'oeuvres. The hors d'oeuvres seemed to be home made, small Chinese dumplings filled with minced, spiced meat and tiny egg-rolls full of chopped vegetables and baby shrimp. They were terrific. He remembered what Lenore had said about the likelihood of mountains of good food and hoped she was right.

A few minutes later, David Chao came down the stairs accompanied by a small blonde woman. Chao saw him, smiled widely, and walked over to the couch. "Richard, do you know Carrie? Carrie Owens? She works in the ER."

"I've seen you in the ER but I don't believe we've met," Kurtz said.

Carrie Owens smiled at him and held out her hand. It vanished inside Kurtz'. He was careful not to squeeze too tightly.

"I remember you," Carrie Owens said. She said it with a wise nod, as if she knew a secret.

"Oh?"

"One time a kid came into the ER tripping on something. He went crazy and tried to wreck the place. You knocked him out."

There had been an incident like that. There had been a couple of incidents like that. "These things happen," Kurtz said.

"Not to most people, they don't." Kurtz gave a deprecating shrug.

"Have you met any of the guests yet?" Chao asked.

"Just a few."

"They're mostly in business with my father. His company makes pre-fab office furniture."

"Exciting."

Chao grinned. "You say it as if you don't mean it but he makes more money than you and me both."

Just then, Herb Chao appeared at the head of the stairs and began urging people to come sit down for dinner. "Let's stick together," Chao said. "You and Lily are the only ones here I can talk to."

"Your cousin? Where is she?"

"Upstairs. Lily is helping my mother."

"How about Chris?"

"He couldn't make it. Something to do with business."

Kurtz went to grab Lenore and they walked up the stairs with Chao and Carrie.

"I'm Lenore Brinkman," Lenore said to Carrie.

"Nice to meet you. Are you in medicine, too?"

"Graphic arts."

"How long have you known Dr. Kurtz?"

Lenore grinned. "Doctor Kurtz, huh? You must work with him."

"I'm a resident in the ER."

"You can call me Richard," Kurtz said, "as long as nobody at the hospital finds out about it."

Carrie grinned.

"We've been going out for almost a year," Lenore said.

The dining room table was covered with a green linen tablecloth. It was a very large table and fit the whole party with room to spare. Each place setting had a pair of wooden chopsticks as well as a knife, forks and spoons. Herb Chao, despite what he had said earlier about helping his wife with the food, sat down at the head. "Would anybody like a beer? How about champagne?" he asked as he popped the cork on a bottle.

"Champagne with dinner?" Kurtz said to David.

"It goes really well with Chinese food."

Kurtz must have looked skeptical. David grinned and said, "Trust me."

Kurtz took a beer. Most of the diners, including Lenore, David and Carrie, went with the champagne.

A few moments later, Lily Chang came out of the kitchen carrying a steaming bowl, which she set down on a sideboard.

"Who is she?" Carrie asked.

"My cousin Lily," David said.

"What does she do?"

"She's a student at Barnard. History."

"She looks like a model."

"It's in the genes," David said. "Those are her parents."

David nodded toward a Chinese couple sitting stiffly at the other end of the table. Kurtz could see what David meant. The woman bore Lily a strong resemblance. Her husband was not nearly so good-looking. He had small eyes and a bloated face.

"My Aunt Rose and my Uncle Jack."

Aunt Rose was looking steadily down at the table. Her posture was stiff. Uncle Jack slumped in his chair, not looking at his wife, his expression grim.

Kurtz thought that Aunt Rose and Uncle Jack did not appear very happy. It seemed wiser not to mention this observation.

A pile of soup bowls sat on the sideboard. Mrs. Chao came out of the kitchen and filled the bowls. Lily passed them around the table, then sat down next to David. She smiled at Kurtz and Lenore. "Nice to see you again."

"Velvet corn-soup with crab," Mrs. Chao announced.

The soup smelled wonderful and looked great. Little bits of red crabmeat, green-peas and yellow egg-drop were floating in the clear broth. It had a peppery zing. Kurtz tasted it and closed his eyes.

"Good, huh?" David said with a grin.

"Fantastic."

"Forgive me for not talking too much," Lily broke in. "I'm helping with the food so I've got to eat fast."

"Go right ahead," Lenore said. "We'll talk later."

Lily nodded, quickly finished her soup, rose to her feet and went back to the kitchen.

"Mom was always a great cook," David said. "My grandmother made sure of it. My grandparents were in Nanking during the war when the Japanese devastated the place, and a few years after the Japanese were defeated, Mao took over. Mao regarded people like my grandparents as parasites. Luckily, my grandfather had already moved most of the business to Hong Kong. My grandmother used to say that you never knew when you might lose all your money but if a girl could cook she would always have something to fall back on."

"Your grandmother was a smart woman," Kurtz said.

There were no appetizers as such. After the soup, one course followed another. Mrs. Chao placed bowls of shrimp fried rice at each end of the table and the diners helped themselves to the rice while Lily brought a large platter from the kitchen. "Lobster with chili sauce," Mrs. Chao said. It smelled as good as it looked. Kurtz tasted it. The sauce was flavored with ginger, lime, red pepper and diced tomatoes.

"Pace yourselves," David told them. "There's a lot more coming."

"You bet," Kurtz said. His mouth was watering.

Lenore winked at him and looked smug.

After the lobster came lamb with scallions, eggplant in garlic sauce, orange flavored beef and squab with cashews. Mrs. Chao would periodically disappear into the kitchen and soon after, she and Lily would come back out with another platter.

Lily's father, Kurtz noted, was drinking quite a lot of champagne. His wife sat without smiling, seeming to devote all of her attention to the food on her plate. Nevertheless, Kurtz could see that she was eating very little and she never looked at her husband.

David, noticing Kurtz' interest, frowned and said, "Rose is Uncle Jack's second wife. Chris's mother died from cancer a few years before Jack met Rose. They don't come over very often."

Lenore glanced at David, then looked down the table toward Lily's parents. Obviously recognizing a sensitive subject, she judiciously nodded and returned her attention to the food. David seemed not to notice her reticence. "Aunt Rose is my mother's half-sister. Rose's mother was not my grandmother. She was a concubine."

"A concubine?" Visions of Pearl S. Buck and James Clavell wandered through Kurtz' mind. "I thought concubines went out of style in the Eighteen Hundreds," Kurtz said.

David shook his head. "Not in China. It was the way things were done. A rich man like my grandfather was expected to have more than one wife. Under the British, this was no longer legal but it was tolerated. Customarily, the first wife–in this case, my grandmother– picked the concubines. They were usually women of a lower social class and being a second wife represented a jump in status for them. Of course, the first wife ruled the roost and the concubines' kids were never considered to be equal to the first wife's kids."

Uncle Jack picked that moment to spill a glass of champagne. He looked at it blearily, picked up the glass and refilled it from a bottle perched at his elbow. Aunt Rose gathered together a clump of napkins and proceeded to wipe up the spill. Aside from this, the two ignored each other.

"I think you told me you had four aunts and two uncles?" Kurtz said.

"Yes. My grandmother had five children. My grandfather had two other wives. Each of them had one daughter, Rose and my aunt May."

"Whatever happened to the concubines?" Lenore asked.

"Rose's mother died from cancer a few years ago. May's mother stayed in Hong Kong. She still lives in the old mansion. My uncles would never kick her out. She's very old now."

"And your aunt May?"

"She's in England. Concubines' kids were much more likely to emigrate. My grandfather took care of them and he made sure they got a good education. Aunt May has a Ph.D from the London School of Economics. But why stick around and be a second-class citizen your whole life?

"How old is Lily?" Lenore asked.

"Nineteen."

"She's gorgeous," Kurtz said.

"Like I said, it's in the genes. Concubines were status symbols. Why have a concubine who doesn't look good?"

Kurtz nodded. "Makes sense to me."

He smiled at Lenore. "Hmm …" he said.

She smiled back sweetly. "Forget it, Buster."

"Huh? What did I say?"

"It's not what you said, it's what you didn't say."

"I didn't not say anything."

"Exactly. And see that you don't."

"I was only thinking that it seems like an interesting custom."

"He's saying it," Lenore said to Carrie. "I told him not to but he just can't help himself."

"No, really," Kurtz said.

"You can't have one," Lenore said.

"I didn't ask for one," Kurtz protested.

113

"You still can't have one."

"I didn't say I wanted one."

"If you get one, then I get one too. A big one, with lots of muscles, and he has to grovel at my feet."

Kurtz paused. He gave her a hurt look. "I have plenty of muscles," he said. "And I grovel at your feet all the time."

"*You* don't mean it." She took another helping of squab from the platter. "You're just begging."

Kurtz turned to Chao. "What do you think? Should we go for it?"

"Concubines eat a lot," Chao said, "I think you should settle for a Chihuahua."

Chapter 17

Families sometimes did pretty rotten things to one another but at least they were there when you needed them. In China, for three thousand years, family had been the one thing you could count on. Kurtz thought of what Lenore had said, about culture being a larger reflection of the family. There was a lot more to it than that, he thought. Culture was a *substitute* for family, and vice-versa. The more supportive and stable a nation's social environment, the less important–the less necessary–family became. It was unusual in America to have much contact with the more distant branches of your family. Aside from a cousin or two, maybe a favorite uncle or aunt, most people barely knew their families at all. The same in most of Europe. If you had a reliable government, you didn't need a close, hierarchical, extended family. Poverty, war and tyranny fostered family.

Chao and his father were cordial but they didn't seem to have an awful lot to say to each other.

Kurtz and his own father had even less, not through anybody's fault. It was just that Kurtz couldn't bring himself to care when the harvest was due and the old man hated coming to the city. They talked on the phone every couple of months but the conversations never seemed to go anywhere.

"God, am I stuffed," Kurtz said.

"I told you." Lenore said smugly. She was wearing a wisp of green lingerie that looked as if it had come from the Victoria's Secret catalog. "Would you like some brandy?"

"I don't think so. I had too much beer at dinner."

Lenore stretched out next to him on the bed. "What were you thinking?"

He reached out and touched her hair. "I was thinking about families. I was thinking that everyone, ultimately, is alone."

Lenore looked at him with narrowed eyes and whistled softly through her teeth. "What brought this on?"

"I don't know."

Her hair was long, straight and fine. She had washed it that morning. It smelled faintly of lilac shampoo.

"Maybe it was Chao's cousin, Lily. She has a place in the family. Not much of a place, but a place. It's her place. It always will be. Safe ... secure."

"Degrading?"

"Maybe. I wonder if Chao's parents are even conscious of it. Lily's parents certainly are. They sat there the whole evening, hardly saying a word."

"David said that they don't see them very much."

"Yes, he did. But whatever is going on between them, it's not enough to prevent Lily from coming over and substituting for hired help. David also said that the children of concubines tend to emigrate, which makes perfect sense to me. As he says, who wants to be a second-class citizen? But it doesn't seem fair to go to a new country and have the family that treats you like a second-class citizen emigrate along with you."

"This is America," Lenore said. "In America, you can tell them to go to hell."

"It must be difficult to tell your family to go to hell." Kurtz shrugged. "I imagine that sometimes they manage to negotiate a new relationship and sometimes they fall right back into the old one. Mostly, I think that they wind up drifting apart."

"You're assuming an awful lot," Lenore said. "You don't really know anything about the dynamics of David's family."

"No, I don't."

Kurtz grinned wanly and Lenore grinned back. He stroked her back. "You look good," Kurtz said.

"I thought you'd never notice."

"Oh, I noticed."

"Well? Care to do anything about it?"

"Give me a minute to brush my teeth."

She turned over, raised her arms over her head and slowly stretched, arching her back. She smiled at him and Kurtz felt his heart give a little flutter. "When you come back," Lenore said, "I want you to get down on your knees and grovel at my feet."

"So alright," Barent said, "the kid isn't so bad after all."

Betty sniffed.

Barent smiled at her back as she puttered over the sink and then settled in his chair to read Paul's newspaper. Denise had been able to come down to dinner, though she still looked pale. Barent liked the way Paul hovered over her. "The kid's alright," he said again.

"I'm a little worried about Denise," Betty said.

Barent was, too. But there wasn't much they could do about it. "She's just like you were. She throws up a lot."

"Sometimes these things indicate a problem with the baby."

"She's seeing the doctor in a few days."

After dinner, Denise had gone back to bed. Ten minutes later, Paul excused himself to go check on her. He came out of the back bedroom and sat down next to Barent at the kitchen table. "She's asleep," he said.

Betty was almost finished. She rubbed the last dish dry with a towel and put it in the cupboard. "You better get some sleep, too. Call us if anything changes."

Paul nodded. Barent put down the paper and shook Paul's hand. Betty kissed him on the cheek. "Don't bother coming out with us."

"Okay. We'll see you, then," Paul said.

It had begun to rain and Barent turned on the wipers. "It was a nice evening," he said.

Betty only smiled.

A few minutes later, they pulled into their own driveway. "You want a nightcap before we go to bed?" Barent asked.

"Sure," Betty said. "We have any B and B?"

"I think so."

They climbed up the steps and opened the door. The first thing Barent saw was the little red light blinking on the phone. Wordlessly, he walked over and pressed the button. Harry Moran's voice said, "Lew, give me a call as soon as you get in. We've found the guy in the suit, the one who was in Mahoney's neighborhood the day he got killed."

Betty gave a patient sigh and went over to the cupboard. She took a bottle down off the shelf and filled a snifter with a generous portion of Benedictine and Brandy. She didn't ask Barent if he wanted one.

"Duty calls," Barent said, and picked up the phone.

"The routine watch on the neighborhood got him."

Moran was sitting at his desk with his feet up, drinking coffee. His slicked back hair was impeccably in place and he looked pleased with himself.

"Doesn't sound like much."

"Maybe not," Moran said.

"Then why are you smiling?"

"Amused, I guess. People–they're all the same." Moran shook his head in wonderment.

The suspect (if you could call him a suspect) was named Stanley Caruso. He was about six feet (the right height, Barent noted), stout and balding. He wore a rumpled blue suit with a blue and red striped tie and a Homburg. The police had been keeping a surreptitious watch on the neighborhood ever since Rod Mahoney's murder. Two plainclothesmen in an unmarked car had seen Caruso scuttling along the side of a house three doors down from the Mahoneys'. He had evidently come from the backyard, perhaps had been in the house and exited from a back door, or perhaps had been searching for an easy entryway with an eye toward burglary. His evident desire to avoid notice, coupled with the fact that his car was parked a quarter of a mile away down the street, had been immediately suspicious. Adding to the suspicion was the fact that Caruso had attempted to run as soon as the cops approached him.

Stanley Caruso was not exactly in great shape. His wind had given out after a hundred yards and they had marched him back to the house and rung the bell.

"She was certainly pissed off," Moran said.

"I can imagine. Her husband away and all that. Loverboy was not supposed to attract attention."

"It's weird. Her name's Linda Weiner. She's a housewife. She's young. She looks good. She's got a nice house, two nice kids, a nice life. You could see from the pictures in the living room that her husband is a hell of a lot better looking than Stanley. So what's the attraction? 'My husband is a bore,' she said. 'He's not exciting.' Is Stanley Caruso exciting? He doesn't look exciting to me."

"What does he do?"

"The husband?"

"No, god damn it! Caruso!"

Moran chuckled and looked at Barent with an impish smile. "He's an insurance salesman."

Barent scratched his head. Frankly, he couldn't care less about Stanley Caruso, Linda Weiner and their idiotic affairs. "So where was Stanley on the afternoon that Rod Mahoney was murdered?"

"Right there. Getting his rocks off."

"And I don't suppose he saw anything, being engaged in more pressing activities?"

"Well, now ..." Moran definitely looked like the cat that had swallowed the canary. "In that, you would be wrong. He did see something. Stanley always left the same way, out the back door, down the side of the house and out to his car. He always scouted the scene before he walked to the street. If anybody at all was passing by, he would wait until they were gone. Stanly had a healthy desire to avoid detection."

More than Linda Weiner had, apparently. If she had really given a damn, they would have gone to a hotel, because sooner or later, the neighbors always pick up on hanky-panky and once that happens, there's always a busybody who just has to tell the husband–"for his own good."

"So bring him in," Barent said.

Moran pushed a button on the intercom and a few seconds later two uniformed policemen escorted a rumpled Stanley Caruso into the office. Stanley's face was gray. He looked terrified.

"Sit down, Mr. Caruso," Barent said. He nodded to the cops, who left without a word.

Caruso sat down and huddled in the chair. He was shivering.

"I'm not interested in your personal life, Mr. Caruso," Barent said. "I have no intention of telling Mrs. Weiner's husband or your wife or anybody else about your relationship. I'm investigating a murder and it's possible that you may have information that could help us. That's all." Stanley did not look reassured. Barent gave him a second to think about it but Caruso continued to sit silently in the chair, his eyes wide with fright.

"You do have a wife?" Barent said.

Caruso's eyes snapped to Barent's face. His lips barely twitched. "Oh, yeah," he said.

"I don't know what the other policemen have told you but our only interest in you is that you were spotted in the vicinity of the Mahoney residence on the afternoon of November Fourteenth. Do you know the afternoon I'm talking about?"

Caruso looked down and didn't answer.

"November Fourteenth was the day that Roderick Allen Mahoney was murdered."

"I know," Caruso said. He cleared his throat. "I know the day you mean."

"Now that we know about your relationship with Mrs. Weiner, we have no reason to suspect that you were involved in Professor Mahoney's murder," Barent said. "Nevertheless, it's possible that you might have seen something that would help us."

It was not entirely true, Barent thought, that Caruso was not a suspect. People sometimes committed murder for reasons that other people would consider strange, or even trivial. If, for instance, Rod Mahoney had somehow become aware of Caruso's affair with Linda Weiner–or if Caruso suspected that he had–then Caruso might have murdered Mahoney just to shut him up. At least it was a motive.

Come to think of it, Mahoney's severed eyelids might have meant exactly that: you shouldn't have looked at things that were none of your business. But then what did the severed arms and hands and legs mean? Not to mention the penis?

"I did see something," Caruso said.

Moran looked faintly interested. Barent smiled at Caruso encouragingly.

"I always left by the back. I didn't want anybody to see me, you know. …"

Caruso looked at Barent beseechingly and Barent nodded with what he hoped was a look of sympathy.

"A few houses down, I noticed two men coming out the front door. I didn't think anything of it at the time but when I heard on the news later about the neighbor guy getting killed, I remembered."

"Two men," Barent said. There had been one set of footprints. That meant one man did it while the other stood lookout.

Caruso nodded.

"What did these men look like?"

"I couldn't tell much. I didn't want them to see me. My only concern at the time was to wait for them to get out of there so I could leave."

"You couldn't see anything?"

"One of them was wearing a trench coat and a hat. I noticed that. Most people don't wear hats these days."

Caruso himself wore a hat. "Ever since President Kennedy, you know?" Caruso said.

"President Kennedy?" Barent said.

"Before President Kennedy, men wore hats. But Kennedy didn't like hats, so everybody suddenly stopped wearing them." Caruso looked offended. "It's ridiculous. People freeze their heads off and catch the flu every winter because John Fitzgerald Kennedy didn't like hats."

"You like hats," Barent said.

"Yes," Caruso said. "I do."

"And this man wore a hat."

"Yes. I noticed that."

"What kind of hat?"

"A fedora. Black or dark gray." Stanley shrugged.

"How about the other man. What was he wearing?"

Stanley shrugged. "Blue jeans, I think. A casual jacket. No hat or tie."

"How about their shoes?"

"No idea."

"What color was their hair?"

Stanley hesitated. "I'm not sure. I just don't remember. The guy in the jeans might have been a blond. The other one had dark hair."

"And how long was their hair?"

"It was just hair. It wasn't so long that it stood out, if that's what you're getting at."

"What was their race? Were they white?"

"I think so." Stanley nodded. "I'm almost certain of it."

Barent looked at Moran glumly. Moran shrugged. "And that's all you noticed?"

"I noticed the car. It was a dark blue Mercedes."

A Mercedes. A trench coat, a hat and a Mercedes …

"Were these men carrying anything?"

121

Mahoney had been carved to pieces. The instruments with which that had been done had not been left at the house.

Caruso got a far-away look in his eyes. "Yeah," he finally said. "I think that the one with the hat may have been carrying a briefcase."

"Did you catch even the slightest glimpse of his face?" Barent asked.

"I'm sorry," Caruso said. "I couldn't really see. Like I told you, I wasn't real interested."

"How about the Mercedes, then; anything else you can remember about that?"

Caruso squinted his eyes, trying to think. "It was a recent model, but not real recent. The headlights were set into the front and they were parallel to the ground. The older model Mercedes, the headlights were up and down and placed on the front bumpers. I liked those old model Mercedes. They had class. Daimler must agree with me, sort of." Stanley smiled wanly. "The newest models have the headlights set into the front but they're up and down, sort of the modern-retro look." Stanley sniffed. "Frankly, I think the new ones look stupid."

"Setting the headlights into the grill is supposed to be aerodynamic," Barent said. "It promotes fuel mileage."

"A guy owns a Mercedes, he shouldn't have to worry about fuel mileage. He's got a car that's supposed to make a statement."

"So it was a recent model Mercedes, but not too recent. Anything else?"

"No." Caruso shook his head. "I don't think so."

"The license plate?"

"I didn't see it. I couldn't even tell you what state it was."

"How about the hubcaps?" Moran asked. "Were they chrome, or were they painted?"

Caruso looked as if he knew exactly what Moran was talking about, which was more than Barent did. He thought for a moment, then nodded slowly. "Chrome," he said.

Moran nodded and leaned back again in his seat.

After a moment, Barent asked, "Getting back to the men," Barent said, "were they young or old?"

Caruso shrugged. "No idea. I figure, a guy wears a nice coat and a hat and drives a Mercedes, he can't be a kid. But aside from that, I didn't see either of them close enough to tell."

"Could you tell how tall they were?"

"The one in the blue jeans was a little taller than the other. How tall was that?" Stanley shrugged.

"And what time of the day was this?"

"It was two-fifteen. I always left at two-fifteen. After that, the kids start coming home from school. More chance of being seen."

"And you didn't notice when these men arrived, being occupied inside the house."

Caruso gave Barent a wounded look. "Hey, come on," he said. "Give a guy a break, okay?"

"Sorry," Barent said. Strangely enough, he actually meant it. Stanley's hang dog face made him feel guilty.

"The answer is no," Caruso said. "I got to Linda's house around twelve-thirty. I don't think the Mercedes was there when I arrived but I'm not sure. I didn't notice it."

Barent glanced at Moran. Moran shrugged.

"Go on home, Mr. Caruso," Barent said. Caruso looked up at him with sudden hope. "Please don't discuss this with anyone." The admonition was pro-forma. Stanley was getting off lucky, and he knew it.

"Fat chance," Caruso said. "You think I'm crazy?"

Barent sighed. "Go home, Mr. Caruso."

"You bet," Caruso said. "Thanks."

He rose from his chair and left the room, gripping his Homburg in both hands.

"The guy's old-fashioned," Moran said when Caruso had gone. "He likes hats. He likes the old-style Mercedes."

"He likes young housewives."

Moran shrugged. "There is that."

"What was that business with the hubcaps?"

"Daimler-Benz used to paint their hubcaps the same color as the cars. Even when they switched to the modern front grill with the recessed headlights, they continued to paint the hubcaps for another couple of years. They changed to chrome hubcaps a few years later."

Moran frowned down into his coffee. "Doesn't help us much. It's probably been fifteen years since they switched. Maybe more."

"How come you know so much about Mercedes?"

"We're saving up to buy one. I want to make a statement."

"The guy who killed Mahoney was making all sorts of statements. Nice suit, nice car. Carving somebody to pieces and stuffing his penis in his mouth … makes quite a statement, don't you think?"

Glumly, Moran nodded. "Yeah," he said. "But what does it all mean?"

"Isn't it obvious? It means the guy didn't like Rod Mahoney."

"Oh," Moran said. "Yeah. Thanks a lot."

Chapter 18

Kurtz had been a junior medical student, on his very first clinical rotation, when he lost his first patient. The patient was a black man in his early thirties–Kurtz couldn't remember his name–recently released from the ICU and assigned to Kurtz' floor. The patient had advanced cirrhosis compounded by alcoholic hepatitis. Such patients rarely recovered. This patient, however, had responded to steroids and supportive therapy. His few remaining liver cells had groaned and begun to metabolize and his blood chemistries had returned, if not to normal, then at least to a range compatible with life, and so he was moved out of intensive care and into Kurtz' inexperienced but eager hands.

Kurtz' resident at the time, a tall, skinny second-year named Harold Klein, had scratched his head, sighed and gone with Kurtz into the patient's room as soon as he arrived from the ICU. "Oh, boy," Harold muttered. "This guy's a train wreck."

The patient lay on the bed, breathing shallowly and muttering to himself. He was skinny as a rail except for a huge abdomen, swollen with ascitic fluid.

Harold flipped through the patient's chart while Kurtz awkwardly listened to his heart and lungs and percussed the abdomen. The patient, if he noticed Kurtz at all, ignored him and continued to mutter.

"Okay," Harold said. "The first thing to do is draw some blood for labs and start a new IV."

"He's got an IV," Kurtz said.

"Yeah, but it's thrombosed."

Harold was right. The IV site was red, the fluid barely dripping. "They should have changed it a few days ago."

"Okay," Kurtz said.

Harold grinned. "I'll be down the hall. Come and get me when you're done." Harold walked out and Kurtz spent the next twenty minutes struggling to find a vein large enough for a catheter. That was probably why they hadn't changed the IV, Kurtz thought. The guy had really lousy veins.

Absently, Kurtz noticed that the patient had stopped muttering. A few seconds later, Kurtz managed to slip a pediatric size catheter into a vein in the left antecubital. The blood seemed quite dark. Then it hit him. The patient was lying still, his eyes closed, his mouth barely open, his chest barely rising.

Oh, my God, Kurtz thought. He felt unreal, like a character in a TV show. He would always remember thinking, *If this guy is arresting I have to call a code but if I call a code and it turns out that he's just fallen asleep I'm going to look like a grade-A idiot.*

Kurtz reached out a trembling hand and felt for the pulse in the neck. There wasn't one. *Okay*, he thought, *just like the movies*. He stuck his head out into the hallway, screamed at the nursing station and started CPR. Within about sixty seconds it seemed that half the hospital was in the patient's room.

So they ran the code and the patient died anyway, which was the way it happened more often than not, and Kurtz felt miserable.

Kurtz had been at a lot of cardiac arrests since then and the whole thing had long since come to seem normal. Disgusting but normal. He grinned. He thought about it now, not because anybody was dying but because of the feeling he had had at the time. He would never forget that feeling, the sense that the world he moved in was somehow unreal, was simply too strange to be believed.

He had the same feeling right now because someone was obviously following him, just like in the movies.

Kurtz had finished dictating his last chart at 5 PM and then closed the office. His apartment was crosstown but Kurtz liked the exercise and he usually walked. This day, however, had been cloudy and by evening, a fine mist filled the air. For a moment, he considered hailing a cab, but it wasn't actually raining and the temperature was warm. He shrugged and started down the street.

He was strolling along with his hands in his pockets when his foot slipped for an instant on some sodden leaves. He stumbled, and had half turned around before he could right himself. Behind him, nearly the length of the block, he saw a man in a blue down parka walking along. The man stopped for an instant when Kurtz began to fall, then hesitated. Kurtz paid him no mind.

Two blocks later, in the darkened window of a shuttered store, Kurtz saw the reflection of a man in a blue parka. He stopped. The man in the parka stopped also. Was it the same man? He was too far away to tell much about him but Kurtz thought that he was. He was average height and thin. He had dark hair cut short around the sides. He was pale and appeared to be clean-shaven.

"Shit." Kurtz muttered it to himself. He turned left at the corner and walked around the block, then turned right and went another block. He leaned over then, and pretended to tie his shoelace. Far in the distance, a man in a blue parka strolled slowly along behind him.

Kurtz hailed a cab. He gave the cabby his address and within five minutes arrived at the front door of his building. He looked around. No blue parka. Kurtz breathed a sigh of relief.

"He must be an amateur," Barent said. There was a faint crackle of static over the phone. "You would never have spotted a pro."

Amateur or pro, Kurtz was not pleased. "So what do you figure?"

"Hard to say. Number one, the character might have been simply out for a walk. It's possible that he wasn't following you at all."

"He was definitely following me."

Barent went on as if Kurtz had not spoken. "Number two, it might have been some kid who was sizing up his chances, maybe thinking about a mugging, but you kept to well-lit streets and never gave him a chance."

"That's possible," Kurtz said.

"And number three, you've been asking a lot of questions. Maybe you've started to attract attention."

"I've been asking questions but I haven't been getting any answers."

"Maybe you're closer than you think."

"I don't see how. The only people I've talked to about the murder are Nolan and Redding, and they don't know shit."

"How about the drug business? You talk to anybody about that?"

Kurtz shrugged uncomfortably. "A few."

Barent cleared his throat. He sounded reluctant. "Want us to put a man on you for the next few days? Ordinarily, a story like this, it's pretty soft, but I figure you deserve it."

Barent had briefed Kurtz some nights ago about Stanley Caruso. Barent had already decided that Rod Mahoney's murderer had to be an amateur. Caruso's story tended to confirm it. Pros did not use garden implements to carve up their victims. They didn't hit them in

127

the head with a crowbar, either. They shot them in the head with a gun.

The cadavers on Halloween night had been dismembered by more than one person. That was a safe supposition. Too many bodies had been mutilated and too many body parts scattered about the room for the perpetrator to have been one person. Then there was Jerry Rubino, Hickey and Marcia Rice. Two murders plus a whole slew of lesser crimes, all of which might have nothing to do with each other ...

"If you had to guess," Kurtz said. "What would it be?"

Barent was silent for a moment. Then he said reluctantly, "Your involvement with Rod Mahoney's murder is peripheral at best, and despite the fact that you've been talking about the mutilated cadavers, frankly, you're just dicking around. You haven't gotten a thing. If I had to take a guess, I would say Rubino. Your role in that particular incident has been well-publicized."

"You think it's someone in the hospital?"

"I have no idea."

"Great."

"So, you want us to put a man on you, or not?"

"No," Kurtz said shortly. Whoever was doing this couldn't possibly know how much Kurtz knew (which was nothing). If Kurtz were merely curious, then the smartest thing by far would be to let him strictly alone. If Kurtz were more than curious (which of course he was), then it would be even smarter to leave him alone. After all, if Richard Kurtz was the duly appointed agent of the police, then the police were a pretty pitiful bunch (which maybe they were). In either case, the best course of action for the bad guys to follow would be to avoid creating any more of a stir than they already had.

The question was: were the bad guys smart? Bad guys often weren't. It was the cops' greatest weapon, the general stupidity of the criminal mind. People who were smart rarely turned to crime.

"Hell no," Kurtz said again. "As long as they're amateurs, let them nibble. Maybe I can catch one."

Barent grunted. "Be careful," he said.

"You bet."

For the next few days, Kurtz watched his back. He avoided lonely streets. In the evenings, when he was in the habit of running, he ran along avenues crowded with pedestrians. He told Lenore nothing of what was going on.

And, in fact, nothing was going on.

He saw nobody in a blue parka and no matter how closely he peered at the crowds, nobody seemed to be following him. Reluctantly, he concluded that Barent's choice number two must have been the correct one. Most likely it was just a kid sizing up the odds, a chance encounter that would not be repeated.

He wished he could believe it.

It took him a few moments to place the voice. "Detective Barent?" Uncertain, high-pitched …

"Yes?" he said.

"This is Evelyn Richter."

"Of course," he said. "What can I do for you, Mrs. Richter?" He made a shushing motion at Harry Moran, who raised an eyebrow, looked briefly amused but nevertheless stopped speaking to Arnie Figueroa.

"I should have told you the other day when you were talking to us but Jay told me not to." Her voice was a breathy whisper. She sounded distraught. "I know who might have killed Rod."

Might have killed Rod? Any one of the twenty million people in the New York Metropolitan area *might* have killed Rod Mahoney. "Who, Mrs. Richter?"

"Kevin," she said.

Barent paused. "Professor Mahoney's son?"

"Yes."

"Why do you say that?"

"About six months ago, Rod and Kevin had an argument. It was terrible. Afterward, they wouldn't speak to each other for weeks."

"What was this argument about?"

Evelyn Richter's voice seemed to hesitate. "I'm not sure. Jay and I were over for dinner. The argument was in the bedroom and we couldn't hear very much of it. As soon as we arrived, Claire knocked on the door and they shut up. When they came out, they barely looked at each other. It wasn't a very pleasant evening, I can tell you that."

"Did you hear *any* of this argument?"

129

"I heard Kevin call his father a prick."

Really … Evelyn Richter might have something after all. "And you have no idea at all what they were arguing about?"

"I didn't say that. I said I wasn't sure what they were arguing about."

Evelyn Richter, he reminded himself, was not one of the world's great minds. "What do you think they were arguing about, Mrs. Richter?"

"Drugs," she said.

"Drugs," Barent repeated slowly. Moran raised his head and looked at him, a hunting dog on point.

"I'm not certain, but that's what I think."

"Why do you think they were arguing about drugs?"

"Because it *sounded* like they were arguing about drugs."

Sounded … A defense attorney would have licked his chops and torn her to shreds. "And what exactly do you mean by that, Mrs. Richter?"

"I could hear Rod yell something like, 'too stoned to study,' and then he said something about Kevin treating college like 'a summer camp for psychotics.' I remember that distinctly, 'a summer camp for psychotics.' That's a very clever line, don't you think?"

It was clever. Barent would have to remember it. "Was there anything else that you recall, Mrs. Richter?"

"No," she said.

"Did Mrs. Mahoney say anything?"

"No. As soon as we arrived, she went in and shut them up. I told you that."

"Did you ever hear anything like this again?"

"No. Just the one time."

Evelyn Richter and her husband were not exactly close to the Mahoneys, Barent reflected. Quite a lot could have been going on and she wouldn't necessarily have known a thing. "Thank you, Mrs. Richter," he said. "You've been a big help. We'll look into it."

Chapter 19

Kevin Mahoney went to Hanover College, which used to be an exclusive institution for women but had been co-educational since 1971. Hanover was in Ithaca, near Cornell. Barent and Moran drove up the next day and arrived at the college a little after two in the afternoon. The place looked just like Barent imagined a college should, tree lined walkways, ivy-covered buildings. A *college*. Barent himself had gone to NYU, which was a pretty good school academically but which looked more like a series of jails. Then again, there wasn't a lot to do up in Ithaca during the winter. Except study, and maybe get drunk and stoned. Two pretty coeds carrying books under their arms looked at Moran and then at each other, giggling … well, maybe a few other things to do up here, as well.

"Nice place," Moran said.

"Yeah," Barent said.

They had already finished a meeting with the Dean of Students, who had informed them that Kevin Mahoney got good grades and had never–so far as their records went–been in any sort of trouble. They had not even bothered to ask about drugs on campus, figuring that the Dean would have nothing to say. Their next meeting was with Edward Horvath, the senior student who was Kevin Mahoney's floor counselor.

Horvath was a pale, blonde kid with pimples. He was short but built like a weightlifter. The two cops met him in a small office on the Fifth Floor. The office had undoubtedly been converted from a dorm room. It was tiny and had a sink in the corner. The carpet was threadbare. One window that appeared long overdue for a washing looked out on a tree-lined quad. There was barely enough room for two rickety chairs opposite the small, wooden desk.

Edward Horvath looked bewildered. He also looked uncomfortable. He cleared his throat. "The Dean told me to cooperate with you," he said. "What can I do for you?"

"Are you friendly with all of the kids on your floor?" Barent asked.

Horvath shrugged and puffed out his cheeks, thinking about it. "I guess so," he said. "I'm not *unfriendly* with any of them, if that's what you mean."

"But you know all of them?"

"Sure. It's my job."

"How about Kevin Mahoney?" Horvath shrugged again. "Sure."

"Has Kevin Mahoney ever been in any trouble that you know of?"

Horvath still looked bewildered. "What sort of trouble?"

Moran threw Barent a glance that said it was going to be a long day. Barent ignored it. "Mr. Horvath," he said, "did you know that Kevin Mahoney's father was recently murdered?"

Horvath gulped. "You don't think Kevin had anything to do with that, do you?"

"Mr. Horvath, what I think is quite frankly none of your business. I want you to understand that Professor Mahoney was murdered in a particularly gruesome way. He was bludgeoned to death and then torn to pieces. Any questions that I ask you are part of the official investigation into a homicide. So I'll ask you again: has Kevin Mahoney ever been in *any* trouble that you know of?"

Horvath's face had turned red during Barent's little speech. He bit his lip and looked out the window. A bunch of kids down on the quad were playing an impromptu game of football. It all looked very pastoral and collegiate. "No," Horvath said. "I don't know of any trouble at all."

Moran suddenly leaned forward and said, "How about drugs?"

Horvath looked back and forth from Barent's face to Moran's. He cleared his throat. "Drugs?" he squeaked.

"Did Kevin Mahoney have anything to do with drugs?"

"Look," Horvath said. He spread his hands in a helpless gesture. "This is a *college*."

"What is that supposed to mean?" Barent asked.

"Everybody does drugs," Horvath said. "It's part of the experience. You're away from home for the first time. You're on your own. The first thing you do is declare your independence."

"So they do drugs."

"Yeah," Horvath said. He shrugged.

Well, it hadn't been so different when Barent was in college, not really. If you didn't smoke a little pot now and then, you just weren't with it. "And what does the University have to say about this?"

"Nothing."

"Nothing?"

"They know about it. They won't admit it but so long as it's kept quiet and nobody gets hurt, they're not going to do a thing about it. What are they supposed to do? Kick three-quarters of the students out of school?"

"And where do you fit in? You're the floor counselor."

"More like the Master of Ceremonies. Look, not too long ago I was at a frat party. Professor Lobert was there, the Dean of Students, you know?"

Lobert was the one Barent had spoken to earlier, a frosty little man with slicked down hair and an unsmiling face. "I've met him," Barent said.

"I went into the kitchen to get myself a beer and there's Lobert, passing a joint back and forth with the President of the fraternity, discussing the relative merits of Glenlivet and Chivas Regal. The Dean of Students, you'll be interested to hear, prefers a premium blended Scotch to a single malt."

This did not exactly conform to Barent's conception of the Dean of Students. Just goes to show. "I will certainly cherish that information," he said.

Horvath grunted. "So what am I supposed to do? I smile and tell them to smoke it their rooms, not in the halls. We know we can't eliminate it. We just try to keep it so no-one gets hurt."

"How about other drugs? Cocaine? Heroin?"

"Cocaine is big, but not as big as it used to be. It's no longer a rich man's drug. Too many associations with crack houses and AIDS. Heroin, interestingly, is making a comeback."

Barent looked at Moran, who shrugged and stared out the window. "A comeback?"

"It used to be, by the time heroin got to the street, it had been diluted a dozen times over. It was maybe two, three per-cent real heroin. The rest was powdered sugar or cornstarch or some other crap. The only way you could use the stuff was to shoot up. Now, college kids aren't into pain and needles are definitely not cool. But things are different today. Now the heroin you see is at least sixty per-cent pure, sometimes ninety or above. You don't have to shoot it up, you can smoke it or even snort it. It's so much more genteel."

"Genteel ... tell me," Barent said. "Where do you stand on the Glenlivet versus Chivas Regal controversy?"

"Huh?" Horvath looked at him suspiciously.

"Never mind," Barent said. "Forget I asked. So heroin is making a comeback and cocaine is not as big as it used to be. Where does Kevin Mahoney fit in?"

Horvath leaned back in his chair and thoughtfully frowned. "Well, so far as I know, he doesn't use any more than the average."

"Great. A fine upstanding citizen."

Horvath looked hurt. "Look, this is the way things are. When did you go to college? The sixties? Were things so different then?"

A ghostly smile briefly hovered over Moran's face. Barent decided to ignore both Moran and the question. "So there's nothing unusual at all about Kevin Mahoney?"

"I didn't say that. I said he doesn't use any more than the average." Horvath shook his head. "I'm not going to get in trouble here, am I?"

"For what? Possession of narcotics? What are we supposed to do? Put three-quarters of the school in jail?"

Horvath smiled crookedly. "I didn't mean that. I mean for slander, or libel, or something. You know, for talking about people."

"You're more likely to get in trouble for *not* talking about people, as in accessory after the fact to a homicide."

Horvath did not seem impressed by the threat. "Fine," he said. "Well, I'm not certain, but I suspect that Kevin is a dealer."

"A dealer ..."

"This is the part of it that gets dicey. I mean, the school deliberately turns a blind eye to casual drug use. It's simply too widespread to try to stop. But if you use it, you have to get it from someplace. Using is cool but dealing is definitely not cool. For one thing, the people you get it from are a very sleazy bunch. You can get your head blown off."

"Really?"

Horvath nodded, totally serious. "It's happened."

"You don't say. Around here?"

"About a year ago, some kid came into the dorm and ripped off another kid at knife-point. The kid who was ripped off had half a kilo of coke and two kilos of pot sitting in his closet. This kid was not too smart. He figured that since it was tolerated, it was condoned. He complained to his floor counselor. The floor counselor went to the Dean. The Dean decided that they have to draw the line someplace so they suspended both kids for a semester."

"Cool," Barent said. "So where do you get your stuff?"

"Me?" Horvath looked surprised. "I don't use it. I'm supposed to be more responsible."

"Right. It's your job."

Horvath nodded. "Exactly."

"So you suspect that Kevin Mahoney deals."

"That's correct."

"But you don't know."

Horvath grimaced. He looked embarrassed. "Well, in point of fact, I do know. He deals. What I don't know is how *much* he deals. There are plenty of kids on campus you can go to for an ounce now and then. But where do these guys get their stuff? Who's the next level up the ladder? I don't know that. And I don't want to know that."

Barent leaned back in his seat, thinking. The picture that Horvath painted was one that he recognized, but what did he want to do about it? He could request that the local cops put the whole University under surveillance. They could gather the evidence and as he had not too seriously said, send three quarters of the student body to jail. But for what? An object lesson?

Barent did not for an instant think that drug use, even casual drug use, was a good thing. Nevertheless, he was not in a position to eradicate it and he wasn't about to ruin a bunch of kids' lives because they liked to take a toke or a snort now and then.

He certainly wouldn't mind busting the local dealers, but Ithaca wasn't his jurisdiction and petty drug use, even petty drug dealing, was not his crime. Barent's crime was murder. The only thing he cared about here was whether or not Kevin Mahoney, who might or might not be dealing drugs, had anything to do with the death of his father, which might or might not have had anything to do with drugs.

Barent turned to Moran. "Let's have another talk with Dean Lobert."

Chapter 20

Kurtz felt ill. He was operating on a thirty-two year old named James Severance, an engineer for Allied-Signal. Severance had come into the office complaining of vague abdominal pain. He had an elevated white count and a mild fever. The symptoms could have indicated a number of things but appendicitis seemed most likely. So here they were in the OR and it wasn't appendicitis. It was cancer, what type Kurtz wasn't exactly certain, probably pancreatic. It was a relatively common presentation for a relatively uncommon condition. Pancreatic cancer usually started in the head of the pancreas, where it blocked the bile ducts. The patient got jaundiced. When it started in the tail of the pancreas, like now, it tended to spread far and wide before the patient had any symptoms at all. Severance had a small mass in the tail of the pancreas and the entire peritoneum was seeded with tiny nodules, like millet seeds.

"Oh, shit," Kaplan said.

Most of the time, you had a patient like this, you expected it. You at least *suspected* it. This guy had a wife and three little kids, none of whom were prepared for a death sentence on daddy.

Kurtz grabbed one of the nodules with a forceps and cut it off at the bottom with a scalpel. The scrub nurse held out a jar filled with formalin. He dropped the nodule into the jar, put two sutures around the base of the wound and tied them tight. He repeated the process twice more, with nodules from different quadrants of the abdomen. "Send them for frozen section," he said.

"Why?" Kaplan asked. "We're not going to do anything differently."

Frozen sections were not as accurate as a full pathological prep, but they gave a quick diagnosis, which was important when knowing the type of tumor you were dealing with might affect the type of operation you were going to perform. That was not the case here. Whatever the origin of the tumor might be, there was no possibility of removing all the nodules surgically. Most of them were undoubtedly too small to even see with the naked eye. "I know that," Kurtz said. "But I want to know what he's got. I have to talk to the family."

They inspected the abdomen one last time. Aside from the obvious, nothing else was unusual. "Let's close," Kurtz said.

The closure did not take long. The patient was in the recovery room by the time the results came back on the frozen section. As had seemed most likely, it was pancreatic cancer. Pancreatic cancer occasionally responded to chemotherapy but only for a short period of time. It always recurred. Also occasionally, you had a miracle; a patient with disseminated carcinomatosis went home on his deathbed and by mechanisms totally unknown, cured himself. The cancer vanished. Spontaneous remission, it was called, as if giving it a name helped to explain it. But the odds against that happening were considerably more than one in a million. No, James Severance was going to die and that was that.

The family of course had trouble accepting it. They always did. He spent as much time with them as they needed but it never did a lot of good. The foundations of their universe had been yanked out from under them and the readjustment would not be pleasant.

He left them an hour later in a foul mood.

He changed into his street clothes in the locker room, took the elevator down to the ER exit. He was less than a hundred yards from the hospital when a well-dressed young man with sandy hair, freckles and an eager smile came up to him. "Uh, excuse me," the man said. "Are you Dr. Kurtz?"

"Yes," Kurtz said.

The man bobbed his head and looked apologetic. "I'm sorry to tell you this, Doc, but there's a man behind you with a gun. Don't turn around and don't yell. We really don't want to hurt you but we're going to have to take you for a little ride."

"A little ride," Kurtz said. Just like the movies. That was the trouble with real life. You saw enough movies, real life turned into a cliché.

The man nodded. "Yup," he said. "Right this way."

Dean Lobert wasn't the *Dean*. Dean Lobert was the Dean of Students. The Dean of the College (known in every college and university simply as *the* Dean) was picked by a search committee appointed by the Board of Trustees. The Dean of Students, on the other hand, was picked by the Dean. Though the title was impressive, the position more often than not was given to an academic who was popular with the students but whose publication record was not quite good enough to justify tenure. And so it was with Dean Lobert. By the time his appointment as Dean of Students ran out, he would have enough papers to get tenure or he would be out the door. The academic life, he explained plaintively, was an unforgiving one.

Barent didn't give a shit. "How widespread is drug use on this campus?" he interrupted.

Lobert stared at him.

"Drug use?" he finally said. "What makes you ask about drug use?"

"Look, we don't have all day. I've been told that drug use is common among the students,"–he smiled thinly–"if not among the faculty. I've also been told that Kevin Mahoney may be dealing drugs. How many students are there around here who deal drugs, do you think?"

"Truthfully?" Lobert frowned and gnawed the inside of his cheek. Then he drew a deep breath. "I have no idea. What's more, I don't want to have any idea. The concept of *in loco parentis* went out a long time ago. We're not these kids' parents. It's our job to educate them, not police them. So long as they pass their courses and don't cause any trouble, we have no reason to look any further into their behavior."

He looked sincere. Vaguely disdainful, but sincere. Dean Lobert's own involvement, according to what Edward Horvath had told them, could easily be interpreted as corrupting the morals of a minor, if not child abuse. However, mentioning this fact without a lot more evidence than they had would not be likely to solicit Lobert's cooperation. "But I have," Barent said. "I have a murder to solve. A number of clues point to an involvement with drugs. The fact that the victim's son may or may not be dealing drugs might be no more than a red herring. I hope that it is but I have to find out. How do you suggest that I do that?"

"I don't know," Lobert said.

"I would like to search Kevin Mahoney's room." "No," Lobert said immediately.

"Why not?"

138

"Because it would cause a riot." Lobert gave a frigid smile. "One thing about college, these kids pay tuition. They think that gives them certain rights. Whether or not it does is debatable, but it most certainly gives them the ultimate right from the University's point of view, which is that they can vote with their feet. There are plenty of colleges around and our students are an elite bunch. They can go anywhere they want."

He had a point, not one that Barent cared too much about, but a point. A more important point was that Edward Horvath's opinion was not what a judge would call evidence, which meant that they had no real chance at getting a search warrant.

Moran leaned forward. "Let's go talk to Kevin Mahoney."

Barent cocked his head at Lobert. "That okay with you?"

Lobert puffed up his cheeks in thought. "I believe so, as long as you remember that you have no jurisdiction here. I'll ask you to be discreet, and don't make any threats that you can't carry out."

"Fine," Barent said. "It's a deal."

Déja vu all over again. This was not the first time that Kurtz had been abducted at gunpoint. On the previous occasion, he had been an unlucky bystander. The real target had been Harrison Thomas, Lenore's former fiancé, whose father had been involved in a money laundering operation. Kurtz had just happened to be there when it happened.

This time, it appeared, he was simply unlucky.

"What's this all about?" he asked (speaking of clichés).

There were three of them. The one who had originally accosted Kurtz sat up front with the driver, who kept his eyes on the road and never said a word. The third man, the one with the gun, sat in back with Kurtz. All three wore suits. The car was a dark blue Lincoln with tinted windows. The first man turned around. His face looked troubled. "You can call me Simms. And that's Rico."

He nodded his head at the gunman. "It's simple. You've been poking your nose into things that don't concern you. We've been asked to tell you to stop."

Offhand, Kurtz could think of a number of things he had been poking his nose into, none of which had yielded him a scintilla of information.

Nevertheless, the general message was clear. "I see," he said.

"I hope you do." Simms looked as if he meant it. "I want you to understand that we're doing this the easy way. You're a doctor. Doctors aren't stupid. You should realize without my having to tell you that we can kill you just as easily as we can pick you up off the street. More easily, in fact."

"Like you killed Rod Mahoney?" Kurtz said. He couldn't stop himself. It just slipped out.

Simms blinked at him and slowly shook his head. "Who?" he said. Then he sighed. "I can see we've got a problem here. You don't think we're serious. Maybe you're not as smart as I thought you were."

Maybe he was right. Kurtz didn't feel too smart right now. What he felt was pissed off.

Rico looked like a professional. His eyes never left Kurtz. He held his gun resting comfortably across his lap, pointing at Kurtz' chest. The gun never wavered.

"Rico doesn't say much, does he?"

Rico smiled slightly.

Simms looked worried. It occurred to Kurtz belatedly that if Simms was worried, then maybe Kurtz should be worried also. "Look," he said. "I get the message. Believe me."

"I hope you do," Simms said. "I really do."

The car, which had been driving aimlessly around midtown, pulled up to a stop in front of Kurtz' building. Simms gave him a thin smile. "But if you don't, it's going to be your problem, not mine. We know where you work and we know where you live. We can get you any time we want you. Do yourself a favor and remember that. Have a nice day."

Rico raised an eyebrow and made a shooing motion with the gun. Kurtz looked back and forth between Rico and Simms. They both were smiling now. Kurtz shrugged, opened the car door and got out. He watched as the Lincoln pulled sedately away.

Lenore will not be pleased, he thought.

Chapter 21

Barent and Moran left Hanover at a little after five. Barent was in a lousy mood. Moran, as usual, seemed unperturbed, even sleepy. "Big time drug dealer," Barent said. "Shit."

He reached into his jacket, pulled out a cigar and lit it. Moran only looked at him.

They had taken the direct approach and informed Kevin Mahoney that certain of the clues in the case were pointing at him. They had mentioned drugs. Mahoney had quietly begun to cry. "You want to search the room?" he demanded, his voice trembling. "Go ahead. Search it."

They did. In one drawer of his desk, they found a small plastic bag containing what appeared to be a few grams of marijuana. That was all.

"I smoke pot now and then. Most of the students do. I don't deal drugs. I once bought a couple of extra ounces for some friends. That's all. I didn't make a profit on the deal." Mahoney sat slumped on the bed, his shoulders hunched. "Who told you this, anyway?"

Barent glanced at Moran and didn't answer.

"Aunt Evelyn, wasn't it? He raised his head and looked at them. Moran scratched his head. Barent found himself unable to look Mahoney in the eye.

"Our sources are confidential, I'm afraid."

"Aunt Evelyn is a complete idiot."

Barent pretty much agreed with this assessment. "Look," he said. "I'm sorry if we've made this tougher for you. You have to understand that we're going to follow up on whatever evidence we have. That's the way it works."

"Sure," Kevin said bitterly. "She probably told you that Dad and I had a fight. Well, we did have a fight. Dad was a pretty straight-laced kind of guy. I don't do a lot of drugs. My grades are good. I stay out of trouble. I had just come back for Christmas vacation in my freshman year. It was my first time home after starting school. I made the mistake of bringing a joint and smoking it in my room. Dad smelled it. He went nuts. After that, I was smart enough to keep it out of his way. That's the way parents want it. As long as you don't throw something that they disapprove of in their face, they won't make an issue of it."

"Alright," Barent said. "I understand. I'm sorry to have bothered you. We'll let you know if we discover anything."

"Sure."

Barent nudged Moran, who nodded, and they left. Twenty minutes later, on the road back to New York, Moran said, "The fact that we only found a little pot doesn't mean he's not dealing. He admits he's a user. I don't see any reason to believe him."

"You want to bust him?" Barent said.

"The thought had crossed my mind. Possession of marijuana is still a crime."

"It's a misdemeanor. The kid gets a fine and the judge puts him on probation. So what? His father just got murdered. He's got enough problems." Barent frowned at his cigar. It tasted like a swamp. "You ever smoke a little pot when you were a kid?"

"No," Moran said. He glanced at Barent from the corner of his eye. "You?"

Barent grunted. Moran frowned and glanced away.

"The latest surveys say that approximately twenty-five per-cent of all the high school kids in the country have at least tried marijuana. I don't know what it is for college but it's got to be a lot higher." Barent trailed off into a moody silence. A few minutes later, he sighed. "You're right, of course. We haven't cleared the kid of anything. I'll alert the local cops to keep an eye on him. If he goes anywhere off the campus, or meets anybody suspicious, they'll let us know."

"Good," Moran said. "Better to be certain."

Lenore was spending the evening with her parents. At about nine, she called and told Kurtz that she would be staying over. Her mother, it seemed, was being difficult. Kurtz wondered how she could tell but he was just as happy. He wasn't looking forward to explaining Rico and Simms to Lenore.

Barent, Kurtz was informed, was away on business. "How about Harry Moran?"

"He's with him." The voice on the phone sounded amused.

"Could you please leave a message for either one of them to call Richard Kurtz when they get in?"

"Sure," the voice said.

"Thanks."

The voice hung up without answering.

It was nearly midnight before Barent called. By this time, Kurtz was asleep. "What's up?" Barent asked.

Kurtz told him. Barent was silent for a moment. When he answered, he sounded more resigned than upset. "I should have known, with you."

"What do you mean by that?" Kurtz was irritated. "Remember Rod Mahoney's body? Remember you asking me if I was 'in or out'? You remember that?"

"Jeez, calm down," Barent said.

"Why the fuck should I?"

"Okay, don't calm down, but don't take it out on me. I'm just trying to help."

Kurtz took a long, deep breath. "Fine," he said gruffly. "So what do you suggest that I do?"

"I suggest that you come down to the station house in the morning and look at some photos. Maybe we can figure out who Rico and Simms really are."

"You think they were phony names?"

Barent gave an audible snort. "Yeah," he said. "I think they were phony names."

"Okay," Kurtz said. "I'll be there around eleven-thirty. Anything else?"

"Yeah. I think you should do what the man suggested. Stop asking questions."

Kurtz had only one case the next morning; he was assisting David Chao on a laparoscopic cholecystectomy. The patient was a typical gallbladder patient, fat, forty, fertile (she had had three kids) and female, the four f's which taken together, predispose to gallstones. Once the patient was asleep, Chao made a small incision inside the belly button; a small steel tube was pushed through into the abdomen and hooked up to a carbon dioxide infuser. Within a minute, the patient's abdomen was as large and tight as an inflated beach ball. Then the pump was withdrawn, a metal trochar was put in and the scope inserted through the trochar. "That's it," Kurtz said. On the TV screen next to the patient's head, the gallbladder could be clearly seen, nestled beneath the liver.

Chao's face was intent behind his mask. His hands were sure. The gallbladder came out with a minimum of fuss. The scope was withdrawn and the incisions closed. A few minutes later they were in the locker room, changing.

"Will you be at the club tonight?" Chao asked.

"I wasn't planning on it."

"I haven't seen you there in a couple of weeks. You'll get out of shape."

Kurtz wasn't worried about getting out of shape. He still ran three miles every other evening and walked home from work. Nevertheless, Chao was right. Karate, like any sport that depended on timing and reflexes, needed to be practiced. "Maybe you're right," he said. "I'll think about it."

"My mom said to thank you, by the way."

"For what?"

"For coming to dinner the other night."

"I should thank her. It was a great meal." He had thanked her, actually. He and Lenore had sent a card. He hoped it hadn't gotten lost in the mail.

Chao pulled on his shirt and tightened his tie. "She's driving me nuts. She doesn't like Carrie."

"Why not?"

Chao gave him an incredulous look. "She's not Chinese. You know what Chinese call you pale, occidental types?"

"No. What?"

"*Lo-Fong*. It means 'foreign devil.' It's fine to do business with the barbarians but you're not supposed to marry them."

"Marry?" This was the first Kurtz had heard of it. "You've been going out for what, three weeks?"

Chao shrugged. "It's never too soon for a mother to worry."

"What does your father think?"

"It's fine with him, but Mom is from the old country. She disapproves. Not from any prejudice, you understand. She just thinks I should find a girl with whom I have more in common." Chao rolled his eyes.

"I know what you mean," Kurtz said.

"You do? How?"

"Lenore is Jewish. I'm not. Her mother is not exactly the live-and-let-live type."

"Really?" Chao grinned. "I thought her mother introduced you?"

"She did introduce us."

"Then what's the problem?"

"From what I understand, this is typical lunatic behavior. They need to control whatever is going on. First she gives Lenore a hard time because she's not producing grandchildren. Then she harasses her because we're living in sin. Then she decides that I'm not her sort and she should find somebody who's Jewish."

"Good luck," Chao said.

Kurtz shrugged. "Lenore knows when to ignore her mother. I imagine you do, too."

"Oh, yeah. I learned that a long time ago."

"Then you don't have a problem."

"Are you kidding? I still have to listen to her."

Kurtz, who was nervously anticipating a lifetime of dealing with Esther Brinkman, could definitely sympathize. "You do have a point."

Chao grinned. "I figure I'm lucky. My parents are occasionally a pain but they're relatively normal. You remember my Uncle Jack? Chris and Lily's father?"

"Sure."

"He's an alcoholic."

At the party, Uncle Jack had gone through well more than a bottle of champagne by himself. "I had sort of figured that out."

"Usually he's a quiet sort of drunk but every once in a while, he gets violent. I don't know what the story is with him. My parents talk about it sometimes but not with me."

Chao grinned wanly. "I think they figure I'm still too young not to be shocked by the family secrets. As near as I can tell, Aunt Rose got pregnant and so they decided to get married. This was in Chicago. Rose worked as a receptionist for Northwind and Uncle Jack was an executive."

"They didn't look too happy together," Kurtz said.

"No. It's sad."

"Why don't they get divorced?"

"Damned if I know." Chao shrugged. "It was tough on Chris and Lily, I can tell you that, particularly Chris, since Rose isn't even his mother. I was pretty close to Chris and Lily when we were kids. We went to High School together. Chris used to talk every once in a while about what it would be like to live in a normal family, one where you could bring other kids over to the house without worrying that the old man would be passed out on the couch or have to listen to the parents screaming at each other. He was pretty bitter about it."

"I can see why," Kurtz said. "How about Lily? Did it affect her the same way?"

"No. Lily is one of those people whose outlook on life comes from the inside. Lily is genuinely happy. She has an infinite capacity for looking on the bright side."

"A useful attribute."

"You bet."

Kurtz finished knotting his tie and headed for the door. "Maybe I'll see you later at the club."

Thirty minutes later, Kurtz was sitting with Harry Moran, going through a computerized list of known felons. On the fifty-seventh picture, Simms' sheepish grin looked out at him from the computer screen. "Him," Kurtz said.

Moran pressed a button. The picture vanished and then reappeared at the top left corner of the screen. The rest of the screen was filled with the subject's history and vital statistics. Moran pursed his lips as he read. "Alfonse Simonetti. Twenty-eight years old. Two arrests for assault, both charges dropped when the alleged victims refused to cooperate. One arrest for armed robbery, dismissed when a key witness failed to testify. A four year sentence in Clinton for grand theft, auto, reduced to eighteen months for good behavior."

Moran's lip curled as he read the next part. "Suspected of the murder of Georgio Serretti, a known member of the Genovese crime family, shot twice through the head. That was in 1992. He seems to have stayed out of trouble since then."

"You mean he hasn't gotten caught."

"Exactly."

"So now what?"

146

"That's up to you," Moran said. "We could pick him up for forcible restraint, even kidnapping, but it would be your word against his and there aren't any other witnesses. He'd be out in less than an hour and the charges would go nowhere. Meanwhile, he would know that you weren't paying attention to his little warning."

"So what do you suggest?"

"I suggest that you lay low. Lew gave you good advice. Stop asking questions. We'll see what we can dig up on Mr. Simonetti's recent activities."

Kurtz pondered this. He hated the idea of running away from a fight but he knew when he was out of his league. "Okay," he said.

Moran turned back to the computer. "Let's see what we can do with Rico."

But with Rico they were not so lucky. Kurtz reviewed photographs for another hour but could find nobody who resembled the gunman. Moran was not discouraged. "You've given us a good lead," he said. "I imagine that once we start looking into Simms, Rico will turn up."

Kurtz shrugged. "Lenore and I are going away for a few days. I'll give you a call when I get back."

Chapter 22

Lenore's parents were going to California for Thanksgiving to visit Lenore's sister, who was married to a producer of documentary films and had recently given birth to her second baby. Kurtz, who figured he had a lot to give thanks for, had rented a cabin on a lake in the Poconos and planned to spend a four-day weekend with his lady love. Lenore, a city girl born and bred, expressed some uncertainty regarding this plan. "What are we going to do there?"

"Oh, the usual," Kurtz said. "Hunt, fish, play a little golf, relax around the fire with a good book and a bottle of wine, fuck our brains out."

Lenore looked thoughtful. "I've only been fishing once. Daddy took me and my sister on a party boat out of Sheepshead Bay. Do they have flounder in the Poconos?"

"I don't think so. Trout, I think. Maybe bass."

"Do you have to put worms on the hook? I don't put worms on hooks. It's a rule."

"No worms. We'll use lures."

"Well, maybe I'll try the fishing," she said grudgingly, "but forget about hunting. I can't make love to a man who shoots baby ducks."

Kurtz gave her a hurt look. "You don't shoot the babies. You attract them with a duck call and when they get close enough to grab them, you jump out and wring their necks."

"Whatever."

"How about the rest of the itinerary?" he asked.

She shrugged. "I guess I could get into it."

The cabin had two bedrooms and a comfortable den with a fireplace, pine floors and a bearskin rug. The kitchen was well-stocked, the furniture new. There was a satellite dish on the roof and a twenty-seven inch Magnavox TV in both bedrooms. "Not bad," Lenore said. "I was afraid we were going to have to rough it."

"You ever do any camping?" Kurtz asked. He hauled both suitcases up onto the king-sized bed and opened them.

"No," Lenore answered.

"When I was a kid, I used to camp out all the time. We should try it."

148

Lenore gave him a smile that said Kurtz was sadly misguided. "I hope what I'm about to tell you isn't going to disillusion you, but this is as rustic as I intend to get."

"Oh, well," Kurtz said. Within ten minutes they had unpacked.

"Would you like a drink?" Lenore asked.

"What do they have?"

A cabinet in the den contained glassware and an assortment of bottles. "Almost everything."

"Brandy?"

She peered inside. "Hennessy V.S.O.P."

"Good enough."

She poured a generous amount into a snifter, then poured a glass of Amaretto for herself. "So what shall we do first?" Lenore asked, sitting down in a soft chair.

"We could try the trout stream."

The cabin was situated less than a hundred yards from a sizeable creek. Kurtz had been assured that it was well-stocked.

"We could," Lenore said. She sipped her drink and made no move to rise from the chair.

After a moment, Kurtz said, "But maybe we should wait until evening when the fish will be more likely to bite. Why don't we find something to occupy ourselves with here?"

She smiled at him. "Let me take a shower."

"How's the investigation going?" Ted Weiss asked. Weiss was an assistant DA. He was as tall and thin as a beanpole, with sandy hair and jug ears.

"Lousy," said Barent.

"That's what I figured. It's been more than two weeks."

"You figured right. So far, every lead we've had has gone nowhere."

Weiss nodded. The fact was that the majority of murders were easily solved, simply because the majority of murders were crimes of passion committed by friends or relatives of the victim, whose efforts to cover their tracks were more often than not laughably inept. A murder like this, where the motive was obscure, the method bizarre and the family ostensibly uninvolved, was very different.

"We have one witness. According to what he told us, it doesn't look like a professional hit. On the other hand, a known wiseguy named Alphonse Simonetti may have been involved."

Weiss's ears perked up.

"Why do you think so?"

Barent told him. When he had finished, Weiss frowned into his coffee cup. "Kurtz again."

"He's a friend of mine," Barent said. "He was also a friend of the victim."

"He's a pain in the ass."

"He gave us good advice on the Lee case. We couldn't have broken it without him."

Weiss made a non-committal sound. "Kurtz is a bull in a china shop. He doesn't know when to butt out."

Barent gave a slight smile.

"You know that," Weiss said. Barent said nothing.

"He has no business mucking around a police investigation."

Barent spread his hands. "Look, I agree with you. What's more, Kurtz agrees with you. He has no intention of screwing things up."

"I hope so," Weiss said.

"He doesn't," Barent said.

An hour later, Barent and Moran were sitting in a coffee shop in Queens. They had been waiting for twenty minutes and Barent was beginning to wonder if their contact was going to show, when the door opened and a little man with a bald head, a harassed expression and a rumpled trench coat came in the front door. He spotted Barent immediately, came over to their booth and sat down next to Moran. Looking at Barent with a sad expression on his face, he said, "I haven't heard from you in a while. I was hoping you had forgotten about me."

"I have a memory like an elephant," Barent said. "What can you tell me about Alphonse Simonetti?"

The little man winced. "Simonetti?"

Barent sipped his coffee. Moran smiled.

The little man's name was Gregorio Peschi. He was a well connected member of the Genovese crime family. About five years before, his son had had the misfortune to be present at a party that was raided by the police. They had found cocaine, methamphetamine and phencyclidine on the premises. There was no real evidence that Jonathon Peschi was involved or even knew about it (and no real evidence that he didn't) but he was Gregorio Peschi's son. He was taken in for 'resisting arrest' and somehow wound up with a broken nose and a detached retina in the left eye that ultimately required surgery to repair. Barent, when he found out what had happened, was furious. He arranged for the kid to be released immediately and ever since then, whenever he needed a special bit of information, he called Gregorio Peschi.

Peschi sipped a cup of coffee and glanced over at the waitress, who was chewing gum and flipping through the pages of a newspaper. "Hey," Peschi said.

The waitress looked up.

"You got any cheese Danish?"

"I think so. Sure."

She went over to a display case and brought Peschi a sticky looking pastry on a white plate. "You gentlemen want anything?"

Barent said, "No, thanks."

Moran just shook his head. The waitress went back to her newspaper.

Peschi carefully sliced his pastry into eight pie shaped wedges and began to eat the wedges with a fork. "You did me a favor once, Barent, but that doesn't mean you own me."

Barent said nothing. Moran sipped his coffee. "I do this for you, I figure we're quits."

Barent nodded. "If you say so."

"I've heard of Simonetti. He's a Luchese. I hate the Lucheses. I'd tell you to go fuck yourself, it was one of our own. You know that?"

Barent shrugged.

"What exactly is it that you want to know?"

When Barent had told him, Peshci nodded his head thoughtfully and said, "I read about that guy Mahoney. It was in all the papers. They wouldn't show the pictures, said he was chopped up pretty bad. Is that true?"

"Yeah," Barent said.

Peshci's jaws moved stolidly as he chewed. "You know Gotti? John Gotti?"

"What's he have to do with this?" Moran asked.

"Gotti's son Frank, he was only thirteen, maybe fourteen at the time, he got run over and killed by a neighbor. It was an accident but that didn't matter any. A few months later the neighbor disappeared. Word is that he got himself chopped up very slowly before he vanished into a landfill."

"Rod Mahoney didn't kill anybody," Barent said. "Accidentally or on purpose."

"Maybe not. But you don't get chopped up into little pieces because somebody likes you." Peschi sighed. "I'll find out what I can about Simonetti and Rico, if there is a Rico. After that, don't call me again unless you can do something for me. You understand what I'm saying?"

Barent smiled into his coffee. "I understand perfectly. I wouldn't think of it."

Chapter 23

"Anybody ever tell you you got shifty eyes?" Moran asked.

Barent looked at him. The car rocked slightly from side to side as a gust of wind caught it. Moran looked glum.

"My wife," Barent said.

"Sort of strange I never noticed that before but I noticed it when you were talking to Peschi. You got shifty eyes."

Moran kept both hands on the wheel as he drove. It was one of the things Barent respected about Moran, without necessarily admiring it. Everything that he did, he did well and by the book.

"So?"

"You ever think that maybe there's not much difference between us and the people we're after?"

The thought had occurred to Barent, now and then. He had always dismissed it. "You mean the feeling that the dirt sometimes rubs off?"

"Yeah," Moran said.

Barent lit up a cigarette before answering. "You want one?" he asked.

"No, thanks."

"We're not just like them. I'll admit that sometimes it feels like we might be. A guy like Peschi, we meet him in a diner, have a little conversation, share a cup of coffee …" Barent shook his head and blew a smoke ring up to the roof of the car, where it dissipated in a current of air. "We'll put Peschi away in an instant when the opportunity presents itself, and he knows it."

"So why don't we?"

"Because we have nothing on him. It's as simple as that."

Moran grunted.

Ten minutes later, they pulled up to the curb by the Mahoney house. Claire Mahoney met them at the door. "Come in," she said. "Please sit down."

Claire Mahoney had rearranged the furniture in the living room. The chairs, which used to face the fireplace, were now clustered by the window. As they talked, her eyes would drift constantly to the street.

She barely looked at their faces. Her posture was stiff, her expression tense. "How are you, Mrs. Mahoney?" Barent asked.

She shrugged. "Getting along."

Moran glanced at him. He gave an imperceptible nod. "Perhaps it's not my place to give you advice," Barent said, "but after what's happened to you, people sometimes find that they're no longer comfortable in their old homes, that familiar surroundings no longer seem secure or even familiar. Sometimes they remind people of things that they would rather not dwell on."

Claire smiled faintly. "Go someplace new and start a new life? Is that the idea, Detective?"

"I was only thinking that perhaps you might feel more comfortable in different surroundings."

She frowned at the street. "You might be right. I'll think about it. Now what can I do for you, Detective?"

"You had told us that Evelyn Richter owed you some money, not an enormous amount but at least a couple of thousand dollars."

She nodded. "That's true."

"And that she never paid it back."

"Yes."

"You also told us that your husband had decided not to pursue the claim."

"Yes," she said again.

"Had he ever told the Richters that?"

"I don't know." Her eyes flicked to Barent's face, then back to the street. Two boys were riding by on bicycles. "What do you mean?"

"I mean that so far as the Richters knew, they were still obligated to pay back the money."

"Are you suggesting …?"

Of course he was suggesting. That was the way the game was played, but he wasn't going to admit it. "I'm not suggesting anything," he said. "I'm only asking."

She frowned at him. "It's not a very pleasant business, is it?"

"No, Ma'am."

"I don't know if Rod ever told her. I have a feeling that he didn't. Evelyn was like a bottomless pit for money, and Jay wasn't any better … isn't any better, so far as I know. If they have a million

154

dollars, they'll spend a million and ten. Rod had loaned them money … oh, maybe three or four times. Each time they would pay back a little but then before long they would ask for more and the debt kept increasing. The last time, he told Evelyn that there wouldn't be any more, ever. Knowing Evelyn, she probably didn't entirely believe him but Rod liked the idea that the debt was there. He felt it protected him."

"Protected him? How do you mean that?"

"From himself. He hated the way Evelyn lived. He hated the way Evelyn *was*. Never quite coping, never quite able to deal with life. Evelyn is the most totally self-indulgent person you can imagine. She simply cannot control her impulses. If she sees something that she wants, she'll buy it. She'll have a million excuses and a million rationalizations but the result is always the same. She's always short of cash. Evelyn was Rod's sister. He wanted to help her. It took him a long time to realize that he couldn't help her. It's not as if another loan was going to put her back on her feet. It's not. It never will. It's just money down the drain. The debt was a constant reminder of that fact."

So the Richters were off the hook but they probably didn't know it. Barent tried to keep his personal feelings out of it, but even objectively, he found the Richters to be hard to like.

"Do they have other debts that you know of?"

Claire Mahoney smiled frigidly. "This is an amazing society that we live in, Detective. Evelyn and Jay declared bankruptcy about three years ago. Within months, they began getting solicitations for credit card applications. It used to be you had to have a credit rating to get a loan." She shook her head. "I doubt very much that Evelyn and Jay were the slightest bit concerned about the money that they owed my husband. They owe a lot more to people who are far more likely to go after them."

She was probably right. Certainly there was no evidence to link the Richters to the crime. Too bad.

"Thank you, Mrs. Mahoney," Barent said. "I appreciate your taking the time to talk with me."

She shrugged and smiled wanly. "It's not as if I have anything better to do, Detective."

"No," Barent said. "I guess not."

Lenore, as it turned out, had a talent for fly-fishing.

"Which is this one again?" she asked, holding up a green and red wisp of feathers.

"Royal Wulff."

She had just caught a fifteen inch brookie on it and she didn't even know its name. "Tie on a new one. Even if you spray it with sealant, once you've caught a fish on it, it'll be too wet to float. Give it a chance to dry out."

They were standing knee deep in the stream. Kurtz, in a leap of extravagant faith, had purchased Lenore a whole outfit from Cabelas, including neoprene waders, fishing vest and a graphite fly rod. Lenore had looked at the outfit doubtfully when Kurtz had presented it to her but as it turned out, she was a natural. "How about this one?" she asked.

"Adams Irresistible."

"I like the sound of that." She tied it to the end of the tippet, snipped off the loose end of fishing line with a nail clipper and sprayed the fly with silicon sealant.

"Why don't you try a streamer?" Kurtz asked.

The end of November was late in the season. By rights, the dry flies that Lenore was using shouldn't be working now. There weren't any real bugs around for the flies to imitate and trout, wily though they might be, were still creatures of instinct. You had to use instinct when your brain was the size of a raisin.

"I'm doing just fine with these."

Lenore made a graceful backcast and allowed the fly to delicately land in an eddy next to a sunken log. Ten seconds later she whooped, "I got one!"

A nice little brookie had dimpled the water under her fly and then hit the air in a series of leaps. She let the fish run until it was tuckered out and then reeled it in. It was her fourth. Kurtz, who had caught only one on his streamer, shrugged and put on a dry fly. The trout, evidently, were using a different brand of instinct than Kurtz thought they were.

In the next half hour, Lenore caught two more and Kurtz reeled in three. By then, the sun was almost below the horizon. "Had enough?" he asked.

"I think so," Lenore said. "This was great."

The moon was starting to rise as the sun was setting. Tiny ripples were glowing on the stream. Somewhere, an owl hooted. Lenore's blond hair, tucked up under a baseball cap, gleamed. Kurtz held out a hand to help her over the embankment. Her hand, when he took it, was strong and held his firmly. Rico and Simms and everything to do with the real world seemed suddenly very far away. "Would you like to get married?" he asked.

She blinked at him. "I've been wearing the wrong perfume," she said. "You country boys prefer raw fish."

He waited.

She cocked her head to the side and made a clicking sound between her teeth. "When?" she asked

"Anytime you say."

"How about May?"

"I always liked May," Kurtz said. "Sure."

Kurtz took a deep breath, knelt down by the bank and took out a curved filleting knife from his creel. "May would be perfect," he said, and slit one of the trout up the belly. He smiled at her. "You want to help me clean these fish?"

Lenore looked down at him. "It occurs to me that this is not the most romantic way in which to make a proposal."

The stars were shining overhead. The moon was bright. Crickets were chirping in the trees. "I thought it was," Kurtz said. "And anyway, somebody has to clean the fish."

"Cleaning fish is gross," Lenore declared.

"Yup."

"You just asked me to marry you so I would feel guilty, didn't you?"

"Nope. Actually, I wasn't planning on it. It just sort of slipped out."

"I'll bet." She sighed, and then grinned wanly. "Show me how."

The problem with Thanksgiving is that even crooks take a break. The Richters stayed home but did nothing suspicious, at least according to the tail the police had placed on them. Barent heard nothing from Georgio Peschi. Betty was planning a family dinner and Barent, morose but with nothing better to do, helped her do it.

Denise was feeling a bit better. The nausea hit her only in the mornings now and didn't last too long. She and Paul were both planning to come, along with Paul's parents. William, the Barent' son, was in school on the West Coast. He had a new girlfriend who lived in San Diego and he had been invited to her parents' for the holiday. Barent had never met the girl and this evidence of a serious relationship made him nervous. Betty was more sanguine.

"What do you expect?" she said. "They only get four days off. You don't fly home from California for four days."

"You do if you want to introduce your girlfriend. She's taking William home to her parents. How come he's not bringing her here?"

"Because they can't be in two places at once and it's a six hour flight to New York."

"I suppose so," Barent grumbled. Then he added, "I'm in a bad mood."

Betty, who knew his moods well, placidly kneaded a pile of dough. "You always get like this when a case isn't going well," she said.

"I know. I can't help it."

"I thought you had some clues."

"They've led nowhere. There seems to be a link to organized crime, but it's weak."

Jerry Rubino's family had come from Naples. The Mafia in the United States had two main branches, the Sicilian and the Neopolitan. The two branches had never entirely gotten along. Simonetti was Sicilian. There might be something there but getting inside the Mafia was a job that took whole teams of professionals and years of effort. Look how long it took to get Gotti. If Gregorio Peschi didn't come up with something, the lead toward the Mafia was going to be a dead end because Barent did not have sufficient resources to pursue it.

"Even the Mafia takes a break for Thanksgiving," Betty said, echoing what Barent had been thinking. "Try to take your mind off it for a little while. Why don't you set the table? It'll help you relax."

"Sure," Barent said, and did as he was told.

The dinner was nice. The food was good. The conversation never flagged. Barent tried not to let his sour mood affect the general tone and generally, he thought he succeeded. Nevertheless, he was not unhappy to see the company drag itself home at the end of the evening.

The next morning, groggy and still feeling low, he arrived at the office to learn that Kevin Mahoney had been arrested in Ithaca, New York, in possession of fifty-thousand dollars worth of heroin and cocaine.

Chapter 24

Mosby was large, black and middle-aged. He had a brush moustache, jowls and sleepy-looking brown eyes that seemed to miss very little. A solid cop. He reminded Barent of Moran, in a way. Ithaca was not Manhattan but Mosby had obviously been around.

"He's not talking," Mosby said.

"Tell me again how it happened."

"We watched him. Yesterday evening he left the campus and drove into town. He went to the apartment of a man named Charles Royce. Royce is a known felon, three years in Clinton for armed robbery. He currently works as a waiter in a place called the *Town House Bar and Grill*. So far as we knew, he'd been clean since getting out, a little over a year ago. After fifteen minutes the kid came out and we moved in."

"Why?" Barent asked.

"What do you mean, '*Why?*'"

Barent drew a breath. "I mean it's not against the law to visit somebody, even a known felon. You had no probable cause. The kid claims unreasonable search and seizure and you're left with no case. Why?"

Mosby grinned faintly. "The kid was smoking what appeared to be a joint."

"On the street?"

Mosby shrugged. Barent looked at him. Mosby appeared excessively pleased with himself. "And was it a joint?"

"As it turned out, it was a perfectly ordinary cigarette. A *Marlboro Light*, I believe. But it looked like a joint. It *could* have been a joint. In any case, it gave us probable cause."

"Sure," Barent said.

Mosby looked at him searchingly. "What's got you so pissed off?" he asked.

Guilt, Barent thought. Christ, he was trying to solve a murder. Claire Mahoney had enough to feel shitty about and now this. "Why the hell did he do it?" Barent said plaintively.

Mosby gave him a cynical grin. "Money," he said. "Why else?"

"But he doesn't need the money."

"Everybody needs money. The kid's father was a teacher. Teachers do not get rich. Let me tell you, no matter how much you have, there's always somebody down the block–or in this case, the next dorm room– who drives a nicer car, takes better vacations and has more money in the bank than yours truly."

This, of course, was true. Barent knew it. He had seen it a thousand times. "Sure," he said glumly.

Mosby shook his head, amazed at Barent's innocence.

"So the kid won't talk …?" Barent said.

"Not a word."

Barent rose to his feet. "Let me try?"

Mosby puffed out his cheeks and looked thoughtful. "Remember you've got no jurisdiction here. Don't push too hard."

"No problem."

Mosby nodded. He led Barent across the hall, knocked on a door and opened it without waiting for a response. Inside, Kevin Mahoney sat at a wooden table, his face pale. He looked sick. Sitting across from him was a stocky man with a blue business suit, a bald head and a red face. "This is Carl Braun," Mosby said, "Mr. Mahoney's attorney."

"Mr. Braun," Barent said. He looked down at Kevin. "I don't suppose you would be willing to leave me alone with your client for a little while."

It was a statement, not a question.

"I suppose you're right," Braun said. His voice was scratchy, as if he had spent years with a cigarette in his mouth.

"Kevin?"

Kevin shrugged, not looking up from the floor.

"Alright," Barent said. He sat down in a chair and pulled it up to the table. The chair was hard and felt unsteady. "We'll do it by the book." He glanced at Braun, who returned his gaze with a thin, crooked smile. Mosby, observing all this, smiled thinly, stepped back out of the room and closed the door. Barent said to Kevin, "You were caught with a considerable amount of narcotics in your possession. How do you account for that?"

Kevin opened his mouth. Braun put a hand on his arm and Kevin closed his mouth, frowning.

"I don't know if they've told you," Barent said, "but on the strength of the evidence that they obtained from you, the Ithaca police raided the apartment of Mr. Royce. They found more than two kilos of cocaine and almost three of heroin. They also found a number of automatic weapons including an AK-47 assault rifle and an Uzi."

"My client knows nothing about the activities of Mr. Royce," Braun said.

"Oh? He just happened to wander into Mr. Royce's apartment looking for directions and inadvertently picked up the wrong briefcase?"

Braun smiled. "The nature of our defense will be made clear at trial. If it gets to a trial, which I doubt. The State's case will clearly hinge on the illegal seizure of evidence."

"Really?" Barent shook his head. "You supposed legal hotshots always amaze me. You might be able to argue that they searched your client without sufficient evidence but Charles Royce is a very different kettle of fish. They had plenty of evidence to go after him and Mr. Royce is not going to substantiate your client's story. Whatever it is."

Barent hoped not, anyway. In reality, it depended on who was orchestrating the defense. "Who's paying your fee, by the way?"

"That is privileged information," Braun said.

"Is it? You appeared on the scene awfully fast. Kevin is nineteen years old. Did his mother authorize the payment of your fee?"

Braun appeared unruffled. "Mr. Mahoney has authorized my defense, including payment."

Barent turned to Kevin. "Is that right?" Kevin hung his head but nodded.

"What do I have to do to get through to you?" Barent asked. "The presumptive suspicion is going to be that you killed your father. You were overheard arguing about drugs. Now you're arrested for possession of narcotics with intent to sell. How is that going to make your mother feel?"

Kevin looked up at him, his face red. "I had nothing to do with killing my father!" His voice was desperate. "Nothing!"

"That's not what they'll say."

Braun scowled at him, and for the first time appeared less than in total control of the situation. "The death of my client's father is not a factor in this case. Any apparent connection is completely coincidental."

Barent gave Braun a contemptuous look. He said to Kevin, "Whatever fatso here might have told you, you are in deep shit. You're going to go to trial, you're going to be found guilty–of possession of narcotics at the very least–and you're going to have a record. The only real question in this case is how much time you're going to have to serve. If you cooperate, it will probably be less. But that means telling everything you know about your friend Royce and it means telling everything you know about the death of Rod Mahoney."

"I don't know anything about my father's death," Kevin said again. "Nothing. Believe me."

Barent looked at him. He looked scared. He looked like a whipped dog. He also looked like he was telling the truth.

Braun's face had returned to its usual calm expression. Why not? It was no skin off his nose. Whatever happened to Kevin Mahoney, Braun was going to go home, eat dinner and sleep soundly.

Barent shrugged. "Good luck," he said to Kevin. He didn't add that Kevin was going to need it. He figured the kid already knew that. And if he didn't, then his scumbag lawyer did.

It was a wonderful vacation. Kurtz managed to put Rico and Simms to the back of his mind. They relaxed around the fire, played a couple of rounds of golf at a local course, ate at the best restaurants in town and celebrated their engagement in bed. Lenore was serene and Kurtz was effervescent. Every time he looked at her, he broke out into a smile. He couldn't help himself. Lenore seemed to find this absolutely adorable but she didn't seem to mind it in the slightest. "How can I deprive my man of the pleasure of worshipping me?" she said one night. "It wouldn't be right."

"I'll worship you as much as you want. Just don't ask me to grovel at your feet."

Lenore pouted. "I don't think that's fair. Other girls have men who grovel at their feet. Why shouldn't I?"

"We country boys prefer more wholesome pleasures than groveling at a woman's feet."

"Oh? Like what?"

"Like tickling them."

Lenore, as he well knew, was ticklish. He grabbed one foot and she pretended to shriek. Then they made love.

On Sunday afternoon, they drove back to the city.

Lenore leaned her head back against the seat and closed her eyes. "How are we going to tell my parents?" she said dreamily. A tiny smile hovered over her lips.

"What do you mean? Just tell them."

"But should we make a big production out of it or should we play the whole thing down?"

"No matter how you tell them, your mother will make a big production out of it. You can bet on that."

"True," Lenore said. "Why don't we wait until next Saturday. You're coming to dinner anyway. We'll surprise them."

Kurtz shrugged, the back of his neck prickling at the very thought of dinner with Lenore's mother. Lenore's mother had always reminded Kurtz of a vampire–a little, Jewish one. "Fine with me," Kurtz said.

Chapter 25

"Kevin?" Kurtz said. "Oh, man ..."

Barent sadly nodded. "Yeah. It's a shame. His mother was pretty broken up about it, I can tell you that."

Kurtz sipped his beer, wiped the foam off his upper lip with a napkin and thought that he should give Claire a call. But what on Earth could he say to her? Sorry about Kevin, but hey, it's only a little heroin. "You don't really think he had anything to do with killing Rod, do you?"

"No. I don't. The papers will see it differently, however."

"Do the papers know?"

"If they don't by now, they soon will. It's too good a story to keep hidden."

"How about this guy Royce? What is he saying?"

"Nothing. Royce knows what will happen to him if he sings. Even if he gave them some names, by the time the cops got there, there would be no evidence to find. It would be Royce's word against the word of whoever is higher up the line. Meanwhile, the operation gets underway again with a new guy at the end of the gravy train. Guys like Royce are small time."

"And guys like Kevin Mahoney?"

Barent looked disgusted. "A dime a dozen."

"How do you ever do anything about drugs?" Kurtz remembered what Hector Segura had said, that Barent could not stop the drug trade.

Barent apparently knew it. He shrugged and looked even more disgusted. "The only way to do it is all at once. You get some evidence on one guy, you *don't* make an arrest. You wait. You get the evidence on the guy above him, and then the guy above him and so on. You only move when you can take out the whole ring. Otherwise, there's no point. They're back in business in a day."

"And if you do get the whole ring, how long does it take until they're back in business then?"

"Maybe a month. Because you *don't* get the whole ring. You can't. Or at least *we* can't, which is pretty much the same thing. Most of the organization is out of state. The biggest parts are out of

165

the country. You need the cooperation not only of the feds but of half a dozen foreign governments."

Barent sipped his beer. "The drug business is like a cancer. You can excise it locally, but it spreads back almost as soon as you do."

"Then what's the point of even trying?"

"Good question. You know my feelings on the subject."

Kurtz did. Barent believed in legalization. Take the profit out of it, the criminal underclass would vanish. Of course, that would still leave society with a lot of people who abused drugs but that was a different, and in Barent's opinion, a much less socially disruptive problem.

Kurtz said, "I doubt very much that Kevin had anything to do with killing his father."

"I agree with you, but I've been wrong before."

"Anything new yet on Rico and Simms?"

"At the present time, Alphonse Simonetti works for a man named Vincent DeNegri. Ever heard of him?"

"No."

"He owns an estate in Rye, on the water. His company imports Pecorino Romano, extra-virgin olive oil and Prosciuotto da Parma from the old country."

"A lucrative business?"

"Apparently. He reports an income in the high six figures." "The business, I suppose, is a front."

"Sure. The guy is as dirty as they come."

"What exactly is it that Simms is supposed to do for him?"

"Supposed to do, or *does* do?"

Kurtz smiled wanly. "I have a pretty good idea of what he does do. What is he supposed to do?"

"The occupation listed on his tax returns is Sales Manager."

"I see ... and why is Vincent DeNegri interested in me?"

"We don't know. I've got somebody trying to find out but I haven't heard from him yet. I hope to soon."

Kurtz looked at him sourly. "Don't keep me in suspense."

"You'll be the first to know." Barent grinned. "And by the way, congratulations about you and Lenore."

Kurtz grinned back at him. "Thanks," he said. "We're telling her parents on Saturday. I can hardly wait."

166

They were missing the boat completely. He knew it. He could feel it. He suspected that Barent did too.

"Make your incision a little bigger," Kurtz said to Kaplan.

Kaplan gave him the usual wounded look but he did as he was told.

"According to the classical textbooks," Kurtz said, "the ideal incision is in layers. The incision through the skin is a little longer than the incision through the subcutaneous fat. The incision through the fat is a little longer than the incision through the fascia, and so on."

"Why?" Patel asked.

Kurtz shrugged. "I have no idea. That's what they used to teach. Maybe they thought it healed better that way. Or maybe it was more esthetic."

"I would think," Kaplan said, "that it would be more esthetic the other way around. You make a tiny incision through the skin and make it bigger as you go deeper. That way you leave a smaller scar."

"I don't think they were too worried about the scar," Kurtz said, "since most of their patients died anyway."

The patient this morning was a teenager named Michelle Davis, a pretty girl with a nodule on the thyroid. The thyroid scan had revealed the nodule to be 'hot', meaning that it took up radioactive iodine and therefore appeared as a large blip on the scanner. This was a good sign. A 'cold' nodule was more likely to be cancer. Still, whatever it was shouldn't be there. The thing about thyroid surgery was that the thyroid sat in the front of the neck, just below the larynx. There were a lot of structures there you had to be careful to avoid.

"What nerve controls the innervation to the cricothyroideus?" Kurtz asked.

"The superior laryngeal nerve," Kaplan said.

"And how about the rest of the larynx?"

"The recurrent laryngeal nerve."

"And what happens if we accidentally cut the recurrent laryngeal nerve?"

"The vocal cord on that side will be paralyzed."

"So?"

"So the patient will have a hoarse voice."

"How about if you cut it on both sides?"

"Then both vocal cords will be paralyzed."

"And what will happen if you do that?"

"The patient won't be able to breathe. She'd need a trach."

They were only removing one half of the thyroid, the half with the nodule, so they didn't have to worry about the patient living the rest of her life with a hole in her neck. Still, a hoarse voice was not an insignificant complication and surgeons had been sued plenty for less. "Make the incision big enough so we won't have any trouble finding the nerves."

Kaplan grunted. Patel smiled.

All this stuff with Rico and Simms and even Jerry Rubino, they were just distractions. Kevin Mahoney was an idiot, a larcenous idiot to be sure, but that didn't make him a murderer. Hatred, Barent had said, that was the key. The way Rod Mahoney was torn to pieces, the arrogance of it, the *contempt*. Somebody had hated Rod Mahoney, hated him enough to turn the manner of his death into a mockery of his entire life. Anatomy, the structure and function of the human body … it was a job that most people would find gruesome but others found fascinating and even beautiful. Rod Mahoney was one of the latter; no reason to kill somebody because they taught anatomy. Who could have hated Rod Mahoney, hated him enough to do that?

And why? So far as they knew, Rod Mahoney had led a perfectly inoffensive life.

Except that he pretty obviously had offended somebody, which clearly meant that there were things in his life that nobody knew about. Kurtz remembered a philosophy professor in college who had once remarked that almost everybody would have spent some time in jail if everything they had ever done had only come to light. Kurtz remembered something else, something that Barent had once told him; the secret to any premeditated murder lies with the victim, and when the moment comes and the knife is descending toward his chest, the victim is almost never surprised …

Barent was thinking the same thing.

"No prints …" he said to Moran, and sighed.

"No prints. You know that."

"No fibers. No hair …"

"Bermuda grass. Six feet tall, approximately. One hundred ninety to two hundred pounds. Reebok DMX, a dark gray or black fedora, a briefcase, a trench coat and a Mercedes."

"Not poor," said Barent.

"No. A business type. An executive."

"Jerry Rubino worked for a computer company."

"Jerry Rubino didn't drive a Mercedes. He hadn't been down South and his shoes were from Thom McCann."

"Jay Richter wears a fedora. And he owed the Mahoneys money."

"Jay Richter is too short and too light and he's out of shape. No way he could have done it."

Barent moodily grunted. "And the murder weapon, or weapons, have vanished."

"Yup," Moran said. He was reading the New York Times. He did not look up.

"I can't believe this guy Mahoney. You know what I mean?"

Moran nodded.

"I mean, nobody drifts through life without causing at least a few ripples. His family loves him. His friends love him. Nobody dislikes him. How can you trust a guy that nobody dislikes? There's something wrong there."

Moran gave a negligible shrug, sipped his coffee and re-folded the paper.

"Particularly an anatomy professor. Jesus, what a grisly occupation."

Moran squinted one eye at Barent and yawned behind his palm. Just then, the phone rang. Barent gave it an annoyed look but picked it up. He recognized the voice instantly. It was Georgio Peschi. "Hello, Barent?"

"Yeah," Barent said. "You got something for me?"

"Simonetti works for Vincent DeNegri. You know that?"

"Yeah."

"So does Rico. His real name is Romano, James G. Romano."

"Good," Barent said. "Thanks. What else have you got?"

"Vincent DeNegri has recently gotten himself a new associate. He's been working with Carlos Esquivel. You know him?"

Barent did. This was not happy news. Already, he could see legions of bodies lying in the city morgue. "What do the Families think of that?"

"They think it's business. Maybe it will work out. Maybe it won't. They're going to wait and see."

"Wise," Barent said.

"You bet."

"Is that it?"

"Yeah," Peschi said, "that's it. And remember what I told you. We're quits."

"I'll remember. Don't worry about it for an instant."

Peschi gave a harsh little laugh. "You bet," he said again.

Barent put down the phone and drew a deep breath. Moran, who had been sitting quietly in his chair during Barent's conversation, said, "Something?"

"Yeah," Barent said. "It's something. It's the Colombians."

Chapter 26

"She did what?" David Chao asked incredulously.

Kurtz looked up. David listened to the voice on the phone and visibly winced. "I'll be right there," he said, and hung up.

"What is it?" Kurtz asked.

They were sitting in the office, sharing a quick lunch, Boston Chicken for David, a corned beef on rye for Kurtz. David rose to his feet. "That was Chris Chang. He says Aunt Rose is hurt. She may have broken her cheekbone. She's down in the ER. I've got to go."

Kurtz glanced at the clock. Neither of them had any patients scheduled for the next hour. "Okay if I go with you?"

"Sure," David said. "Come on."

They walked across the connecting bridge from the Hampshire Building, where most of the staff had their office space, into the hospital itself and took an elevator down to the emergency room. "What exactly happened?" Kurtz asked.

"Chris didn't say but I can guess."

Kurtz looked at him sharply. David shrugged. Uncle Jack, he remembered, was a drunk–a violent drunk.

They found Rose Chang in a small treatment room, with an ER resident fluttering about. She had a handkerchief pressed against her cheek and she was staring at the resident with openly hostile eyes.

"Mrs. Chang," the resident said, "would you please let me look at it?"

"No," she said.

"I can't help you if you won't let me look."

"Go away," she said.

The resident looked up imploringly as Chao and Kurtz walked in.

"It's okay," Chao said. "I'll take care of it."

The resident looked back and forth between their faces. "You bet."

Rose Chang looked at Kurtz. The look was not friendly. "I'll wait outside," he said.

"Thanks," David said.

Kurtz found Chris Chang sitting in the waiting room. He was wearing a rumpled blazer and blue jeans. His face was pale and he was trembling. He smiled wanly when he saw Kurtz.

"How are you?" Kurtz asked.

"Not bad," Chang said. "How is she?"

"David is in with her. Offhand, it didn't seem too serious."

"Good." Chang nodded stiffly.

"How did it happen?" Kurtz asked.

Chang grinned with one half of his face. "She slipped in the kitchen and hit herself on the stove."

"I see. One of those routine accidents. By the way, where was your father while this was going on?"

Chang shrugged. "I don't know. When we left him, he was sitting in the den, drinking beer and crying."

Kurtz hardly knew what to say to that so he nodded his head in what he hoped was sympathy and said nothing.

His expression evidently said it for him. "Don't concern yourself," Chao said bitterly. "This has been going on for years."

Just then, the door to the examining room opened and David walked out. "I've ordered an x-ray. She may have a fractured zygoma but I think it's just a bruise."

Chris nodded curtly and stared down at the floor.

Kurtz' presence did not seem to be helping. "I hope she's alright," he said. Then, to David, "I'll see you back at the office. Take as much time as you need."

David nodded gratefully. "Thanks."

"Oops," Kurtz said. It was an hour after he had left David in the ER with his aunt and Chris Chang. David had not yet returned to the office but Lew Barent had. Kurtz was not thrilled by what he had to say.

Barent looked at him. "What do you mean by that?"

"Nothing," Kurtz said hastily. "Nothing at all."

"I know for a fact that they teach you guys not to say *oops* in medical school. A surgeon says *oops* at the wrong time, he could get himself in serious trouble. You know what I'm saying?"

"Yeah," Kurtz said.

"So tell me. What do you mean?"

"Hector Segura," Kurtz said.

"Segura? The name is familiar. … What about him?"

"He's supposed to be a Colombian drug kingpin. He's been at Staunton for months."

"Really?" Barent said. His eyes narrowed. "I remember him. I didn't know he was at Staunton."

"I talked with him," Kurtz said.

Barent blinked at him. "You talked with him … about the weather, I suppose?"

"Not exactly."

"Oh, boy …" Barent rose to his feet, filled his coffee cup and sat back down. "I'm going to need this," he said. "Now tell me."

Kurtz told him.

At the end, Barent drew a deep breath and lit a cigarette. Kurtz gave him a hurt look, which Barent ignored. "So you told him what was going on and asked him about the heroin trade."

"Yes."

Kurtz did not enjoy feeling like a dope. He stirred uncomfortably in his seat. "I didn't tell him anything that wasn't in the newspapers."

"Still, it never occurred to you that Segura might somehow be involved?"

"Involved in what? The Halloween party was supposed to be a joke, remember? I had no reason to think Segura had anything to with Mahoney's death. I still don't. And as for Vincent DeNegri, Jerry Rubino and Carlos Esquivel, you haven't established any sort of link to Segura. There must be hundreds of Colombians involved in the drug trade."

"There may not be a link." Barent leaned back in his seat and stretched his hands over his head. He looked pleased with himself. "But then again, there may. From what I know about it, which wasn't very much, Esquivel and Segura operated in different parts of the city. They weren't competitors. Segura had a section of the lower West Side. Esquivel had a part of the Bronx. When Segura was shot, his organization dissolved. Esquivel wound up with a part of it. A man named Joaquin Almodovar got another. The rest …"

Barent shrugged. "I don't know."

"There used to be a police guard outside Segura's room. It hasn't been there for months."

"That's interesting." Barent picked up the phone. "Let's find out." Two phone calls later, Barent was speaking with a Lieutenant Thaddeus Jones, who had been in charge of the watch on Hector Segura.

"He asked us to leave," Jones said.

"He give any reason?"

"He said we were making him nervous."

Barent puffed on a cigarette. A perfect smoke ring floated up toward the ceiling and dissolved. "And so you left."

Jones voice sounded as if he frankly didn't give a damn. "He was the victim. We were there to prevent whoever tried it from trying it again. If he wasn't going to worry about it, why should we?"

"Sensible," Barent said.

"We thought so."

"Okay, thanks."

Jones hung up.

"So," Barent said. "Give it to me again. You asked Segura about the heroin, how the stuff got into the country."

"Yes. He said the Colombians didn't deal in heroin."

Barent snorted. "That might have been true at one time but the Colombians will deal in anything that makes a profit. So will anybody else who ever thought about making an illegitimate buck. There are over twenty-million Americans who have at least tried cocaine, twice that who've sampled marijuana. In New York City, one citizen out of every ten regularly uses some sort of illicit drug, and for every ten people who use, there is at least one person who sells. We've got Jamaican gangs, Dominican gangs, Colombian gangs, Irish gangs, Vietnamese gangs, Chinese gangs, black gangs and good old American white gangs. There are no national boundaries on criminal behavior.

"What else did he say?"

"He said I should mind my own business and not get involved."

"Good advice."

"He said that the police didn't have a chance of stopping the drug trade, that it was too big."

"Did he now?" Barent frowned into his coffee cup as if noticing a bug. "Well, the son-of-a-bitch is absolutely right on that one." He looked up at Kurtz. "Anything else?"

"No."

Barent shook his head. "You," he said, "are a dummy."

"So sue me."

"How in the hell could you go to a guy like Hector Segura, a guy who has murdered more people than you can count, with this shit?"

"It's hard to think of him that way," Kurtz said defensively. "For as long as I've known him, he was just a patient. Actually, he always seemed like a perfectly pleasant sort of guy."

"As drug kingpins and mass murderers go, he's probably as pleasant as any."

Kurtz shrugged. He didn't, to be perfectly frank, see what Barent was acting so smug about. If Kurtz was a dummy, and Hector Segura turned out to have something to do with Rod Mahoney's murder or the heroin that had been brought into the medical center, then the police had not exactly covered themselves with glory.

"I don't suppose they keep a visitor's log?" Barent said.

"Are you kidding?"

"Forget I asked," Barent said. "It doesn't matter anyway. Nobody important would use his right name. But I think we have to consider the possibility that Hector Segura is back in business."

"So now what?"

"Now?" Barent grinned with one side of his mouth. "Now we watch. I will be very interested to see who comes calling on Hector Segura. Rico, maybe? Simms?"

"You said that Segura had no link to Carlos Esquivel."

"That was then, this is now."

"I suppose it's possible," Kurtz said.

"Anything's possible." Barent picked up the phone and began to punch the buttons. "Let's go get some evidence."

Chapter 27

David's aunt had a hairline fracture of the zygoma but it was non-displaced and would heal without surgery. After briefly telling Kurtz what had happened, David did not seem eager to discuss the situation further. Kurtz was not inclined to pry. It was none of his business and as Chris Chang had said, the whole thing had been going on for a very long time.

The Union Square Cafe was–and is–one of New York's premier restaurants, renowned for both food and service. Kurtz had waited nearly a month to get reservations. The Friday after Thanksgiving weekend, Kurtz, Lenore, Carrie Owens and David Chao ate dinner at the Union Square Cafe. They were seated up on a balcony, from which vantage they could watch the crowd down below at the bar.

"So that's the latest," Kurtz said. "The murderer is approximately six feet tall, weighs about a hundred ninety pounds, probably has a house in the country and is well off." Kurtz did not mention Hector Segura. It seemed smarter not to.

David didn't even glance at him. He and Carrie were sitting close together, playing little touchy-feely games with their fingertips, smiling with wide, dewy eyes into each other's faces. David seemed to be having trouble following the conversation. Lenore smiled at them with benign amusement, looked at Kurtz and arched an eyebrow.

"So Carrie," Kurtz said. "How are things in the ER lately?"

She looked at him. "What was that?"

"How's work? Any interesting cases?"

"Oh," she said, and shrugged. "The usual. A few heart attacks, a stabbing, some MVA's."

"The stuff of life," Kurtz observed.

"You bet," Carrie said. ER work had a high turnover rate. A lot of docs were attracted to the ER, mostly because of the regular hours and the fact that you didn't get stuck with long term care. The end of your shift came, you packed up and went home. After awhile, however, it started to get to you. The work was ultra-high stress, one life and death situation after another–and it never stopped. In percentage terms, more patients died in the ER than any other part of a hospital except maybe the cancer ward or the cardiac care unit and

176

when they went, they never went quietly; it was always the full court press.

Some people thrived on it, however. Carrie, apparently, was one of these.

Chao leaned over and whispered something in Carrie's ear. Carrie giggled.

"We never acted like that, did we?" Kurtz asked.

"I think it's sweet," Lenore said.

"You," Chao said, showing that he had at least paid some minimal attention to the conversation, "are an old fart."

"I agree with you," Lenore said virtuously. Kurtz only grunted. He was having trouble keeping a straight face since Lenore's hand was at that moment caressing the inside of his thigh.

"No drug overdoses in the last couple of days," Carrie said.

"That's good," Kurtz said.

Lenore smiled innocently.

"How did you get to be so friendly with Detective Barent?" Carrie asked.

"It's a long story," Kurtz said. Lenore coughed.

"Something the matter?" Carrie asked.

"No," Kurtz said.

"Not at all," Lenore put in.

"Honestly," Carrie said. "And you think we're sappy."

"I haven't the faintest idea what you mean," Lenore said. Her hand drifted higher.

Kurtz felt his face turn red.

At that moment, the waiter chose to arrive with their appetizers. Kurtz gave him a disappointed look, which the waiter seemed not to notice.

"What is he like?" Carrie asked.

"Who?" Kurtz said.

"Barent?"

"Yes."

"Detective Barent," Lenore said, "has a nasty habit of dragging Richard into awkward situations. Aside from that, he's a very nice man."

"Lenore is referring to the fact that two mafia hit men recently waved a gun in my face and told me to stop asking questions." Kurtz sighed, picked up his fork and began to eat. "Barent is planning on paying Rico and Simms a little visit," he said. "Hopefully, after that, they'll have bigger things to worry about than me."

Barent was one of the few New York City cops who still preferred the old style .38 to the new nine-millimeters. At the moment, the barrel of his .38 was pointing at Alphonse Simonetti, a.k.a. Simms.

Simms was visibly sweating. "What's going on here?" he whined. "What do you think you're doing?"

"I'm delivering a little warning."

Barent smiled widely. This was just like the old days. Police work rarely offered such simple satisfactions anymore, not since Miranda, Escobedo. … Slowly, he put the tip of the barrel against Simms' head, right between the eyes. He cocked the trigger. Simms gulped and tiny droplets of sweat broke out on his forehead. "Richard Kurtz," Barent said, "is my friend. You understand what I'm telling you here?"

Simms gave a tiny nod of his head. Barent ignored the gesture and went right on speaking. "Anything happens to Richard Kurtz, you're not going to live long enough to enjoy your pay. I don't care who does it. I don't care if he stubs his toe on a piece of dog turd, falls down and skins his knee. *Anything* happens to Richard Kurtz, I'm going to be coming after you. *And* Mr. James G. Romano. Understand?"

Simms gave another tiny nod. Barent smiled. "Excellent," he said. He pulled the gun back about an inch. Simm's eyes never left its tip. "So tell me," Barent said, "how is Mr. Vincent DeNegri doing these days? Is his health okay?"

Barent could see Simms jaws tighten. "And how about Mr. Carlos Esquivel? Is he feeling good? I gotta tell you, I'm concerned about Mr. Esquivel, I really am. I hear things. You know what I'm saying? I hear Mr. Esquivel isn't too happy with the terms of his arrangement. After all, the Colombians are taking the majority of the risks. Why shouldn't they take the majority of the dough? At least, that's the way Carlos Esquivel is supposed to see it."

Barent uncocked the .38 and smiled at Harry Moran, who was leaning against the wall of Alphonse Simonetti's apartment, looking bored and pretending to file his nails. "I hear a little accident is being planned for a shipment due in next week. I hear that maybe it's going to disappear." Barent chuckled. Oh, he was enjoying this. He really was.

"You understand?" he said to Simms.

Simms looked at him, his face very pale. "I understand."

"Good," Barent said. He put the gun back in his holster, smiled once more and went out the door. Harry Moran followed him. Neither of them looked back. Once they were in the car, Moran said, "What shipment due in next week?"

Barent made a clucking sound with his tongue, a sound meant to convey gentle reproach. "You know how much heroin goes through New York City every single day? There's got to be a shipment due in next week. Shit, there's probably a dozen shipments due in next week."

Moran lit up a cigarette. Finally, he nodded. "They'll figure you were bluffing."

"Maybe they will," Barent said. "And maybe they won't."

Putting a police guard back outside the room would have been a bit too obvious. Barent sent a request down through the ranks. He needed somebody who had some experience with hospital work, somebody who could hang out on the floor and be inconspicuous. Within a day, he had five names. He chose Louisa Kelly, a stout, middle-aged policewoman with a round, motherly face and dyed red hair.

Mrs. Kelly had worked summers as a file clerk at Bellevue, back when she was putting herself through college. She didn't need to fake it, and so a long unfilled request for additional secretarial support was unexpectedly granted. Mrs. Kelly arrived on Monday morning and immediately set to work collating patient records. The work had been piling up for weeks and would take at least a few days to finish, which suited Mrs. Kelly just fine.

On Tuesday afternoon, a well-built young man with dark skin walked onto the floor and into Hector Segura's room. Mrs. Kelly, working at the nursing station, took his picture with a miniature camera and made an entry in her notebook. The young man stayed for about fifteen minutes and then left. Two hours later, an attractive woman with a streak of gray in her hair appeared with a young boy

179

in tow. The boy appeared to be about ten years old. He was wearing a white shirt with a tie and had a rebellious expression on his face. They stayed for nearly an hour.

The next day, an elderly man, small, thin, with a bald head and dark eyes, wearing an expensive looking charcoal suit, walked into Segura's room and left after approximately thirty minutes.

Nobody on the floor paid these visitors the slightest attention. Mrs. Kelly did not find this strange. The visitors obviously knew where they were going. In her experience, nobody who was well dressed and carried themselves with assurance was ever questioned as to their whereabouts.

The next day, the same elderly man returned and again stayed for approximately thirty minutes.

The day after that, Mr. Segura was scheduled for surgery. He went down to the OR at the appointed time and re-appeared about three hours later. A half hour before his return to the floor, the good-looking lady with the streak of gray came into his room, this time with a little girl in tow. The girl wore a yellow dress and a bow on top of her head. She carried a doll, a coloring book and a box of crayons. They were still there when Segura returned. They stayed for an additional hour and then left.

On Friday afternoon, Mrs. Kelly took a bus downtown to the Precinct House and met with Barent.

"Ricardo Sanchez and Jaime Escobar," Barent said with a smile.

"Are these names I should recognize?" Mrs. Kelly asked.

"They're the guys you took pictures of. Sanchez is the young one. He's been linked to at least a dozen murders, both here and in South America. Escobar is Segura's right hand man."

"How about the woman and the children? His wife and kids?"

"Yeah."

Mrs. Kelly smiled. "It's nice to know he's a family man."

"Oh, he's all heart, you can bet on that."

"So what do I do now?"

"Continue doing what you're doing."

"What's the point? We already know he's maintained his contacts."

"After Segura was shot, his organization broke up and supposedly dissolved. Esquivel got the largest chunk of it. Segura still has his money and obviously he's maintained some contacts but he shouldn't have much left to work with. What I'm concerned about is the possibility that he's involved with somebody else's organization. Like Vincent DeNegri's." Mrs. Kelly pursed her lips and looked more than ever like a kindly Irish grandmother (which she was).

"I see," she said. "And how long do you want me to stay there."

"I'm not sure." Barent shrugged. "I planted a little seed. Let's see what happens."

Another of the unpleasant things that Esther Brinkman occasionally reminded Kurtz of was a predatory bird, an owl maybe. She had the same round cheeks and bright, unwinking gaze. Instead of claws, she used words. "More fruit salad?" she asked.

"Please," Kurtz said.

She passed Kurtz the bowl and he helped himself. Lenore's mother was quite a good cook. The chicken had been excellent. She had a lot of redeeming qualities, he told himself; offhand, however, this was the only one he could think of.

"So tell me," she asked, drawing herself upright in her chair, "why didn't you decide to specialize?"

"Excuse me?" Kurtz said.

"My friend Libby Siegel's husband is a vascular surgeon. She tells me that a surgeon has to specialize to get anywhere today. She says that general surgeons are a dime a dozen."

"She does?"

Mrs. Brinkman nodded firmly.

"Oh," Kurtz said.

Kurtz looked at Lenore, who smiled at him serenely.

"She says that people only go to surgeons who are experts on their particular type of problem, like head and neck, or colon and rectal. Nobody wants a jack-of-all-trades."

"I like to do a little bit of everything," Kurtz said.

Esther Brinkman sniffed.

"Some wine?" Lenore's father asked. Stanley Brinkman was a fat man with a bald head and a round, sad face. Since this was the first night of Chanukah, he wore a yarmulke. The yarmulke was too small and at the moment had slid to the side of his head, where it perched like a precarious beret.

"Thank you," Kurtz said, and held out his glass. Kurtz also was wearing a yarmulke, which he knew was the custom but which made him feel stupid. The wine was Baron Herzog, kosher but pretty good.

Esther Brinkman looked at her husband imperiously and sat back in her seat with a tiny frown. "So I imagine being a surgeon you know something about colitis?" she said.

"Colitis? Ulcerative colitis?"

She nodded. "I've suffered from the colitis ever since Lenore was born. She never told you?"

Kurtz glanced at Lenore, who rolled her eyes and gave a tiny shrug. "No, she didn't."

"They told me to try this stuff, *sulfa* something. It didn't help a bit. Sometimes it's all I can do to keep going through the pain."

Lenore gave a barely audible sigh and continued to eat her fruit cup.

"Azulfidine?" Kurtz said.

"That's it."

"Azulfidine sometimes helps. Have they tried steroids?"

"They've tried everything. Nothing works."

"That's too bad. Nobody knows what causes ulcerative colitis but there's an obvious genetic component. It tends to run in families."

Esther Brinkman nodded wisely. "My mother had it."

"Aside from azulfidine and steroids, there's not too much that can help."

Esther Brinkman sniffed again. Kurtz resisted the urge to ask her if she had a cold. "For this sort of advice," Esther Brinkman said, "they charge an arm and a leg, I can tell you that. I think the way you doctors make money off of helpless patients is a scandal. A car mechanic only charges if he fixes the problem."

Kurtz said, "We're not car mechanics."

The metronomic regularity of Lenore's spoon halted for an instant, then resumed. Kurtz smiled at Esther Brinkman. Lenore's mother looked at him with lowered brows. "That doesn't make me feel much better," she said. "I'll remember it the next time I'm writhing in agony."

Writhing in agony. The last time Kurtz had run across this particular expression had been in a Victorian novel. The heroine had been dying of cancer. "Tell me, these times that you're writhing in agony, do you ever have fever?"

Esther looked momentarily uncertain. "No, I don't think so."

"How about weight loss?"

She shook her head.

"They must have done some blood tests. How about your white count; was it elevated?"

Lenore made a face at a piece of cantaloupe, seemed about to say something, then thought better of it. She put the cantaloupe in her mouth and proceeded to chew.

"If it was, they never told me."

"If you really had ulcerative colitis," Kurtz said, "you would have had an elevated white count. If it was a bad case, you would have fever and weight loss. You probably don't have ulcerative colitis. You probably have irritable bowel. Irritable bowel comes from stress. Maybe if you calmed down a little, you wouldn't have a problem."

Irritable bowel was an annoying but not serious medical condition. One of Kurtz' professors had once joked that it was 'a simple pain in the ass.'

Esther Brinkman ought to know.

Esther's face turned red. Stanley Brinkman looked back and forth between Kurtz and his wife, his mouth hanging open. Lenore had finished her fruit cup. She gave a tiny sigh and sat there, tapping her spoon on her plate.

"Furthermore," Kurtz added, "you're not my patient and it's not my job to make you feel better. Believe me, I wouldn't do it for free."

Lenore cleared her throat. "Is there any more fruit salad?" she asked.

Her mother ignored her. "You ..." she pointed a trembling finger at Kurtz.

"Yeah?" Kurtz said.

"Oh, well," Lenore muttered.

"How dare you speak to me like that!?"

Pretty lame comeback, Kurtz thought. He doubted that the worm turned very often. Esther Brinkman wasn't used to it. He smiled. "We surgeons like to lay it on the line, so there aren't any misunderstandings later. You know what I mean?"

Esther continued to glare at him, then, almost miraculously, the corner of her mouth twitched. She coughed, and patted her lips with a napkin. What might have been the tiniest hint of a smile seemed to cross her face. Without looking, she picked up the bowl of fruit salad and passed it to Lenore, who calmly took it and refilled her cup. Stanley Brinkman continued to stare, first at Kurtz, then at his wife.

Kurtz was the first to break the silence. "That's very good fruit salad," he said.

Esther Brinkman's face was by now a neutral mask. She looked at Kurtz for a moment before answering. "I hope you like cheesecake," she said.

"Cheesecake?" Kurtz nodded his head warily. "I love cheesecake."

"By the way," Lenore said brightly, "have I mentioned that Richard and I are getting married?"

Chapter 28

The rest of the dinner went peacefully enough, though Lenore's mother did seem a bit stiff. When the meal had finally ended, Stanley Brinkman helped his wife clear the table. The silence when they left the room was palpable. Lenore was the first to break it. "You didn't have to say that," she said.

"You're right," Kurtz replied.

"Well?"

"Well, what?"

"Are you going to apologize?"

"Nope," Kurtz said. Lenore had broken up with her former fiancé, Harrison Thomas, at least partly because of the way Harrison had reacted to her mother. Harrison, according to Lenore, had been 'ashamed' of her. Lenore had told Kurtz later that she could have stood it if Harrison had merely disliked her mother, or even despised her mother, but he wasn't allowed to be ashamed of her mother. Well, Kurtz wasn't ashamed of Esther Brinkman but he had no intention of letting her push him around. He just hoped that Lenore would understand that.

Lenore gave a small smile. "Good."

Kurtz sat back and drew a silent sigh of relief.

The rest of the visit passed uneventfully. Esther Brinkman said almost nothing. Stanley Brinkman looked as if he were waiting for the cataclysm, glancing with apprehensive eyes back and forth between Kurtz' face and his wife's. Kurtz said as little as possible. Only Lenore seemed serene. After another half-hour or so, Lenore rose to her feet. "Well, it was nice," she said. "But we'll have to be going."

Her mother merely grunted. Stanley stood up. "Let me get your coats."

Kurtz shook hands with Stanley and smiled vaguely at Esther, who barely nodded her head. Lenore kissed them both.

Outside in the elevator, Lenore leaned her head against Kurtz' shoulder and snuggled up to his side. "I think she's beginning to like you."

"Really? How could I be so lucky?"

"Don't be sarcastic. The evening went about as well as could be expected."

"That well?"

Lenore chuckled. "Poor Mother." She shook her head regretfully. "She's getting old and she feels useless. She's a smart woman but she's got absolutely nothing to think about except her family. And her family doesn't need her, not the way they used to."

"She ought to get a job."

"At what? She has no skills."

"That's too bad, but I'm not going to let her use me for a punching bag."

"No. I wouldn't want you to." Lenore grinned. "You upset her preconceptions. People like my mother only get away with it because other people let them." She chuckled. "I think after tonight she'll be different."

"I hope so," Kurtz said morosely. "The prospect of beating up on your mother for the next fifty years is not one I'm looking forward to."

Lenore shrugged. "She'll either change or she won't. It's up to her. If she doesn't, then you might as well amuse yourself."

On a Monday evening, two weeks after Thanksgiving, Carlos Esquivel sat at a table in a restaurant called *Meson Castillo*. *Meson Castillo* specialized in South American cuisine, things like charbroiled Argentine steaks marinated in garlic and rack of lamb with mole and black bean salsa.

Carlos Esquivel was thinking that he disliked stereotypes. He resented the fact that everyone he met automatically assumed that he was involved in the drug trade, just because he was Colombian. Why didn't they assume he imported coffee? Wasn't Colombian coffee famous the world over? Whatever happened to Juan Valdez and his stupid mule? Or emeralds? The fact that Colombia produced the finest emeralds in the world didn't register with people. People thought Colombia, they thought cocaine. It was a reflex. The fact that he was involved in the drug trade didn't matter. People shouldn't assume things. Unlike a lot of his friends and competitors in the trade (as he liked to think of it), Carlos Esquivel was naturally a peaceful man with a placid disposition, more than willing to let

186

bygones by bygones. That didn't mean he was going to let anybody push him around or treat him with disrespect. Not at all. But he didn't believe in murdering people who looked at him cross-eyed or in killing the wives and children of those who had betrayed him. Killing the offending party himself was quite enough. Carlos Esquivel believed in an eye for an eye and anything more than that was crude and excessive.

Vincent DeNegri was a large man with a hooked nose and thick black hair. DeNegri had a smile on his face and sleepy looking eyes. As always, the look on DeNegri's face annoyed Carlos Esquivel but Esquivel knew the man well enough to know that DeNegri–despite the look–missed very little that went on around him.

"Almodovar is pressing me," Carlos Esquivel said. "There have been three incidents in the past month between his people and mine. I don't want a war. Wars are bad for business."

"Do tell," murmured DeNegri.

"He's undercutting my price."

DeNegri shrugged. "He can charge his customers anything he likes. So can you. If he's eating into your market share, you'll just have to take less profit."

"I would be in a better competitive position if my overhead weren't so high. You're charging me five times what the stuff costs you."

DeNegri yawned.

"Your profit is exorbitant," Esquivel complained. "I'm the one taking all the risks here."

DeNegri puffed up his cheeks thoughtfully and allowed his eyes to wander about the room.

"Are you listening to me?" Carlos Esquivel demanded.

DeNegri looked at him. "You're full of shit. I have to get the stuff into the country. My risks are at least as high as yours. You don't like it, try to get the stuff from somebody else. You'll find my prices are the best you're going to get."

No, Carlos Esquivel did not like Vincent DeNegri. He did not like him the least little bit. It was a pity that Esquivel needed DeNegri, or needed the organization that he represented, which was pretty much the same thing. Fleetingly, he wondered what the repercussions might be if DeNegri should simply disappear one night. Was it worth it to him?

Reluctantly, he decided that it probably wasn't, at least not yet.

"I would like to take delivery two nights from tonight," Esquivel said. "Will that be acceptable to you?"

DeNegri smiled fleetingly. Esquivel thought of the look on a shark's face and almost shuddered. "Certainly," Vincent DeNegri said.

"Hold it, buddy," the little man said. He carried a long curved knife. The knife looked sharp. The little man had stringy black hair that looked like it hadn't been washed in the last ten years, a weathered, reddish face covered with old acne scars, and he wore a blue parka.

Jesus, Kurtz thought, why do I live in this city?

"Richard?" Lenore said uncertainly. The little man's knife swung in Lenore's direction and then swung back to point at Kurtz.

They were right outside the lobby of Kurtz' building. It was late at night but Kurtz lived in a busy neighborhood. The street was hardly empty. The passersby could not help but see what was going on. Most of them sped up as soon as they noticed. One or two momentarily slowed down and looked like they might have been thinking about interfering. None actually stopped.

So where was a policeman when you needed one?

Community policing was reserved for "communities," which meant by definition poor and crime-ridden communities. This was an upscale neighborhood, which meant that any cop who happened by would be riding in a car, not walking the beat, which meant more specifically that the chances of one wandering by right at this moment were laughably slim.

"Don't tell me," Kurtz said. "You want my money, right?"

The little man nodded and looked for a moment uncertain. "Right. Just hand it over and there'll be no trouble."

"Lenore," Kurtz said. "Would you please step over to the side?" The knife moved back and forth again between Kurtz and Lenore.

"Just stay right there, lady."

"Move over to the side, Lenore." Kurtz' voice was flat.

Lenore sighed and shook her head as if she knew she was going to regret this. She took two steps to the side. Kurtz took one step forward. The little man took one step back. "Hey," he said. "I'm warning you."

"Warn me again," Kurtz said. In a way, he was enjoying this. Somewhere deep in his psyche, that fact worried him. It must have been Lenore's mother. She must have annoyed him more than he had thought.

"I'm telling you, I'll use this. I swear I will!" The little man's voice was desperate. He took another step back. Kurtz took another step forward.

Should he let the little cretin go?

He smiled and shook his head. The little man must not have been used to his victims smiling. He moaned. For an instant it looked to Kurtz like he might turn and run, in which case Kurtz fully intended to tackle him from behind. Then the little man obviously changed his mind. He swallowed, pointed the knife at Kurtz' chest and charged.

Kurtz pivoted as he came in, trapped the knife and the arm holding it against his side and raised his knee. Kurtz felt a crunch as the little man's elbow shattered. He screamed. The knife fell out of his fist and tumbled away. Kurtz kicked the little man's legs out from under him and he fell to the ground heavily, where he lay curled into a ball, clutching his elbow and sobbing.

For a moment, Kurtz actually felt sorry for him. "Lenore," he said. "Would you please go inside and call the police?"

Lenore puffed up her cheeks and looked at Kurtz as if trying to decide how she was supposed to feel about what she was seeing. Finally, she shrugged and smiled with one side of her mouth. "You bet," she said.

Blue parka. Barent had been right, Kurtz thought. Just another asshole down on his luck looking for a cheap score. Too bad, in a way. But then, Rico and Simms would not have been this easy.

"That elbow is going to need surgery," Kurtz said. "I hope you have some insurance." *Fat chance*, Kurtz thought.

Chapter 29

"No luck, huh?" Ted Weiss asked.

"Not yet," Barent said.

Weiss squinted down at the piece of paper in front of him on the desk and grunted, his mind apparently somewhere else. "Well, I'm not surprised."

Barent gave him a hurt look. Weiss was supposed to be surprised. Finding criminals was supposed to be something you could depend on. This, of course, was the ideal. Barent knew as well as Weiss did that the odds on solving the Mahoney case were getting slimmer by the minute. Still, the guy could at least pretend. "The case isn't over yet. We still have leads."

"You've got nothing," Weiss said. He had folded the sheet of paper into an airplane, which he picked up between the thumb and forefinger of his right hand and threw across the room, where it landed in Barent's lap. "For one thing, you've got no connection that you'll ever be able to prove between the Mahoney kid and either Segura or the mob. You've got one unreliable witness who saw two guys drive away from the murder scene but he wasn't close enough to get a good look and he couldn't identify them if they spat in his face."

Barent picked up the plane, briefly considered throwing it back, instead dropped it in the wastebasket. "We know that Esquivel and DeNegri are working together. We know that Segura is still in business."

Weiss shrugged. "When you find the connection, call me."

It was sad, in a way. A generation ago there would have been more pressure. Pressure from the public, pressure from the press, pressure from City Hall. Prominent scientist gruesomely murdered and savagely mutilated. There would have been a public outcry and demands for immediate (if futile) action. Now?

It was a nine-day wonder (and nine was pushing it), swiftly shoved into the back pages by more immediate events. Almost a thousand murders a year in New York City, most of them forever unsolved, were too much of a burden for the public psyche to bear. It was not that they didn't care; it was more like the collective soul of the City had gone numb.

"Like I said, we still have leads."

Weiss shrugged. "How about the reward offer? Anything?"

"Hard to tell," Barent said. "We've had phone calls."

"You always have phone calls."

Barent shrugged. "We're looking into them."

Weiss smiled thinly. "You will let me know if you come up with anything?"

"No," Barent said. "I've decided to prosecute the case by myself. That way, we might get a conviction instead of a plea bargain."

"Ouch," Weiss said amiably.

The calls, in fact, had long since dwindled to a trickle. They still got one or two a day, every one of which Moran and Figueroa dutifully followed up on, but none of them so far had turned out to be useful.

At two o'clock in the afternoon, however, the phone on Figueroa's desk rang. The voice was hesitant, a woman's voice. "Is this Officer Figueroa?"

"Yes," Figueroa answered. "How can I help you?"

"I saw a story in the paper the other day. About the man who was murdered?"

Which man who was murdered? There were only about a dozen unsolved homicides on Figueroa's desk at this particular instant. "Yes?" he prompted.

"I don't read the papers much," the voice said apologetically. "I drive a cab. I'm too busy."

"I understand. What's your name, Miss?"

"Nancy Lester."

"Go on, Miss Lester."

"Anyway, I saw this story. About the reward?"

Ah, *that* murder … "Of course," Figueroa said.

"I saw the picture of the murdered man. I'm sure it was him. Mahoney?"

Figueroa made an encouraging noise.

"I picked him up on the day he was murdered."

"Really?" This was interesting. So far as they knew, Rod Mahoney had gone nowhere on the day he was murdered except to work and then home. "Where was this?"

"Uptown, near 80th and Broadway."

191

That was not too far from Staunton. ... "How many fares do you pick up each day, Miss Lester?"

"On a good day? Maybe forty to fifty."

"How many of them do you remember, Miss Lester?"

"Not too many, that's for sure."

"Then why do you remember this one?"

"He was carrying a bouquet of flowers and he looked sad. I broke up with my boyfriend, not too long ago. I remember thinking that he looked just the way I felt."

"I see ... was there anything else about him that struck you?"

"No. Just that he looked sad."

"What was he wearing?"

"A jacket and tie, I think. I'm not too sure."

"And would you remember exactly where it was that you picked him up, Miss Lester?"

"Not really. Somewhere near 80th and Broadway, like I told you. He was standing near the curb. He waved me down."

"And where did you take him?"

"To Mulberry Street. In Little Italy."

"Any particular place? A shop? A restaurant?"

"No. He said to drop him on the corner."

"And what time of the day was this?"

"About twelve noon."

"Thank you, Miss Lester. We'll certainly look into it."

"Wait a minute. Am I gonna get a reward?"

"If the information that you've given us turns into anything useful, then you might. Why don't you give me your phone number and address?"

She did so. Figueroa dutifully wrote them down. "Thank you again, Miss Lester," he said. "We'll get back to you when we know more."

"Mrs. Mahoney?"

It was a lousy connection. Claire Mahoney's voice was scratchy and difficult to hear. "Yes?"

"This is Detective Barent."

"Oh, yes, Detective. What can I do for you?"

192

She sounded tired. It was nice that she was still being polite to him. It would have been easy for her to blame him for the troubles that her son was going through. Kevin was still keeping silent, his lawyer relying on a defense of illegal search and seizure. That, at least, was the public posture. In reality, a plea bargain would probably soon be struck. As Barent had suspected they would, the newspapers had loudly trumpeted the supposed connection between Rod Mahoney's death and his son's involvement with the world of organized crime. To date, however, no real evidence to support such a connection had surfaced and Barent sincerely hoped that it never would.

"Mrs. Mahoney, did your husband give you flowers very often?" Her voice seemed to hesitate. "No, I can't say that he did. Perhaps once or twice a year, on my birthday or our anniversary."

"Did he bring home flowers on the day he was killed, Mrs. Mahoney?"

"No. He didn't."

"You're certain?"

"Absolutely. What's this all about, Detective."

"Probably nothing, Mrs. Mahoney. Thank you for your time. I'll get back to you when I know more."

"Dr. Pang?"

Elvira Pang's office was barely large enough for an old mahogany desk and two rickety chairs. The desk was scarred with cigarette burns and cluttered with papers and manila folders. Against the wall stood a bookcase filled with textbooks and journal reprints and a gray metal filing cabinet with a lacquered human skull sitting on top of it. Elvira Pang looked tired. She glanced up, seemed for a moment uncertain, then her face cleared. "Detective Barret?"

"Barent."

She looked briefly embarrassed. "Yes, of course," she said. "Sorry about that."

"Don't mention it. I have a few questions you might be able to answer."

She glanced at the clock. It said 10:55 AM. "I only have a few minutes. I have a lecture to give."

"This won't take long. You told me that Rod Mahoney ate lunch every day at 12:00 noon."

"Yes." She nodded her head. "That's correct."

"When would he get back?"

"Exactly? I'm not sure. I never paid it too much attention."

"You told me that Professor Mahoney spent the afternoons either proctoring the anatomy lab sessions for the medical students or in his own, private lab."

"That's true."

"If he wasn't with the medical students, how did you know he was in his own lab?"

She shrugged. "Sometimes I heard him. His lab is down the hall from mine. I would pass by the door and hear sounds from inside."

"Other times?"

She squinted her eyes. "I don't know."

"So if you didn't see him or hear him, then you just assumed he was in his lab?"

"We would talk. Every once in a while, he would mention that he had been doing something in the lab."

"But not all the time?"

"No."

"So it's entirely possible that on some days when you thought he was in the lab, he might have been somewhere else?"

"Yes, if you put it that way. It is possible. I mean, it certainly wasn't my business to keep track of him."

Elvira Pang was a good-looking woman. She and Rod Mahoney had worked closely together for a number of years …

"He ate lunch at 12:00. Where did he eat lunch?"

Elvira Pang looked at the clock and frowned. "Could we talk on the way to the classroom?"

"Sure."

They walked down the hall, out the door and down the stairs to the street. Elvira Pang said nothing for a little while, evidently thinking about Barent's question. "Things have been difficult for us lately," she finally said. "First Rod, and then this thing with Howard … there's a lot more work for the rest of us."

"Howard?"

"Howard Clark. He was killed in a car crash over a week ago."

194

Howard Clark. Barent barely remembered him, a skinny post-doc with unruly brown hair and bad skin, one of Rod Mahoney's lab assistants. "Where did this happen?" Barent asked.

"On Long Island. Howard was visiting his parents for the weekend."

"I see ... well, I'm sorry to hear that."

Elvira Pang shrugged. "Anyway, to answer your question, Rod ate lunch anywhere he felt like. Sometimes the faculty club, sometimes, if he was in a hurry, the school cafeteria. Usually he would go out. There are only about a million restaurants in Manhattan."

"Did you ever go with him?"

"Now and then." She shrugged, her manner suddenly cool, as if suspecting where the conversation might be heading.

"We've received information that Professor Mahoney may have been spending time in the afternoons with a woman other than his wife."

That was stretching it, Barent thought, but why not go for broke? "Would you have any information about that possibility, Doctor Pang?"

They had reached a ten-story building with marble steps and an arched doorway. Students clutching books under their arms were streaming in and out. Elvira Pang turned toward him and smiled. "Do you mean were Rod and I shacking up somewhere during lunch hour?"

She seemed amused at the thought. Barent waited and said nothing. "No," Elvira Pang said, "we weren't."

"You were his friend, though. You worked together for years. Do you have any idea who he might have been seeing?"

"No," she said. "I don't. And frankly, I doubt that your information is correct. I just don't believe it. Rod was not the type."

Barent sighed. "Thank you, Doctor Pang. If you can think of anything else that might help us, please give me a call."

"Of course."

She said it in a perfunctory fashion, already dismissing the notion, turned on her heel and vanished inside the building. Barent watched her go, wondering.

"Howard Clark ..." He muttered it to himself.

"Mister Dixon?"

The motorcycle shop looked the same. The big Suzuki was gone from the back. A Harley with black leather seating and chrome trim had taken its place.

Dixon held out his hand. "How's it going?"

Dixon's hand was like a slab of concrete. "Not bad," Barent said. "How's the wife and kid?"

Dixon grinned. "Not bad. What's up?"

"You had told me that Rod Mahoney seemed pre-occupied lately. That something was on his mind. A number of other people have told us the same thing."

"Go on," Dixon said.

"We've received some information indicating that on the afternoon he was murdered, he might have met someone, probably a woman."

Dixon whistled between his teeth and looked thoughtful. "I don't know …" he said.

Barent waited.

"You think that Rod was having an affair?" Dixon had a doubtful look and a skeptical tone in his voice.

Barent said it again: "I think that he met someone, probably a woman."

"If Rod was having an affair …" Dixon shook his head. "I don't know," he repeated.

"He never said anything to lead you to believe he might have been involved with someone other than his wife?"

"No. Never."

"So far as you know, had Professor Mahoney ever been involved with anyone other than his wife?"

"You mean since he was married?"

In point of fact, Barent *did* mean since he was married, but now that Dixon mentioned it … "Ever," Barent said. "Since he was married, before he was married, ever."

"If he ever cheated on his wife, I wouldn't know it, but Rod was in love with a girl before he met Claire–when he was in graduate school."

"What happened?"

"I don't know, exactly." Dixon shrugged. "It didn't work out. Rod didn't like to talk about it."

"What was her name?"

"Mei-Ling," Dixon said. "Mei-Ling Yan."

There were probably a hundred stores and restaurants within a three-block radius of Mulberry Street. Moran and Figueroa spent the afternoon going into each one, showing a picture of Rod Mahoney and asking questions. It was a tedious and, at least initially, a futile job. They came up with nothing. At each restaurant or store, they would leave a picture and let people know that there was a reward involved.

People sometimes took vacation. They called in sick or they took the day off. It was possible that somebody who might have noticed Rod Mahoney, with or without a woman in tow, might come in to work later, or the next day, or the day after that.

Maybe. If they were lucky.

Chapter 30

"What was he like?" Kurtz asked.

"Howard Clark?"

"Who else are we talking about?"

Barent usually didn't drink on duty but he had gratefully accepted the shot of Bourbon that Kurtz had offered him. "What is this?" Barent asked.

"Blanton's Single Barrel. The best."

Barent gingerly sniffed, then sipped. "It tastes like Old Crow to me," he said doubtfully.

"You have no taste buds. You burned them out years ago from too many cigarettes and cigars."

"Is it expensive?"

"Fifty bucks a bottle."

Barent stared at the glass. "It's ridiculous to pay fifty bucks for a bottle of Bourbon."

Which might be true, but the price wasn't keeping Barent from drinking it. "Anyone ever tell you you're an old prude?"

"My wife. My kids …"

"I'm not surprised. So what was he like?"

"A loner," Barent said morosely. "His neighbors didn't know him. He kept to himself. Elvira Pang says he did a good job. His folks live in Roslyn, out on the Island. It was a hit and run in broad daylight. The witnesses say he was crossing the street and a red Corvette came around the corner, ran him down and kept on going."

"An accident," Kurtz said.

Barent shrugged. "Maybe."

"You sound skeptical."

"Could you do something for me?"

Kurtz sighed. "Here we go."

"You did say you wanted to help." Barent grinned faintly. "Now's your opportunity."

"What is it?"

"He was brought to North Shore. DOA, so not much was done for him. He was cremated two days later. I've asked the Nassau cops to look through the medical record but there's nothing in it. North

Shore is the biggest hospital on the Island. Do you know anybody there?"

At least two of the guys Kurtz had trained with were at North Shore. "Sure," he said.

"Could you give them a call? See if there was anything funny about the body?"

"Funny?"

"Ask if there were any needle marks."

"Why would you think there might be?"

"Because Howard Clark had a lot more money in his bank account than he should have."

"Maybe he was frugal."

"A post-doc in anatomy earns about forty thousand a year. The guy had over a quarter of a million sitting in six-month CD's."

"That's a lot," Kurtz said.

"Yeah."

Barent drained his glass in one gulp and then held it out for more. Kurtz winced but filled it.

"I'll call North Shore," Kurtz said. He smiled. "So tell me, whatever happened to the cadavers that were mutilated on Halloween?"

Barent stopped with his glass half-way to his mouth. "I don't know. Why?"

"Isn't it obvious?"

Kurtz grinned. Barent was usually quicker on the uptake than this. "Howard Clark would have had the keys to the safes, the ones where the cadavers are kept."

"So?"

"I think you should find out where they are and have the Medical Examiner take a look at them."

"You think …"

Kurtz held up a hand. "It doesn't look so much like a joke, anymore, does it? Howard Clark had too much money. Obviously, you suspect the source of the money was drugs …"

Barent put down his Bourbon and picked up the phone. "I'll get right on it," he said.

"Relax," Carlos Esquivel said.

199

Jose Torres shot him an annoyed look. It was Jose Torres' job to make certain that Carlos Esquivel arrived at his destination unharmed. It wasn't Torres' job to relax. It was his job to worry. This time, he had plenty of reason. "We're going onto their turf," he said. "I understand why we have to do it but I don't have to like it."

Carlos Esquivel shrugged. "A gesture of good faith."

"A gesture of stupidity. You can't trust these people. They're crazy."

"Who trusts them? I don't have to trust them. I have you." Carlos Esquivel favored him with a wide, placid smile.

"Thanks a lot," Jose Torres said sourly. "I really appreciate that."

The Mafia had existed as an organization for at least seven centuries and had tentacles in every country on the globe. Their own organization, the Colombians, they were newcomers. Carlos Esquivel was not intimidated by this fact but Jose Torres was. The Mafia had a long, long history of dealing with newcomers and the Mafia was still doing business.

"If they wanted to try something, they could do it anywhere," Carlos Esquivel said. "You have men on the streets?"

"Of course."

"These men are anonymous? Nobody can spot them as belonging to us?"

"Of course not."

Carlos Esquivel beamed.

"Well, then."

"I still don't like it."

"Relax," Carlos Esquivel said again.

The car–a big Lincoln–slid around a corner and smoothly accelerated. The driver was an Indian, a man whose grandparents had killed invading missionaries with curare-tipped darts, prior to shrinking their heads. He wore a chauffeur's cap that was much too small for him. The cap annoyed Jose Torres. It made the driver look like a clown, which could not reflect well upon his employers.

"Take off that hat," Jose Torres said.

The driver briefly turned and gave him an impassive look.

"Take off the hat," Torres said again.

The driver shrugged and placed the cap on the seat.

He drove well, though. He kept his eye on the road and his enormous hands moved the wheel with capable assurance.

The driver suddenly grunted. The car swayed, then lurched toward the shoulder before veering back onto the pavement.

Carlos Esquivel's breath hissed through his teeth. "What's happening?"

The driver muttered something in Spanish. Jose Torres leaned forward and the driver looked at him, his small black eyes glittering. "The car in the next lane, behind us, just tried to run us off the road." The car was a Cadillac sedan, maroon, tinted windows. As JoseTorres watched, the car accelerated suddenly, its windows rolled smoothly down and some tubular objects that looked just like the barrels of submachine guns poked out. "Shit!" Torres yelled.

The guns opened fire. The Lincoln swayed and rocked from side to side. Carlos Esquivel threw himself to the floor and huddled in a tight ball, moaning in Spanish. Jose Torres felt something strike his left shoulder with a dull thud and then, suddenly, an awful pain blossomed in his side and he screamed.

A tire blew with a bang. The car shuddered and the driver cursed, fighting the wheel. Where was their escort?

Behind them, that was where. And the big Caddy was next to them, calmly shooting bullets through the windows. They lurched off the road and spun to a stop. The Caddy made no move to follow. The gun barrels went back inside, the windows rolled back up and the car drove smoothly, almost sedately, off with the traffic.

Their escort roared up behind them and three men jumped out, ineffectually waving pistols in their fists. The leader, a thin man with a tiny black moustache and slicked back hair, named Ramon, came running up, cursing. He stopped when he saw Carlos Esquivel, still lying on the floor of the car, and Torres, the shoulder of his shirt soaked through and dripping red. "Are you alright?" Ramon asked.

An idiot, Torres thought, truly an idiot. Esquivel, seeing Ramon standing there and the shooting apparently over, groaned and sat back up. "He's fine," Torres said, and gave Esquivel a disgusted look. "Get me to the hospital."

Five hours later, Carlos Esquivel was sitting in the library of his house in Stamford, drinking slowly but steadily from a bottle of Cardinal Mendoza brandy and trying to think. Carlos Esquivel was in a daze. Jose Torres had come out of surgery and was now resting comfortably. The crisis, for the moment, was over. Esquivel's surroundings, familiar, secure, helped him to regain his bearings. Despite the violence that always seethed beneath the surface of his business, it had been years since Carlos Esquivel himself had come so close to violence. In his younger days, first as a mule and then as a soldier in the Miami drug wars, he had seen his share of the action, but that was a long, long time ago.

Once, it had been Carlos Esquivel's job to hold down the young wife of a rival courier while three of his fellow soldiers kicked the man to death. The woman had seemed strangely paralyzed under his hands, her flesh rigid. Her breath had come in ragged gasps while her husband screamed and then whimpered and then faded into silence. After the husband was dead, they had taken turns raping the wife. She had screamed a few times herself then, struggling violently. Carlos Esquivel still remembered how she had raked his face with her fingernails. He hadn't enjoyed the whole experience as much he thought he would. He felt a little bad about it, actually.

Another time, it had been Esquivel's job to do the beating. Their victim was only eighteen, a skinny kid who had pleaded frantically and then cried for his life. Carlos Esquivel shook his head sadly at the memory. The kid should have known better. You played the game, you took the penalty. Carlos Esquivel would never forget the way the bones of the kid's face had crunched under his fists.

Once, he himself had been shot during a raid on a rival's apartment, taking a bullet in the thigh that had laid him up for almost a month.

In all, he had been a participant in six shootings, one bombing and more acts of extortion than he could remember. But for many years now, Carlos Esquivel had been giving the orders, not carrying them out. He had forgotten what it was like to feel that sick thrill as bullets came whizzing by his ears and comrades on either side screamed suddenly, stared with disbelief at their own blood and then slumped to the ground like limp, empty sacks, the light fading from their eyes.

Had he grown soft?

Perhaps he had. Perhaps his pretensions to living a more civilized life had been perceived by his rivals as weakness, and perhaps his rivals were right. He didn't think so, though. The men who had tried to murder him tonight had failed and the penalty for failure was death. Carlos Esquivel was going to see to it.

Almodovar or DeNegri?

He thought Almodovar. DeNegri would have waited until he arrived at the rendezvous and taken the money before opening fire. Why not?

Yes, he thought, Almodovar. He stared into the bottle of brandy and thought dreamily of the many ways he was going to take his revenge on Joaquin Almodovar.

The bottle was almost empty. He pressed the button on the intercom. "Another bottle of brandy," he said. It had been a long time since dinner. His stomach felt raw.

"And bring me something to eat."

Five minutes later, the door opened and Luis, his butler, stepped into the room. Luis was a young man with a ready, gentle smile and liquid, brown eyes. He wore a white uniform and carried a silver tray with a covered platter and an unopened bottle of brandy.

Tiredly, Carlos Esquivel looked up at him. "Put it on the desk," he said.

Luis smiled and placed the tray where he was told. He removed the cover from the platter, reached down, picked up a long, thin dagger from the plate and plunged it into Carlos Esquivel's chest. Esquivel stared at the knife, then looked upward into Luis' sad, regretful eyes.

There was a rushing sound, a ringing in his ears. Luis' face seemed to balloon in and out and then blur. Carlos Esquivel tried to speak but his lips felt numb, his tongue heavy. The words faded. Somewhere, he could hear a radiator dimly rattling.

"Hector Segura sends his regards," Luis said.

Chapter 31

The killing of Carlos Esquivel may or may not have had anything to do with the murder of Rod Mahoney. Barent was for the moment withholding judgment on the question. The story in the papers was sketchy. The local police were obviously keeping things tight to their chests. Barent called them up and got the details. Apparently, the butler did it–and then vanished. Barent smiled faintly as he replaced the phone in the receiver. Thankfully, Esquivel's killing did not add to Barent's caseload. Stamford, Connecticut was far outside his jurisdiction.

For the moment, at least, Barent had enough to occupy his mind. Chinese immigrants, or so he had been told, usually changed their name to something more American. Mei-Ling Yan was a Chinese name. The woman who had once gone by that name could now be Trudy Goodheart, or Murphy Brown. INS would probably know. He had filed a request for the information the day before. It should arrive any time. He wondered briefly if Mei-Ling Yan had not turned into Elvira Pang. It seemed an unlikely possibility but in any case, he would soon know.

The cadavers were his immediate problem. It took Elvira Pang only a few minutes to track them down. "The bodies were left to the Medical School," she said. "They're in the basement. It seems that Rod had decided to save them until the end of the semester. We always need a lot of parts for the final exam."

Barent could think of nothing to say to this statement except, "Oh."

The police crime unit had taken them away to the ME's offices and it wouldn't be long until they had some answers, if there were any answers to be found.

Two hours later, Barent was sitting in his office, eating lunch with Harry Moran.

"So how's Denise?" Moran asked.

Barent took a bite out of his turkey and cheese sandwich before responding. "She's finally stopped throwing up. The doctor says the baby is doing fine."

Moran poured himself another cup of coffee, added two sugars and milk, then settled back in his chair and lit a cigarette. "I'm glad to hear it," he said, and blew a haze of smoke to the ceiling. "Maria thinks she's pregnant."

Barent's sandwich stopped halfway to his mouth. "That's great," he said.

Moran did look pleased with himself. "I hope it's a boy this time."

"Congratulations," Barent said.

At that moment, the phone rang. It was the Medical Examiner. "We found what you were looking for, Barent."

The ME's voice was grim. "Her name was Joyce Silverstein. According to the records the school sent over, she was a widow from Brooklyn, seventy-three years old with a history of angina. The presumptive cause of death was an acute MI."

The ME hesitated.

"Yeah?" Barent prompted.

"It wasn't an MI. She's got so much heroin in her blood she was almost pickled."

"Then I guess she died happy," Barent said.

Moran's ears pricked up.

"She was a mule, Barent. A courier. I found shreds of latex in her intestines."

The ME sounded bitter.

"She had swallowed condoms filled with heroin. At least one of them must have popped and it killed her. A little old lady from Brooklyn. Can you believe it?"

Barent could believe almost anything. So, he would have thought, could the ME. Apparently, the ME had a soft spot in his heart for little old ladies from Brooklyn, probably because his wife was one and his mother, now in a nursing home, was another.

"So she swallowed a bunch of condoms full of heroin. Where are the rest of them?"

"We've got four bodies here that were chopped to pieces, including the intestines. Whoever did it must have taken them then."

"Which is presumably why they were chopped to pieces in the first place."

"I suppose so," the ME said morosely.

"What's the world coming to?" Barent said. "When you can't trust a little old lady from Brooklyn?"

"You bet," the ME agreed.

Mrs. Schapiro peered around the edge of the door to Kurtz' private office. "I'll be going now, Doctor," she said, and sneezed. Kurtz, who was dictating the last of his charts, glanced up at the clock. It was almost five o'clock.

"I'll see you in the morning," he said. "And take care of that cold."

"Oh?" she said, and grinned wanly. "What would you suggest? Chicken soup?"

"It couldn't hurt."

She barely cracked a smile. Mrs. Schapiro was a great secretary: smart, efficient, self-possessed and almost always cheerful.

The cold must be really getting her down.

"Make sure you lock up when you leave," she said. "You bet," he said. "I'm almost done."

Five minutes later, Kurtz was putting the last of the charts into the file when the phone rang. He let it ring. The answering machine would get the message and he wanted to go home. The machine beeped and Mrs. Schapiro's voice said, "This is the offices of Easton Surgical Associates. (Kurtz' former partner, Edward Ornella, had picked the name *Easton Surgical Associates* years before. Kurtz was happy to keep it. It made them seem like a much larger and more important organization than two general surgeons.) Nobody is in the office at the moment. Please leave a message after the tone and we will get back to you as soon as possible."

Another voice said, "This is Lew Barent. Could you please ask Doctor Kurtz to give me a call? There have been some developments–"

Kurtz didn't hesitate. He grabbed the phone. "Lew? This is Richard. What's up?"

"Oh. Well, you were right about the cadavers. One of them, a widowed lady from Brooklyn, had been carrying heroin. Her name was Joyce Silverstein. She had a daughter and a couple of grandkids in Miami. She used to fly down to see them a few times a year."

"And I don't suppose Mr. Silverstein left her much of a pension."

"No. Mrs. Silverstein did not have a lot of disposable cash. It's hard for the elderly on fixed incomes to make ends meet these days."

"Airfare to Miami isn't cheap."

"Nope." Barent's voice sounded amused. "But there's more. Before he married Claire O'Brien, Rod Mahoney was engaged to a girl named Mei-Ling Yan. Her parents broke it up. Mahoney ever mention Mei- Ling Yan to you?"

"No," Kurtz said. "He didn't."

"Word from INS came in an hour ago. It seems that Mei-Ling Yan changed her name to Rose and married a guy named Jack Chang. They live in Westchester. How about Rose Chang?"

"Rose Chang?" Kurtz said. He cleared his throat. "Holy shit."

"What do you mean? You know her?"

"Yes, in a manner of speaking. I do."

The next morning, neither David Chao nor Mrs. Schapiro showed up at work. There was a message on the answering machine from Mrs. Schapiro. She had a fever and could barely get out of bed. She had called the secretarial pool and a replacement would be coming in at nine. Kurtz glanced at the clock. It was already 8:30.

There was nothing from David. This was disturbing. David usually came in before eight. He liked to catch up on his paperwork before the patients arrived.

An hour later, he had still not arrived. At ten o'oclock, Kurtz asked Mrs. Slater, Mrs. Schapiro's substitute, to call Chao's apartment. There was no answer. It was possible that Chao had gotten involved in an emergency case and was simply too busy to call in. Kurtz asked Mrs. Slater to contact the OR's at both Easton and the Medical School. Chao was not operating. Kurtz hesitated, then picked up the phone himself, called the ER at Staunton and asked for Carrie Owens. A few seconds later, she came on the line.

"Hello? Can I help you?"

"Carrie, this is Richard Kurtz. David hasn't shown up at the office this morning. Have you seen him?"

"Not since last night. Is something the matter?"

"Only that he hasn't shown up. He has office hours. The patients are getting restless."

This was not exactly true. Kurtz had instructed Mrs. Slater to call David's patients and re-schedule their appointments.

"Oh," Carrie said. "Well, I haven't seen him. Maybe you should call his parents."

"I'll do that."

"Let me know, will you? Now you've got me worried."

"Sure," Kurtz said.

Chao was not at his parents', and he had still not returned to his apartment. At least, nobody was answering the phone. Briefly, Kurtz considered calling Barent. He had a bad feeling about this, but what could he say? People dropped out of sight all the time, for all sorts of reasons, and then re-surfaced. You had to be missing for a lot longer than twelve hours before the police would bother to show an interest.

Kurtz worked through the morning, took a quick break for lunch and then returned to the office to see more patients. He did the job mechanically, finding two inguinal hernias and a probable gallbladder, scheduled colonoscopies for the hernias and liver functions for the gallbladder. David had still not shown up. Kurtz called his apartment twice more through the afternoon and Carrie called Kurtz once. Nothing. Then he called Barent.

"We'll get right on it," Barent said. His voice seemed to hesitate. "How well do you know David Chao?"

"Well enough to know that he wouldn't commit murder, if that's what you're asking."

Barent grunted. "We'll let you know if we find anything." He hung up.

At 3:30, Kurtz finished with his last patient, washed his hands, put on his coat and headed for the door. Outside, the wind blew in chill, icy gusts. Clouds scudded by overhead and it looked like it might snow. Kurtz had walked no more than a block when a voice from behind him said, "Keep walking straight ahead and don't look back. I've got a gun on you. If you try to run, I'll shoot you."

What was it with these guys. Kurtz sighed. "Again?" he muttered.

"What was that?" the voice said.

"Nothing."

"Turn left at the corner," the voice said. Kurtz did so. "Now," the voice said, "the middle of the street, you see the blue Mercedes?"

"Mercedes ..." Kurtz murmured.

"The back door is unlocked. Open it and get in."

It could be worse, Kurtz thought. The guy could have just shot him on sight.

Kurtz grasped the handle and twisted it open. A large, blonde, young man sat in the back. He looked familiar. He smiled at Kurtz. "Get in," the voice repeated from behind. Kurtz stepped in and sat down next to the blonde young man. The door closed. The blonde young man smiled wider and hit Kurtz on the head with an iron pipe.

Barent didn't know if the old stereotype about Oriental impassivity was true in general, but after five minutes, he was prepared to state that it applied in full to Rose Chang. She was a beautiful woman. She must have been close to fifty but she looked no more than thirty-five; her face was heart-shaped, smooth and unlined, her hair glossy and deep black.

She readily admitted having seen Rod Mahoney. She denied any knowledge regarding his death. She also denied any recent affair.

"I was young," Rose Chang said. "I was working as a receptionist at the offices of Northwind, in Chicago. Do you know Northwind?" She barely smiled.

Barent had heard of the company. "Nothing specific," he said.

Rose Chang shrugged. "It doesn't matter. My parents objected. He wasn't Chinese. I stopped seeing him. I never saw him again until this past August, when I noticed his picture in a Medical School faculty list that David brought home."

"David Chao? Kurtz' associate?"

"That is correct."

Barent grinned at Moran. Moran kept a look of distant interest on his face and otherwise sat quietly on his chair.

"And then what?" Barent asked.

"I called him," Rose Chang said.

"Why did you do that? You hadn't seen him in twenty-five years."

She shrugged. "I wanted to," she said simply.

She wanted to ... "What did you hope to achieve by that?"

She smiled then, very faintly. "Perhaps nothing," she said. "I had thought of Rod many times over the years. I was unhappy with the

209

way our relationship ended. I wanted to see him, to speak with him."
She shrugged. "To apologize."

Bullshit. Rose Chang was a married woman with a grown daughter of her own. You didn't just call up a guy you used to be intimate with and hadn't seen in a quarter of a century, not unless you were hoping for something more than a little chat. "What does your husband do, Mrs. Chang?"

"He is an executive. With Northwind."

"Do you have a good relationship with your husband, Mrs. Chang."

She grinned with one side of her face, a cynical grin. "I would not say so," she said. "No. My relationship with my husband is not everything that I might wish."

And she admitted it very readily. Most women at least pretended. Rose Chang quite obviously didn't give a damn.

"So you called up Rod Mahoney. Then what?"

"We had lunch together, a few times."

"Where?"

"Once in a place in Chinatown. A couple of times in Midtown. Once in Little Italy."

"And what did you talk about?"

She shrugged again. "Our lives. Our families."

"And what else?"

"Nothing else."

"How long did these lunches take, Mrs. Chang?"

"About an hour, each time."

"For an hour on four separate occasions you talked about your lives and your families."

"Twenty-five years is a long time. We had much to catch up on." Impassive, relaxed and serene. She smiled faintly while waiting for the next question.

"And after lunch, what then?"

"I returned home. Rod went back to work, or perhaps he also went home. I don't know."

All of this may have been true, but what is true today does not necessarily stay true tomorrow. The guy had given her flowers. He had been preoccupied. Everybody who knew him well had noticed it.

"And if Rod Mahoney had proposed an affair with you, what would you have said, Mrs. Chang?"

She answered instantly and without hesitation. "I would have said yes."

"I see ... did your husband know that you were having lunch with Rod Mahoney, Mrs. Chang?"

She wrinkled her nose as if smelling something distasteful. "No," she said.

"You're sure?"

She shrugged. "I said nothing. When I left the house, my husband was at work. How could he have found out?"

That was the question, wasn't it? "Is your husband at home, Mrs. Chang?"

"He is in the den," she said. She smiled and pointed at a door. "In there."

Moran looked as if he were enjoying himself. The expression on his face could have been a mirror, in fact, for the one on Rose Chang's. Both of them looked as if they knew the punch line to some secret joke.

Barent rose to his feet and pushed open the door. On the couch, watching a videotape of an old Western on TV, sat an Asian man with a slack face and red eyes. He held a glass full of an amber liquid in his hand. A bottle that said *Southern Comfort* sat on the table next to him.

"Mr. Chang?"

Jack Chang looked up blearily. He said nothing. Barent came into the room. Moran followed him and closed the door. Jack Chang continued to look at them without emotion, without surprise.

"Yes?" he finally said. A drunk. Rose Chang's attitude toward her husband suddenly became more clear.

"I'm Detective Barent. This is Detective Moran. We have some questions to ask you."

Jack Chang's eyes wandered back to the TV set. On the screen, a man who looked vaguely Mexican was about to shoot it out with Clint Eastwood.

"Mr. Chang?"

Jack Chang shook his head and squinted at the TV screen. "Do you know a man named Rod Mahoney, Mr. Chang?"

Chang smiled, very faintly. Loud, portentous music came from the TV screen. The Mexican squinted his eyes at Clint Eastwood. Clint squinted back. The Mexican went for his gun. Clint was faster. The music swelled to a crescendo as the Mexican grabbed at a spreading red stain on his chest and fell bonelessly to the ground.

Jack Chang staggered out of his seat, made a sound like a garbled scream and swung his fist at Barent's head.

Barent ducked. Chang's fist grazed his cheek and Barent fell backward over a chair. Jack Chang jumped on top of him, grabbed him around the neck and began to squeeze.

The guy's breath could have killed an ox but his grip wasn't strong enough to cause much damage. Barent hit him in the ears with the palms of both hands. Chang groaned and clapped his hands to his head.

The room was a mess. The chair Barent had fallen over lay in splinters. The bottle of Southern Comfort lay on its side and the liquid spread out over the floor. Barent was sitting in it, his pants soaking. Moran looked down at Barent with a look of amused disdain and chuckled.

The door opened. Rose Chang looked in and slowly smiled. Jack Chang began to cry.

Chapter 32

Somebody was moaning. It took him a little while to realize that it was him. When he did realize, he tried to stop but the moaning went on. Oh, well. He was lying on something hard; he realized that much, hard and damp. He tried to turn over. No luck. He opened his eyes. A single naked light bulb hung from a cobwebbed ceiling. He turned his head. David Chao was tied to a metal post. There was tape around his legs and his arms were handcuffed together. Kurtz' own legs were also tied together and chained to another post.

"Richard," Chao said, "can you hear me?"

"I hear you," Kurtz said. "Don't talk so loud."

"Son-of-a-bitch," David said, "I'm sorry."

"What about?"

"For getting you into this."

With his head throbbing the way it was, this statement was beyond Kurtz' ability to figure out. "Huh?" Kurtz said.

"I came in early. Mrs. Schapiro wasn't there. I thought she might have called in. I listened to the messages on the answering machine. I heard you and Detective Barent talking."

Right. Kurtz had neglected to wipe the tape after his conversation with Barent. Mrs. Schapiro's was the only message on the machine when Kurtz checked it in the morning. David must have wiped it before she called. "And then what?"

"Rod Mahoney had an affair with my Aunt Rose. I never knew that. Then I thought of something, something you had mentioned last week when we went out to dinner."

"Go on."

"You said the murderer was about six feet tall, two hundred pounds, drives a Mercedes, usually wears a hat, lives somewhere in the country and just got back from a trip down South, where he most likely played a little golf. I know someone who fits the description."

"Who?" Kurtz asked.

The door opened. Standing in the dim light from the single bulb was Christian Chang. He was carrying a gun in his right hand, a Glock.22, Kurtz noted. The hand was trembling.

He was wearing a blue parka.

"You fucking idiot," Chris Chang said.

Chang (or whoever) had done a good job of tying his arms and legs together. Kurtz could barely move. He thought there might have been just a bit of give in the tape around his legs but it would take him hours to work them loose, if he even could. Nevertheless, there was no point in not trying. He might be here for hours. If they had wanted to kill him, they presumably would have done so already. Slowly, quietly, he flexed his wrists and ankles. Flex, relax … flex, relax …

"Why do you say that?" Kurtz asked.

"Because you just won't keep out of things that don't concern you."

Since this was obviously true, Kurtz did not reply. He looked steadily at Chris Chang and kept on flexing his wrists and ankles.

"You stupid piece of shit," Chang said bitterly, "I couldn't care less about you. But David … He looked at David and swallowed. "I didn't want anything to happen to David, despite that little cunt he's fooling around with. I really didn't."

"I don't suppose you'd mind telling me what this is all about?" Kurtz said.

"No, since I'm going to kill you anyway." He glanced over to his cousin. "David too, I'm afraid. He knows too much."

So much for the idea that the bad guys would have already killed him if that was what they intended. Oh, well …

"Chris," David said. "This is insane. Don't do this. It's not too late."

"It is too late," Chang said.

"You were following me, a week or so ago, weren't you?" Kurtz asked.

"Yes. I could tell you spotted me. After that, I was more careful."

"I recognized the parka."

Chang shrugged. "It gets cold up here. You need warm clothes."

"Where are we?"

"About two hours north of New York, in the Berkshires. I have a vacation home."

"Don't tell me. You use it to store imported heroin, before distributing it to Vincent DeNegri."

Chang blinked at him. "I use it as a vacation home, to relax in, and I don't know anything about heroin. Who is Vincent DeNegri?"

"Nobody important," Kurtz said. "Forget I asked."

"No. What are you talking about?"

"The Chinese Triads are heavily involved in the heroin trade. There have been some incidents at the hospital with heroin abuse and a couple of guys recently warned me not to stick my nose into it. I assumed you were involved."

Chris Chang shook his head in wonderment. "You are totally nuts."

Considering where he was and what was going on, Kurtz couldn't argue. "So what is this all about?" he asked.

"It's about Rod Mahoney," Chris Chang said.

"Oh." He supposed that he should have guessed.

"I killed Rod Mahoney. David there had managed to figure it out." Chang nodded at David. "I was stupid. He had no evidence. Lots of people drive a Mercedes and play golf. It was all circumstantial, but he decided to surprise me. He brought me a hat, a nice black fedora. He said he found it in a dumpster. He said he thought it looked just like one of mine."

Chang smiled wanly. "He was right. It did look like one of mine. I didn't throw it out, though. I burned it. along with everything else I was wearing that day. Still, I looked into his eyes and I knew." Chang was looking at David right now, his eyes almost pleading. David was staring back as if Chang were a snake. "And I knew that he knew."

"So then what?" Kurtz asked.

"I admitted it. We talked about it. He told me about you and your cop friend. Then I hit him on the head."

"He caught me by surprise," David said.

"Yeah," Chang said. "I intended to."

"So why," Kurtz asked, "did you kill Rod Mahoney."

"Mahoney?" Chang smiled with one side of his face. "Because he was fucking my mother."

"Your mother," Kurtz said.

"My stepmother. Twenty-five years ago, my stepmother worked for Northwind, in Chicago. Mahoney was in graduate school at Loyola. I don't even know how they met but they had an affair. She got pregnant. They wanted to get married but my grandfather wouldn't allow it. It's okay to do business with the Lo-Fong but marrying them is out of the question. So she married my father instead. He was a junior executive for Northwind. My grandfather arranged it."

"Did your father know she was pregnant?"

"She wasn't by then. She had a miscarriage."

Chang looked at him scornfully. "My father is an alcoholic but he did his best for me. I wasn't her kid, you see, and she had lost the one she really wanted. She made my life hell, the fucking bitch. And she made my father's life hell, too. When he's not drunk, he sits around feeling sorry for himself. When he is drunk, he feels even sorrier. My stepmother plays on that. She likes the idea that he's a drunk and a weakling. For twenty-five years she's taken her mistakes out on my father."

It sounded like a sad story but at the moment, Kurtz' was not too interested. "So your mother and Rod Mahoney were involved twenty-five years ago. These things happen. What does that have to do with the present?"

"The information packet for staff privileges at Staunton contained a faculty list, with pictures. David left it lying around the house and my mother saw it. She recognized him, Roderick Allen Mahoney, the one that got away. She couldn't resist. She called him."

"Oh," Kurtz said.

"Oh," Chang repeated savagely. "For twenty-five years she never let a day go by without reminding my father of how he didn't measure up. My stepmother, you may have noticed, is gorgeous. She's also frigid, at least with my father. Oh, she did her marital duty but she made him beg for it. She hated him, the poor idiot. He had no idea at all what he was getting himself into when he married her. How could he?

"And then suddenly, there *he* was again, the knight in shining armor, Roderick Allen Mahoney."

He shrugged. "My father is a pretty good executive, when he's not drunk. My grandfather kept his part of the bargain. Dad has a comfortable income and a nice pension fund. My stepmother, on the other hand, doesn't have a penny. The old man figured he had done enough for her by breaking up an unsuitable marriage and then getting her a husband. Also, my grandmother was a concubine,

216

which made my stepmother not quite equal to the rest of his kids. David's mother got a very nice trust fund when the old man died. My mother got a fond farewell. I ask you," Chang finished bitterly, "is that fair?"

"So that's why you killed Rod Mahoney? Because you hate your stepmother?"

"No." Chang grinned. "I killed Rod Mahoney because my father loves her, the dumb fuck. My stepmother has spent twenty-five years making my father and me miserable. My father worked his tail off but he *cared*. He brought me presents. He took us places on the weekends." He looked down on Kurtz and smiled ferociously. "She was just as hard on Lily and me as she was on him. Nothing was ever good enough. Meanwhile, she didn't do much to justify her own existence except critique the rest of the world.

"But there's more than that. There's also the purely mercenary aspect. My father is bankrolling me. A messy divorce would put a nasty crimp in the budget. I can't have that. I need the family finances intact."

The tape, unfortunately, seemed no looser.

"So how did you find out about your mother and Rod Mahoney?"

"She began to go out a lot in the middle of the afternoon. I suspected something was up. She seemed different. She seemed … happy."

Chang shrugged. "I followed her."

"And how did you approach Mahoney?"

"That was easy. I told him the truth. I said I wanted to meet him. The stupid jerk let me into the house and I hit him over the head with a crowbar."

"I see. And why did you cut him into pieces?"

"That business about the cadavers was in all the papers. I figured it increased my chances of getting away with it if I made it look like there was a connection."

"Why Mahoney? If you hated her so much, why didn't you just kill your mother?"

Chang's eyes closed. He shivered as if in pain. "Despite everything, my father still loves her. That's the real tragedy. I couldn't do that to him."

"But you wanted to hurt her."

"Oh, yes." Chang smiled again and licked his lips with a tongue that seemed dry. "And I did hurt her, didn't I?"

David, who had been listening to all this wide-eyed, shook his head slowly.

A door opened. A blonde man, the same one who had been sitting in the back of the Mercedes, walked into the room. He was very tall, his musculature clearly defined through the thin white tee shirt. He smiled.

This time, Kurtz recognized him. "Oh, shit," Kurtz muttered.

"You know Tom Banner, I see," Chang said. Banner gave him a gentle, satisfied smile and bounced a little on the balls of his feet. "Tom was the lookout for me, at Mahoney's. Tom is very good at karate. You remember me telling you that he was turning pro? Tom didn't want to just kill you."

"No," Banner said. His voice was deep and gravelly. "I've heard of you. You used to be pretty good. I wanted to see just how good."

Chris Chang shook his head sorrowfully. He handed Banner the gun, took a small pocketknife out of his pocket, opened it and knelt down by Kurtz' feet. He kept to the side, well out of Banner's line of fire, and slit the tape around his ankles.

Banner handed the gun back to Chang. "Get up," Chang said. Slowly, Kurtz rose to his feet. The situation, to put it mildly, did not look good. Chris Chang had the gun. He also had Tom Banner, who even now was running a practiced eye over Kurtz' anatomy, no doubt searching for the weak points. Kurtz' head still hurt and his hands were tied behind his back.

"Tom," Chang said, "you go first."

He waved the gun toward the steps. "Upstairs," he said to Kurtz.

"Chris!" David yelled. "Don't do this!"

Chang seemed to hesitate, then shook his head slowly. He didn't look at David.

Banner shrugged his massive shoulders and went up the steps. Kurtz followed, with Chang behind.

He found himself in a neat, well-lit room. The floor was made of varnished pine board. The walls were paneled. A buck's head hung on one side of the fireplace and a mounted rainbow trout hung on the other. The fish must have gone a good ten pounds. An enormous window covered one whole wall of the room, looking down on a pine covered valley and, in the distance, a series of mountains.

Chang came up behind him. "Over there," he said. "Through that door."

Banner went first. Kurtz reluctantly followed. The door entered onto a dojo. The floor here was covered in cork. The walls were padded. There was a window on each wall.

"What's the point of all this?" Kurtz asked.

Banner smiled. "Chris has his own reasons for what he's done. My reasons are simple. I want to be the best. You can't be the best until you beat the best."

"Nobody ever said I was the best."

Banner shrugged. "Maybe not, but I like to fight. I figure, you tell a man his life depends on it, he's going to fight a lot harder. Most fights, they're just for show. I score a few points. You score a few points, nothing really riding on the outcome. This,"–Banner smiled wolfishly–"this is different. I like the idea. I like the idea a lot."

A lot of people in the martial arts saw themselves as modern-day Samurai, warriors in a time and a place that no longer had any use for their kind. It was one of the things that had made Kurtz stop fighting competitively. Too much accumulated macho. Banner, in particular, looked like a steroid freak, which was also common in the martial arts and which tended to induce rage bordering on psychosis as well as enlarged muscles. Banner had the look, his chest massive and sharply defined. He also had the telltale bad skin, pasty with a scattering of pimples. "I'll bet your balls are the size of raisins," Kurtz said.

Banner blinked and looked hurt.

Kurtz used to be pretty good, but that was five years ago. How good was he now? Kurtz honestly didn't know, and he hadn't planned on ever finding out. "Beating me still won't prove much."

"Doesn't matter," Banner said. "You're just an obstacle on the way to larger things. Besides, I need the exercise."

"Get it over with," Chris Chang said.

Banner looked at him. "Cut his arms loose."

Chang slit the tape on Kurtz' wrists. Kurtz flexed his arms at the elbows and clenched his fists. He suppressed an urge to giggle.

Well-known surgeon killed by renegade karate ring. How did he get himself into these situations?

Kurtz had not fought competitively in five years. Banner, most likely, did not take Kurtz seriously as an opponent, which was probably Kurtz' only advantage, though not much of one, Kurtz thought, since Banner's low opinion was most probably correct.

Banner moved forward, dropped and spun. Kurtz jumped back. Banner smiled, rose, reversed and spun again, this time the flat of his foot moving toward Kurtz' head. Kurtz barely had time to move away. Banner's foot whizzed by his nose.

Evidently, Banner liked that move. He tried it again. This time, as his leg went by, Kurtz helped it along with a straight punch to the back of Banner's knee. It didn't help him. Banner continued his spin and landed on the balls of his feet, perfectly balanced. He gave Kurtz a little grin, his eyes shining.

Kurtz jumped. The side of his foot connected with Banner's ribs and Banner grunted, then grabbed Kurtz' foot and twisted. Kurtz went with the throw, reversed himself in midair and landed inside Banner's guard. There was an old Ninja move where you came in with your shoulder against your opponent's chest. It could crack a man's sternum if you did it right. Kurtz lunged but Banner was already moving backward. Kurtz managed to get in a quick punch to the abdomen, which didn't do him any good at all since the guys stomach muscles were like stone. Banner stopped, just out of Kurtz' reach. This time, when he looked at him, his eyes held grudging respect.

Respect, but no fear, no doubt at all …

Bruce Lee used to say that the main difference between the winner and the loser was not the strength or even the speed, but the physical conditioning of the combatants. Banner's conditioning might have been purchased from a pharmacy, but he had it all the same.

"Very good," Banner said softly. He moved to his left, his arms circling around his head. Kurtz turned to face him, putting himself to the side of the window. Outside the window stood a small woodpile. Leaning against the woodpile was an axe.

Banner spun, jumped, kicked. Kurtz took two steps to the side. Banner's foot connected with his hip. Kurtz stumbled. His arms flailed. He took another two steps to the side and crashed through the window, shards of glass sprinkling around him.

"Get him!" Chang yelled.

Banner jumped after Kurtz. It was a dumb move–a really dumb move. Kurtz grabbed the axe, stepped in and swung. Banner's stomach muscles were hard but the axe was much harder. It sank in with a solid, satisfying *thunk*. Banner screamed and doubled up over the wound in his abdomen. He fell to the ground and kept on screaming, red blood leaking out from between his fingers, staining the ground.

Chris Chang was leaning out of the window, the gun pointing at Kurtz. "Don't move," he said. "Don't move a muscle."

He raised the gun, aimed it at Kurtz' head. "I'm sorry," he said. "I really am."

He had a split second, no more. Kurtz jumped, rolled. A shot rang out, then three more. Kurtz landed awkwardly behind the woodpile. He heard a slow, sliding thud, like a body falling to the ground, then nothing. Banner's screams had faded to a whimper. Cautiously, Kurtz peered around the side of a log. Chris Chang sprawled unmoving beneath the window, the gun lying on the ground beside his head.

"Don't look so bewildered," a voice said. The voice was amused. "We've come to rescue you."

Kurtz turned and looked up. "Rico," he said. "Simms. How you doing, guys?"

Chapter 33

Chris Chang was dead. Kurtz briefly examined Banner. He was unconscious, his pulse barely detectable. The wound in his abdomen continued to leak blood. There was nothing Kurtz could do for him, not without the facilities of an ER and an operating room, and he didn't bother trying.

"Stay here," Simms said. Kurtz didn't argue.

Rico and Simms went into the house, their guns at the ready. They soon returned with David Chao.

David looked at Banner and at the body of his cousin and shuddered. "Who are these guys?" he asked Kurtz.

Kurtz scratched his head. "Friends," he said.

Simms grinned. He had a can of gasoline in his hand. Smiling lazily and whistling between his teeth, he splashed gasoline on the wall of the house and lit a match.

"Why?" Kurtz asked.

Simms shrugged. "No reason." He touched the match to the gasoline and the flames roared up the side of the house.

Rico smiled. Simms chuckled, just two big kids playing with matches.

"Wait here," Rico said. He walked off down the driveway and came back a few minutes later, driving a Chevy Bronco. "Hop in," he said.

Within minutes, they were bouncing along the road. Behind them, billows of smoke rose into the blue sky.

Kurtz' head was throbbing. He lay back against the seat and closed his eyes. "There's a hospital down the road," Simms said. "We're going to leave you and your friend there. That alright with you?"

Since, until that moment, Kurtz had not been certain that Rico and Simms did not intend to kill him as well, he had no objection. "Yeah," he said. "That would be fine."

Simms reached into his pocket, pulled out a pack of cigarettes. He held the pack out to Kurtz questioningly. Kurtz shook his head. Simms shrugged, lit up and took a long drag, then let the smoke dribble out of his nose.

"Why?" Kurtz said.

Simms looked at him. "Why what?"

"You were following me, weren't you?"

Rico shrugged. Simms only smiled.

Barent and Moran arrived a few hours later. By that time, the little house in the woods had burned to the ground. A pool of blood was still evident where Banner's body had lain, but both he and Chris Chang were gone.

Kurtz had a minor concussion and two cracked ribs. He was transferred by ambulance to Staunton, where his ribs were taped. There was no necessity to keep him in the hospital. He was released and sent home.

Two days later, Kurtz paid a visit to Hector Segura. Segura was sitting up in bed, his hands folded in his lap, when Kurtz entered the room. Segura's one eye looked at Kurtz.

"How are you, Mr. Segura?"

"I am well, Doctor," Segura said.

Kurtz nodded as if Segura had said something deeply important. "I've been thinking," Kurtz said. He waited. Segura said nothing.

"My friend, the policeman, the one I told you about …?" Segura nodded.

"He thinks that you might have had something to do with the heroin that was being used in the hospital."

"Your friend is wrong," Segura said simply.

Kurtz went on as if Segura had not spoken. "It seems that what you had told me was not entirely correct, about the Colombians not being involved in the heroin trade. It seems that a man named Vincent DeNegri had until very recently been selling heroin to a Colombian named Carlos Esquivel. Do you know Carlos Esquivel, Mr. Segura?"

For the first time, Segura stirred. A sigh came from beneath the bandages. "Yes," he said. "I know Carlos Esquivel."

"Then you probably know that Carlos Esquivel has recently been killed."

Segura inclined his head. "I had heard that this was so."

"A few weeks ago," Kurtz went on, "some men who worked for Vincent DeNegri, accosted me outside of the hospital. It was a day or so after I asked you about the heroin trade. These men told me to stop asking questions. They threatened me. Yet these same two men recently saved my life. Did you know that, Mr. Segura?"

Segura's posture radiated attention, but he said nothing.

"There is only one explanation that makes sense to me. Can you guess what it is?"

Segura looked at him.

"You knew Carlos Esquivel. Carlos Esquivel knew Vincent DeNegri. Did you also know Vincent DeNegri, Mr. Segura?"

After a moment, Segura cleared his throat. "I might have," he said.

"You sent Rico and Simms, didn't you, Mr. Segura?"

Segura sighed again. His shoulders seemed to slump. Suddenly, he seemed a very old, very frail little man. "Have you ever heard of the legend of the phoenix, Doctor?" he asked.

"The phoenix is a magical bird who dies, is cremated and then rises from the ashes, every five hundred years."

"That is correct. The phoenix lives for a very long time, but even the phoenix grows old eventually. When the phoenix senses that death is not far away, it prepares for itself a funeral pyre. It prepares its pyre most carefully, of dry wood, and cinnamon, and herbs, and when it has done so, the phoenix places itself onto its pyre and lights it. And when the wood and the herbs and the phoenix have burned to ashes, the phoenix rises, young again, and flies away. The phoenix prepares its pyre most carefully and always in a secret place, for it is during its burning and re-emergence that the phoenix is most vulnerable, and can most easily be destroyed by an enemy."

Segura sighed. "This is my funeral pyre, Doctor, this place …" He raised a hand and gestured at the walls. "This is where I have come to be reborn. I must guard my funeral pyre, Doctor. I must make certain that it is a safe place, a secure place, a place where evil men and evil intentions cannot reach."

Kurtz leaned forward. "You told Vincent DeNegri not to allow heroin into the medical center," he said softly.

Segura only looked at him.

"Joyce Silverstein died after swallowing condoms filled with heroin. Her body was brought to the medical school. Carlos Esquivel arranged for a number of cadavers, including Joyce Silverstein, to be mutilated during a Halloween party. It was meant to seem like a joke. Howard Clark, a laboratory assistant, arranged it for him. Howard Clark was recently killed in a hit and run accident. Both of his arms and both of his legs had needle tracks.

"Did you kill Howard Clark, Mr. Segura?"

Segura said nothing.

"A man named Jerry Rubino worked for Vincent DeNegri. Jerry Rubino was selling heroin at the hospital. Jerry Rubino was shot in the head, gangland style. Was that your doing, Mr. Segura?"

Segura cleared his throat. "A hospital is supposed to be a safe place, Doctor. A place of healing, a place where evil men and evil intentions cannot reach."

"Does that include yourself, Mr. Segura?"

Segura stiffened. His one eye, only for a moment, glared at Kurtz. Finally, he said, "The phoenix is a very wise, very careful bird, Doctor. The phoenix guards his secrets. It is the only way that he can survive." He leaned back against the pillows and closed his eye.

Kurtz opened his mouth to say something, then hesitated. For a long moment, he stared at the man on the bed. Finally he said, "Goodbye, Mr. Segura."

Segura did not open his eye and did not answer. After a moment, Kurtz turned and left.

"So that's it, huh?" Barent sipped his Bourbon. "The rich get richer and the poor get fucked." He shook his head.

Kurtz said, "He didn't confirm much of anything, but it makes sense. DeNegri killed Clark and Rubino and probably Esquivel too, on Segura's orders, and there's not a thing we can do about it."

"No," Barent said, "there isn't."

He didn't look too concerned, however. "You don't care, do you?" Kurtz said.

"Not really. Like I told you, let the animals kill each other. Why should I care? Why should you? Segura was right about one thing; the world is a safer place without them."

"Yeah," Kurtz said. He too, sipped his Bourbon, and shook his head.

"This stuff is starting to grow on me," Barent said. He held his glass up to the light, peered through it and smiled.

"And you never found Chris Chang, or Banner."

"Nope."

"But the murder is solved, and that's the most important thing."

"It is to me," Barent said.

Kurtz looked out the window. In the distance, the sun hung on the horizon as evening turned to night, streaking the sky with orange and purple. Down below, on the Hudson, chunks of ice floated, drifting out to the sea. "Me too, I guess," he said.

Barent only smiled.

One month later, a box arrived by Federal Express. The box was about two feet-square and weighed about ten pounds. It was addressed to Richard Kurtz. Kurtz signed for it, then looked at Lenore. "Did you order anything?" he asked.

Lenore shook her head. "Not recently," she said.

Gingerly, Kurtz peeled away the wrapping. The box was made out of cardboard, with tape around the rim. Kurtz removed the tape and opened it. "Jesus," he said.

Nestled inside the box were two human skulls. Lenore looked in and gulped.

Kurtz took one of the skulls, the smaller, and raised it in front of his face. The skull had been cleaned and lacquered. It gleamed. It was a male skull, Kurtz noted. The teeth were sharp, the temperomandibular joint and the lacy filigree of bone inside the ethmoid sinuses firm and unsoftened by age and arthritis. The second skull was similar; both had belonged to young men, men with good teeth and good bones.

Kurtz sighed. "I'll bring them over to the school tomorrow," he said. "There's a place for them on the shelf. Elvira Pang can use them."

Hector Segura was released from the hospital soon after. He returned to his home in Queens and lived peacefully among his neighbors. It was a peaceful neighborhood, a neighborhood of shady trees and healthy children and clean buildings. No crime ever seemed to occur there. No drugs were dealt on its streets.

Shortly after Carlos Esquivel's death, a man named Joaquin Almodovar entered into a clandestine contract to distribute heroin, which a man named Vincent DeNegri agreed to supply.

It was rumored among those who knew of such things, that Hector Segura had given his blessing to the new arrangement, but nobody ever knew for sure.

Hector Segura died suddenly, two months later. The cause of death was listed as an unexpected myocardial infarction. Since the body was cremated, nobody was able to refute this theory.

Joaquin Almodovar and Vincent DeNegri sat together at the funeral.

—The End—

Information about the Kurtz and Barent Mystery Series

I hope you enjoyed *The Anatomy Lesson*.

The series continues with *Seizure*, in which surgeon Richard Kurtz and police detective Lew Barent delve into the mystery of a decades old conspiracy involving bootlegging, organized crime and murder in order to solve the present-day homicide of a young hospital administrator. Please read on for a preview of *Seizure*.

For updates regarding new releases, author appearances and general information about my books and stories, please sign up for my newsletter/email list at www.robertikatz.com/join and you will also receive a **free short story** entitled "Something in the Blood" featuring Richard Kurtz as a young surgical resident on an elective rotation in the Arkansas mountains, solving a medical mystery that spans two tragic generations.

Preview: Seizure

Chapter 1

It had been raining steadily for most of the day, turning into an intermittent gusting drizzle around sunset, but those inside the operating room were barely aware of it. The operating room, as always, was cool, dry and brightly lit, a perfect artificial environment.

"Give me a tie," Kurtz said.

The nurse handed him a strand of double-0 chromic and Kurtz wrapped it around the serosa at the base of the clamp, knotted it three times and cinched the knot down tight. Adler released the clamp and the two men stared at the wound for a second. No blood.

Kurtz was in a bad mood. He had woken up in the morning feeling groggy, having gone to a boring but obligatory hospital fund-raiser the night before. Now it was almost midnight and he had been operating on and off since eight in the morning. You had days like this, days when disaster followed disaster and you barely had time to think or even catch your breath before you were cutting into the next bleeding victim. Not many, thank God.

The first had been a kid hit by a car, a nameless John Doe, eleven years old and basically dead before they even got him on the table. They had barely begun to operate before the kid went into slow V-tach from lack of blood to the heart. Kurtz had opened him up and tied off the blood supply to his ruptured left kidney but there hadn't been much he could do about the shattered liver except pack the wound and close. It hadn't helped. The kid was dead.

The next one was a jumper. She had a long medical history, most of it centered around trauma inflicted by her abusive boyfriend. Amazing that she had never left him, Kurtz thought. This time she had jumped out of a fifth story window because her boyfriend had gone off to California for the weekend with another woman. Her name was Kimberley Morgan and she was young, pretty and twenty-four, a pretty young woman with her whole life ahead of her. Except that as it turned out, her whole life was behind her because she, too, never got off the table. What happened exactly was uncertain. She had two broken femurs and a ruptured spleen. After Kurtz finished with the spleen, the orthopods were supposed to come in and pin the legs. Unfortunately, while Kurtz and the residents were closing the abdomen, the patient's oxygen saturation fell to zero and she promptly arrested. Again, they ran a code and again, the patient died. Probably a fatty embolus. It wasn't uncommon with broken femurs.

Kurtz had never before lost two patients in a single day.

By now, Kurtz was working on auto-pilot, too tired to think straight but thankfully barely needing to. The latest operation—a sub-total gastrectomy for a bleeding stomach ulcer—was one he had performed a hundred times before and this patient wasn't even dying. Hooray.

Even Adler, the Chief Resident, usually irrepressible, seemed wilted. The only one who seemed to be enjoying himself was the intern, Rodriguez. Rodriguez had just returned from a week's vacation and was comparatively well-rested. Kurtz tied off another bleeder and Rodriguez clipped the ends of the chromic.

Adler sighed and Kurtz grinned tiredly beneath his mask.

Adler's beeper went off. They all stared at it. The beeper was sitting on a small shelf beneath the clock on the opposite side of the OR.

Wordlessly, the scrub nurse went over and pressed a button on the top of the beeper, then squinted down at the number displayed in the tiny screen. "It's the ER," she said.

Adler sighed again.

Not another one, Kurtz thought, and glanced at the clock. "Rodriguez and I can finish closing," he said. "Why don't you go and see what they want."

"Sure," Adler said, and began to take off his gloves.

From the main desk of the Emergency Room, Adler could clearly see the remnants of the storm outside. He could even hear it. Rain pelted against the thick glass doors and the wind made them vibrate. Sheets of old newspaper, empty plastic bags and other bits of garbage too small to make out flew by, briefly lit by the lights in the parking lot, and then vanished.

An ambulance stood backed up against the curb, a ramp leading down from the opened interior to the sidewalk. The ambulance was empty but the paramedics had evidently been in too much of a hurry to close the doors.

A lot of noise was coming from Room 1. Adler walked down the hall and peered in. A crowd of people dressed in scrubs milled about the table. From somewhere inside the crowd, a voice was counting, "One and two and three and four and five. One and two and three and four and five…"

Adler knew what that meant. Whoever was speaking was also pumping on somebody's chest. After each five, somebody else was breathing for the patient.

Adler went up to the head of the table. A respiratory therapist was squeezing an Ambu bag, the clear plastic mask covering the mouth and nose of a little old lady. The lady was obviously dead but since they were doing CPR, perhaps not irreversibly dead. An ER doc named Carrie Owens, small, blond and good looking, was running the code.

"What can I do for you?" Adler asked.

"We can't get a tube in," Carrie said. "She needs a trach."

The code had evidently been going on for quite some time. The patient's stomach was swollen with air. This always happened with mask ventilation. You could squeeze air into the lungs through the nose and mouth but some of it went into the stomach as well. The stomach blew up like a balloon and put pressure on the contents of the chest, making it harder and harder to ventilate. And sooner or later, the pressure got too high and the air surged back up the esophagus, usually bringing stomach contents with it, the main component of which (aside from whatever the patient might have eaten lately) was hydrochloric acid. At least a portion of this would always go down the trachea. If the patient didn't then drown outright, she would wind up with aspiration pneumonia and probably die a few days later as her lungs rotted away.

"Has Anesthesia tried?"

A tall young man dressed in green scrubs and wearing a blue bouffant OR cap said, "I tried. She's got a receding chin and bad arthritis. I can barely open her mouth."

"Okay," Adler said. "Let me get up there."

A permanent tracheostomy required an incision in the neck below the cricoid cartilage. Sometimes you had to peel back a portion of the thyroid gland, which was highly vascular and would bleed if you accidentally cut it. You then cut through the tracheal rings, inserted the trach tube and sutured it down; but with the patient bouncing up and down on the table from all the pumping on her chest and with the respiratory therapist's hands in the way, a formal trach, in Adler's opinion, was not the wisest choice.

A nurse had opened a trach set on a stand and brought it up by the patient's head. The patient was a skinny little thing. You could practically see the anatomy. A cricothyroidotomy was not as stable as a formal trach. The structures were more delicate; sooner or later the tube would erode through the larynx but if the patient lived they could always revise it later and in an emergency, a cricothyroidotomy was the quickest, easiest way to get a secure airway. Adler picked up a number fifteen scalpel and slit the cricothyroid membrane, inserted a pair of clamps between the cricoid and the thyroid cartilage, spread the incision, picked up a 6.0 trach tube from the tray and popped it in. Instead of suturing it, he picked up some umbilical tape (Adler had always wondered why they called it 'tape.' The stuff looked like a pair of shoelaces.), inserted it through the openings in the flange around the trach tube and tied it around the patient's neck. The respiratory therapist took the mask off the Ambu bag, connected the bag to the trach tube and continued to ventilate the patient. "Thanks," he said.

Adler absently nodded. The patient seemed to have an intermittent rhythm but was wandering in and out of v-fib. Probably secondary to an MI. That was how most heart attack victims died—an irreversible arrhythmia.

At that moment, the patient's body grew rigid and began to tremble, then shake. Her shoulders jerked back and forth, her neck arched and her fingers clenched into claws. Adler shook his head. "She's seizing," he said. Lack of oxygen to the brain often did that.

"Give me five of midazolam," Carrie Owens said. A nurse handed Carrie a syringe. Carrie inserted the needle into the IV line, injected the liquid and turned the flow up high. A few moments later, the patient gave a final shudder and grew limp.

The monitor screen still showed v-fib.

"Get back," Carrie Owens said loudly. The man who was pumping stopped and moved away from the metal table. The crowd hastily moved off a discreet two inches. Only the respiratory therapist stayed where he was, since the Ambu bag was made out of plastic and rubber and would not conduct. Carrie put two paddles on the patient's chest and pressed a button. There was a snapping sound and the patient bounced about six inches into the air.

For a moment, the ECG screen showed only a flat line. Then a lone heartbeat wandered through, then another. "Give her some more lidocaine," Carrie said. "A hundred milligrams. And a milligram of atropine." A nurse injected two syringes full of clear fluid into the patient's IV line. The heart rate picked up. The guy who had been pumping on the chest, presumably a resident, looked at Carrie uncertainly.

"Is there a pulse?" Carrie asked.

One of the nurses had her hand on the patient's groin, where the femoral artery could be palpated. "I think so," she said.

The patient's heart rate seemed to have stabilized at around eighty. "You think so," Carrie said.

"She's got a pulse," the nurse said.

Carrie put her own gloved hand on the patient's neck and pressed down lightly on the carotid. Slowly, she nodded. "Okay," she said. "Let's get her up to CCU." A save, Adler thought. For now. Maybe. If she wasn't brain dead and she didn't decide to fibrillate again and if what was left of her heart muscle didn't poop out completely in the next few days. "See you later," Adler said.

Carrie briefly glanced at him. "Thanks," she said.

She had read about things like this but she had never dreamed that it would happen to her. She knew that she was dying, her body flaccid and unresponsive on the cold, metal table but she was totally aware of her surroundings. There was no pain. She floated, serene and invisible, above the chaos and viewed it all, in stark, minute detail, as if some stranger were dying on the metal table, not herself.

Terrible, she thought, just terrible. All this effort. In a way, she was grateful. She had been feeling poorly ever since the dinner party last night. She didn't get out too often. It should have been exciting but something about it...so many things seemed to disturb her these days. Little things, usually. The faces of people she had never met seemed to contain hints of memory, clues to a past that was seventy years behind her and long since forgotten. It was absurd, but then, growing old was always absurd. There had been one young lady in particular, a pretty young woman with light brown hair. She had come up to them at the party. Her name had been Regina Cole. "I'm the Associate Director of Human Resources," Regina Cole had said. "I wanted to meet you." She had looked back and forth between Vincent and herself, smiling. "I wanted to thank you for your donation to the children's wing. It was very generous."

She had been perfectly polite but something about Regina Cole disturbed her—frightened her, even—something in the smile, in the level, intent gaze. Vincent had found the young woman charming but she had been unable to get that disturbing smile out of her mind. She had difficulty sleeping and once she had finally drifted off, her sleep had been troubled by restless dreams. Then, when it was almost dawn, she had awakened with a pain in her chest, a pain which she foolishly had tried to ignore, a pain which had grown steadily worse throughout the day. And now here she was.

All this effort. Ridiculous.

After a little while, she began to lose interest in what they were doing to the decrepit old body. Why, this is fun, she thought. Her awareness floated above the table and the people milling about the room. It was just like flying. She smiled to herself. Seventy years ago, when she was just a little girl, she had once jumped off the roof of her house, flapping her arms, willing herself into the air. She had been so sure it would work, but of course it hadn't. She had fallen to the gravel and broken a leg and the servants had been very cross with her.

But now she could fly. She really could. All it took was the thought. The cabinets around the room were filled with all sorts of exotic things, syringes and medications and tapes and clamps and scalpels and others she couldn't recognize. She peered inside and examined them all but soon lost interest.

If she listened, she could hear voices coming from outside the room. Was it possible? Why not? She concentrated and found herself floating down the hallway, past the old-fashioned windows, past a wooden door that led out to the street. Wonderful! She came to a

233

stairwell and floated up. There were patients here, and nurses and orderlies and a few doctors talking together in hushed voices.

The young man who had put the tube in her throat, the young surgeon, was walking near the end of the hallway. Curious, she followed him, floating invisibly above his head. The young man came to a doorway and knocked. He listened for a moment but heard no answer. He nodded slowly to himself and gave a little smile, then he walked on down the hall, his hands in his pockets, soundlessly whistling.

Curious, she floated inside. It was a bedroom. A woman was lying on the bed. The woman was naked. Her body was young and slim and firm, her face mottled and red. Her eyes were bloodshot and staring. Her mouth was open, the tongue swollen and protruding to the side. Blue and purple bruises circled her neck.

She recognized her at once, without surprise, as if she had somehow known what she would find in this room. The young woman lying dead and naked on the bed was Regina Cole.

Chapter 2

"It seems, Doctor Adler, that you have become involved in a homicide."

"I have?" Adler reached up a hand and scratched his head. "Whose homicide?"

Brody looked at him, gave a knowing smile and nodded his head. "For the moment, I prefer not to say. Why don't you sit down and tell us about it?"

Adler scratched his head again. Sean Brody was the Chairman of the Department of Surgery. He was a good surgeon, a good administrator and a good teacher but he was known to have a morbid sense of humor. He sat on the other side of his desk with a thin smile on his face. Richard Kurtz sat across from the desk, looking at Brody with glum disapproval. "I don't think you should be joking about this," Kurtz said.

Brody raised an eyebrow and gave Kurtz a wolfish grin. "I've asked Doctor Kurtz to be here today because I wanted a witness. This is a very serious business, very serious indeed. You have the makings of a talented surgeon but talent in the OR is no excuse for criminal behavior. No excuse at all. We can't have murder. Murder is bad for the profession, bad for the image, bad for everyone concerned. Why did you do it? You might as well confess."

"I really have no idea," Adler said. He sat down in a chair and glanced at Kurtz. "My mind is a blank."

"A random killing?" Brody made a regretful clucking sound. "Let me warn you, young man, the insanity defense rarely works these days. Juries have grown more cynical. I suggest you save all of us a lot of trouble and simply admit to your crimes. I doubt this was the first. Then we can kick you out of the program, quietly commit you to an institution upstate, sweep the whole thing under the rug and get on with the serious business of saving lives."

"Cut it out, Sean, huh?" Kurtz said.

"You," Brody said, "have no sense of humor."

"It's not that funny."

"What are you talking about, anyway?" asked Adler.

Brody sighed and turned to Kurtz. "Why don't you tell him?"

Kurtz cleared his throat and looked briefly embarrassed. "The lady that you trached last night, the one who was arresting in the ER?"

Adler just looked at him.

"She's doing quite well. Her name is Eleanor Herbert. Her brother is on the Board of Trustees of the hospital. Her family have been benefactors of the place for almost a century. It seems that while she was arresting, she had an out-of-body experience. She claims that she followed you up the stairs where you knocked on a door. You received no answer. You continued down the hallway. Eleanor Herbert then entered the room and found a young woman lying on a bed, strangled."

"I did?" Adler blinked back and forth between Kurtz' face and Brody's.

"So she says."

"Which young woman?"

Kurtz glanced at Brody. "The Associate Director of Human Resources. Her name is Regina Cole."

"Damn." A meditative look crept across Adler's face. "I thought I detected a faint spectral presence hovering over me." He shook his head regretfully. "I should have realized. What a fool I've been."

"Then you admit it?" Brody asked.

"You've got me," Adler said. He held out his hands, the wrists close together. "Put on the cuffs. I'll go quietly."

"Doctor Adler," Brody said with relish, "despite my attempts at levity,"—he eyed Kurtz—"misguided though they might be, I'm afraid that this is not a joke. Accusations of murder are to be taken seriously, particularly when they are made by major contributors and members of the Board of Trustees."

"Okay," Adler said. "I'm serious. What do you want me to do?"

Kurtz shook his head and sighed.

"Nothing," Brody said, his face suddenly tired. "We're just telling you. The woman is obviously a lunatic, but she's a lunatic who's making some serious accusations. If she persists in her delusion, we're going to have to call in the police, if only to satisfy her family."

"In which case," Adler said, "I'll probably sue all of you for slander, discrimination, and everything else my lawyer can think of."

Brody puffed out his cheeks and grimaced faintly. "Hopefully, it won't come to that."

"Don't let it." Adler said. He looked annoyed. He frowned, first at Brody, then at Kurtz. "Jeez, we're talking about my career here. Has anybody turned up missing?"

"Yes," Brody said. "One person has. The Associate Director of Human Resources." He grinned wanly. "She missed her shift and didn't call in."

"No shit," Adler said.

"So tell me about Adler."

Lew Barent was a cop. He was also a good friend of Kurtz. The two men were sitting in a restaurant not far from Easton. Kurtz had given Barent a call and invited him to lunch.

"Not much to tell. He's a chief resident in surgery, good hands, nice guy, conceited—but then, most of them are."

Barent took a bite out of his hamburger and chewed. "Family?" he asked.

Kurtz poured himself a glass of Coke from a small pitcher while he thought about the question. Kurtz was annoyed at himself. The last thing he wanted to do was stir up a hornet's nest but Regina Cole was still missing. "His parents live in Summit, New Jersey. His father owns a car dealership. His mother's a housewife."

"An obvious criminal background."

Kurtz grunted.

"The old lady, she says she saw him knock on the door. She didn't actually see him do it?"

"No. she says that he nodded his head and smiled, like he knew what was in there."

Barent looked skeptical. "Most of the time, you've got a body, your problem is finding a witness. This time, you've got a witness but no body."

"Some witness. The whole thing is nutty. She admits that she was nowhere near the murder that she claims to have seen and all the objective evidence says she was unconscious the whole time."

"Any history of irregular behavior?"

"I don't know."

"So maybe she's always been a nut and maybe what she's been through has driven her over the deep end."

"It's a nutty story. We're supposed to convict a man of murder because of some old lady's mystical adventure?"

"Don't jump to conclusions. You said she claimed to see a body. She didn't see anybody kill her. The old lady might believe what she's saying but that doesn't mean we have to. And it certainly doesn't mean that she actually saw what she thinks she saw. What can you tell me about out-of-body experiences? Is there anything to them? Medically?"

Kurtz sipped his Coke and ate a couple of fries before answering. "They're fairly common among people who've had close escapes from death. About ten per-cent of CPR survivors report having had them. The same with serious car-crash victims, people who've fallen from tall buildings and survived...you get the picture."

Barent nodded.

"The stories are quite similar. There's almost always the feeling of floating, as if they're looking down on their own body. They can see everything that's going on around them. Some have accurately reported on the contents of cabinets that they couldn't possibly have seen from where their body was lying. Sometimes they've even been aware of things going on in other rooms. Almost always they report a sort of hovering light which they feel they have to go to. Many of them claim a feeling of disappointment when their resuscitation is successful. They feel as if they're being pulled back into their bodies and they don't want to go back. They're drawn by the light. That's the name of a popular book on the subject, by the way, *Drawn by the Light*."

"It sounds as if you think there's something to it."

"Do I?" It was another gloomy day, Kurtz noted. A thin drizzle splattered against the window, typical for this time of year. March was lurching creakily toward springtime and Kurtz, like most New Yorkers, was sick of it already. He wanted some sunshine. "Most of the stories have turned out to be untrue. They saw somebody next to their stretcher or walking down the street and they just weren't there. They saw something in the room, maybe a chair, a coat rack, a pair of scissors, anything at all—and there was no such thing. We're talking about people who are dying. Their brains aren't getting a lot of oxygen and they don't function the way they're supposed to. These are not stories that can be regarded as reliable."

"But sometimes they turn out to be true."

"Yes."

"Not a lot of evidence," said Barent.

"I agree."

"And Regina Cole is still missing."

"Yup."

"What's happened with Adler?"

"Nothing. But if Regina Cole doesn't turn up soon, the administration is going to have to go to the police, officially. None of this is going to do Adler's reputation any good."

"Has anybody contacted the girl's family?"

"Somebody in administration put in a discreet phone call. Her mother is dead. Her father lives on Long Island. He hasn't seen her or heard from her in a couple of weeks, which apparently isn't unusual."

"Boyfriends?"

"Nobody knows."

"That's unusual. In this day and age, your co-workers almost always know more about you than your family does. You spend more time with them."

"She kept to herself, apparently."

"And if Eleanor Herbert persists in her delusion, the Board might insist on putting young Doctor Adler on suspension."

"That's what Brody is afraid of."

"I wish I had some advice for you." Barent chewed stolidly on his hamburger. "As you say, there's not much evidence for anything. Regina Cole will probably turn up. If she doesn't, then we'll have to be called in but even then, nobody is going to arrest Adler, not on the basis of a story like this. In my opinion, the whole thing is going to blow over."

"I hope so," Kurtz said.

"Well, we'll soon know." Barent rose to his feet and began to put on his coat. "Thanks for the lunch."

Kurtz nodded gloomily. "Sure," he said.

Made in the USA
San Bernardino, CA
24 November 2019